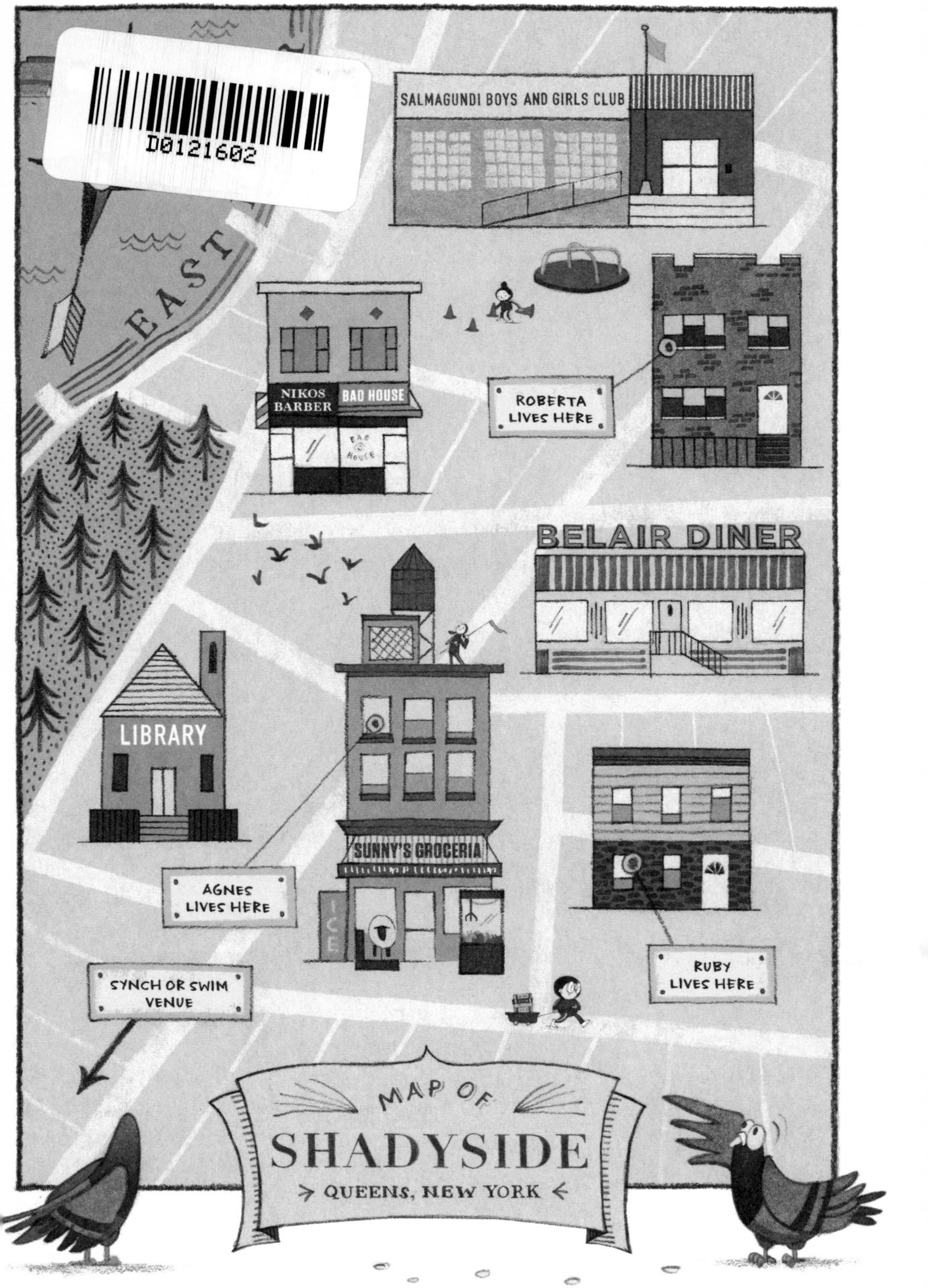
SALMAGUNDI BOYS AND GIRLS CLUB
EAST
NIKOS BARBER
BAO HOUSE
ROBERTA LIVES HERE
BELAIR DINER
LIBRARY
SUNNY'S GROCERIA
ICE
AGNES LIVES HERE
RUBY LIVES HERE
SYNCH OR SWIM VENUE
MAP OF
SHADYSIDE
QUEENS, NEW YORK

For Owen and all the offbeats
who dance to their own tune.

Many thanks to the Squid Squad—Ivanna, Niamh, Ayoola, Joanna, and Satu for your meticulousness, patience, and steady guidance. Special thanks to Sam for having the vision to see a larger Shadyside story.

To my fellow storytellers for their camaraderie and indispensable advice: Mika Song, Minh Lê, Angela Dominguez, Rina and Simon Villalon, Paolo Lim, and Aram Kim.

For all my childhood friends who inspired this tale, keep it weird!

First edition published in 2021 by Flying Eye Books,
an imprint of Nobrow Ltd. 27 Westgate Street, London, E8 3RL.

Text and Illustrations © Isabel Roxas 2021.

Isabel Roxas has asserted her right under the Copyright, Designs and Patents Act, 1988, to be identified as the Author and Illustrator of this Work.

1 3 5 7 9 10 8 6 4 2

Published in the US by Nobrow (US) INC.
Printed in Latvia on FSC® certified paper.

MIX
Paper from
responsible sources
FSC® C002795
FSC
www.fsc.org

ISBN: 978-1-912497-25-6
flyingeyebooks.com

- Isabel Roxas -

THE ADVENTURES OF TEAM POM

SQUID HAPPENS

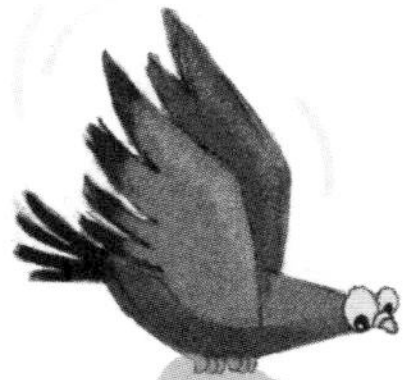

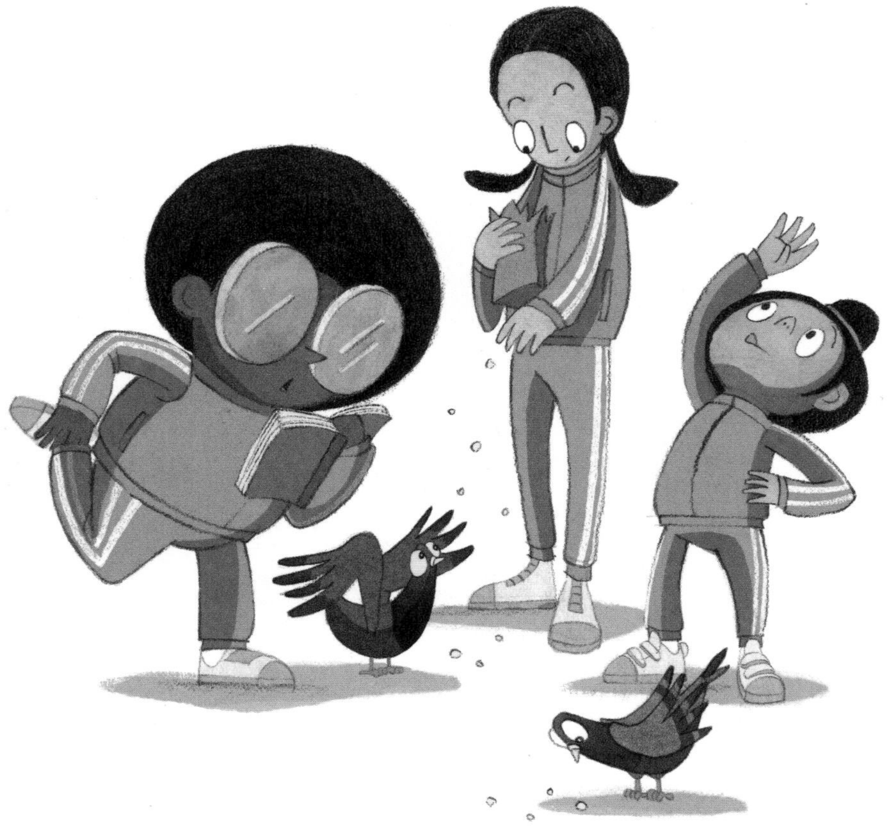

Flying Eye Books
London | Los Angeles

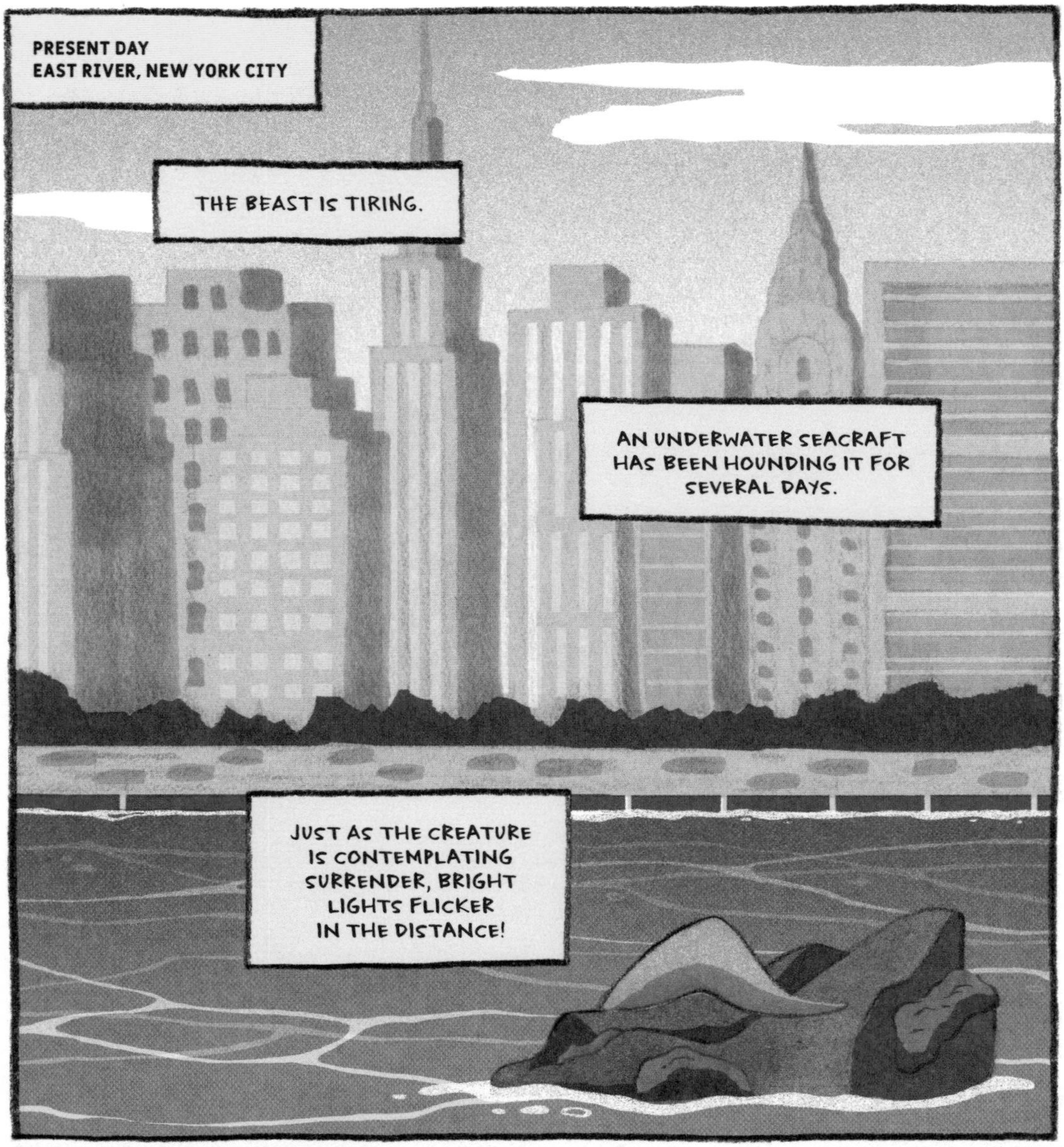
PRESENT DAY
EAST RIVER, NEW YORK CITY
THE BEAST IS TIRING.
AN UNDERWATER SEACRAFT HAS BEEN HOUNDING IT FOR SEVERAL DAYS.
JUST AS THE CREATURE IS CONTEMPLATING SURRENDER, BRIGHT LIGHTS FLICKER IN THE DISTANCE!

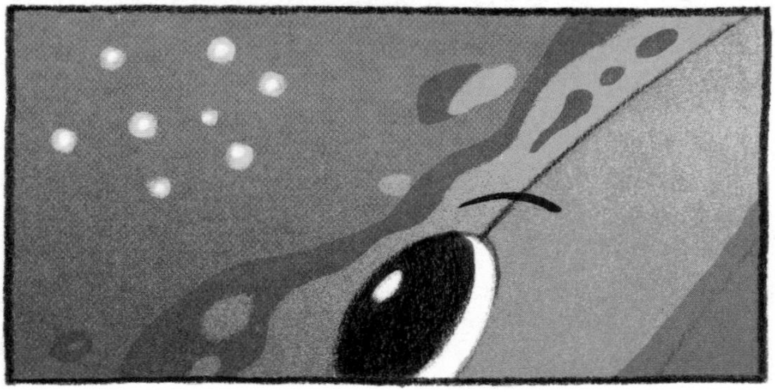

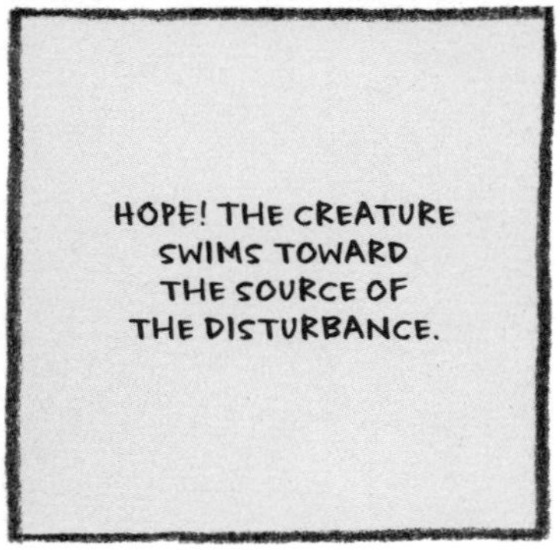
HOPE! THE CREATURE SWIMS TOWARD THE SOURCE OF THE DISTURBANCE.

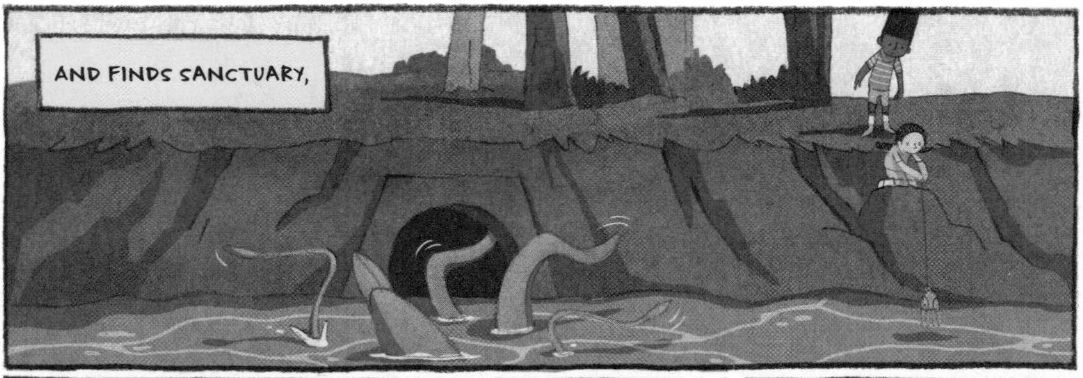
AND FINDS SANCTUARY,

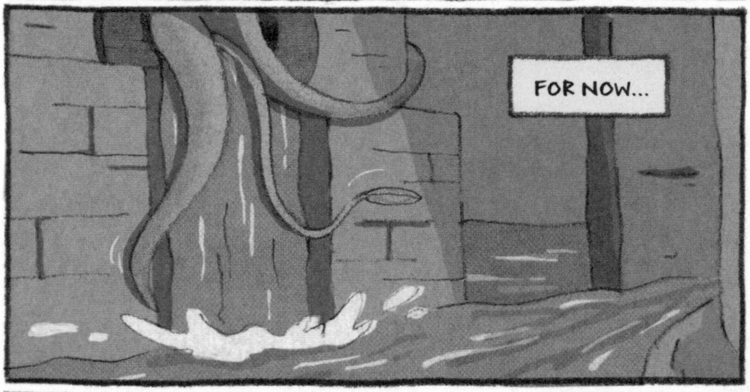
FOR NOW...

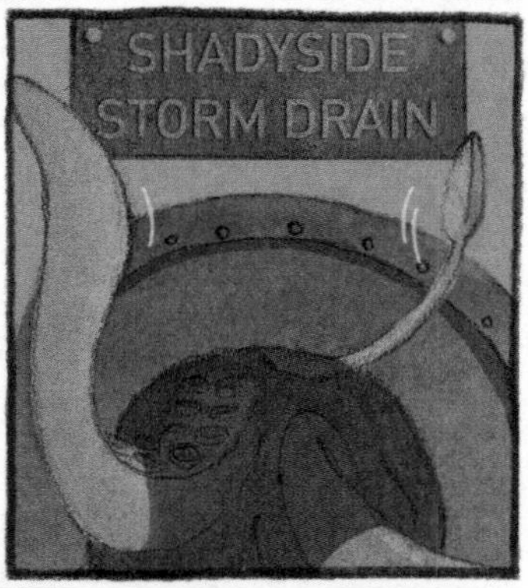
SHADYSIDE STORM DRAIN

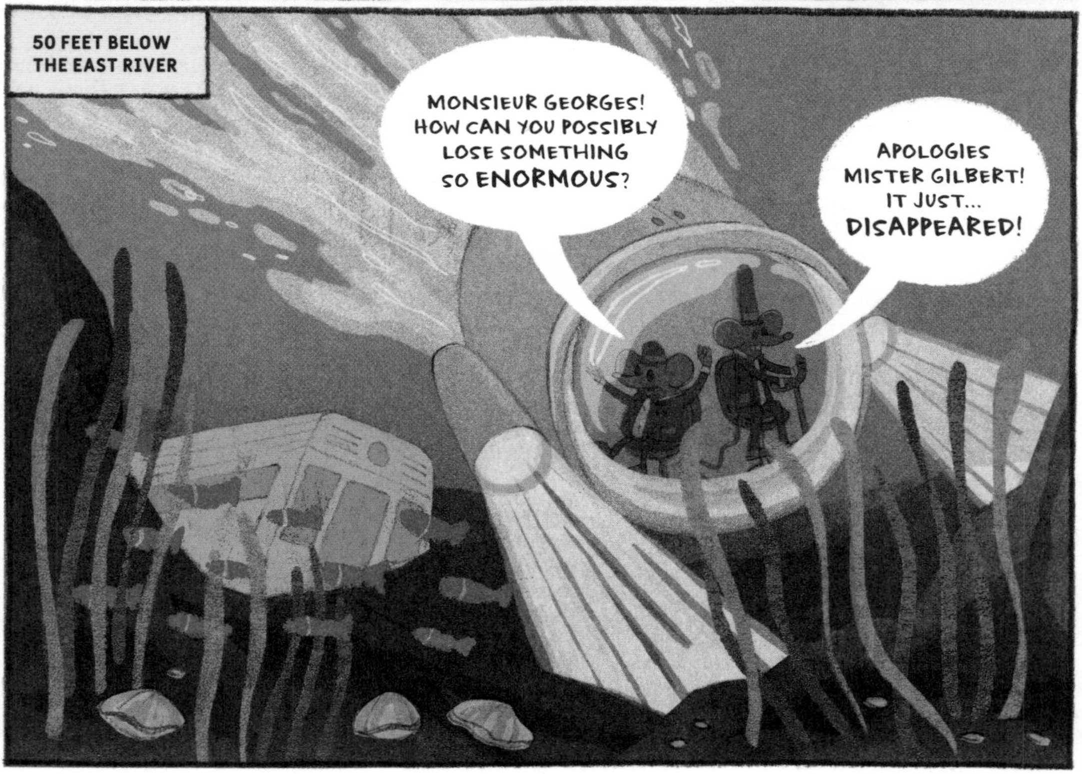
50 FEET BELOW THE EAST RIVER
MONSIEUR GEORGES! HOW CAN YOU POSSIBLY LOSE SOMETHING SO ENORMOUS?
APOLOGIES MISTER GILBERT! IT JUST... DISAPPEARED!

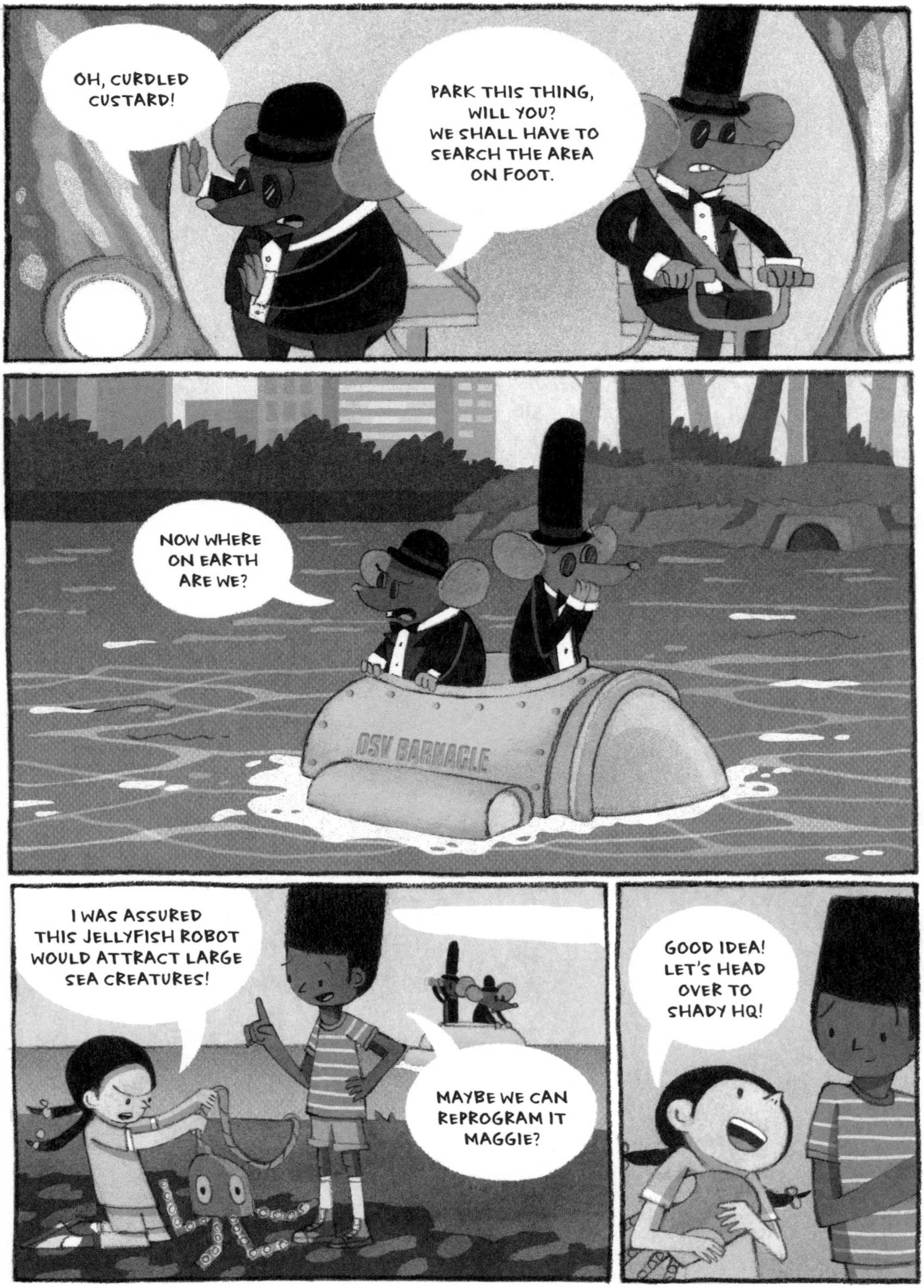
OH, CURDLED CUSTARD!
PARK THIS THING, WILL YOU? WE SHALL HAVE TO SEARCH THE AREA ON FOOT.
NOW WHERE ON EARTH ARE WE?
OSV BARNACLE
I WAS ASSURED THIS JELLYFISH ROBOT WOULD ATTRACT LARGE SEA CREATURES!
MAYBE WE CAN REPROGRAM IT MAGGIE?
GOOD IDEA! LET'S HEAD OVER TO SHADY HQ!

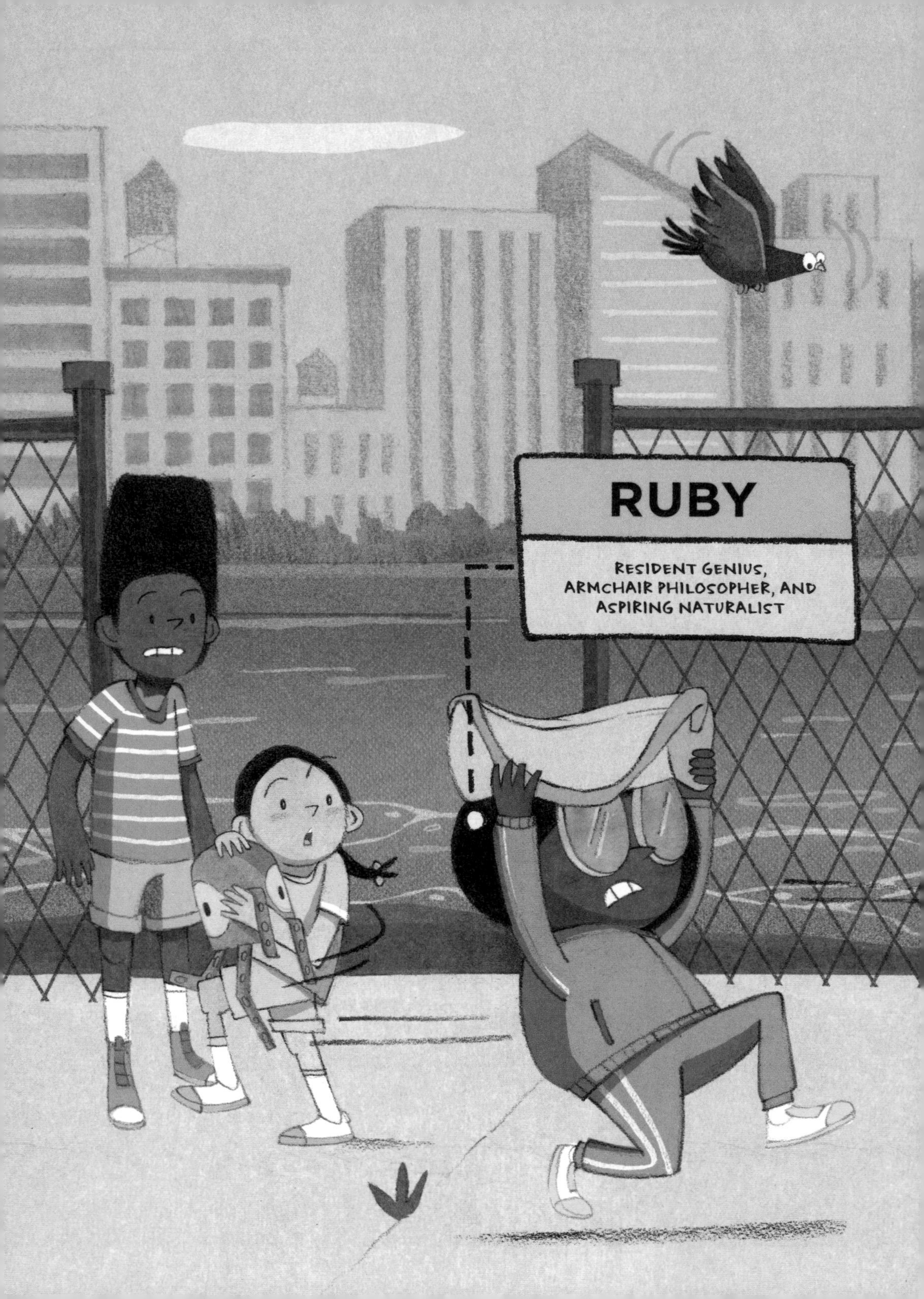
RUBY
RESIDENT GENIUS,
ARMCHAIR PHILOSOPHER, AND
ASPIRING NATURALIST

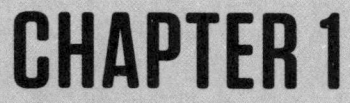

CHAPTER 1

THE BOROUGH OF DREAMS

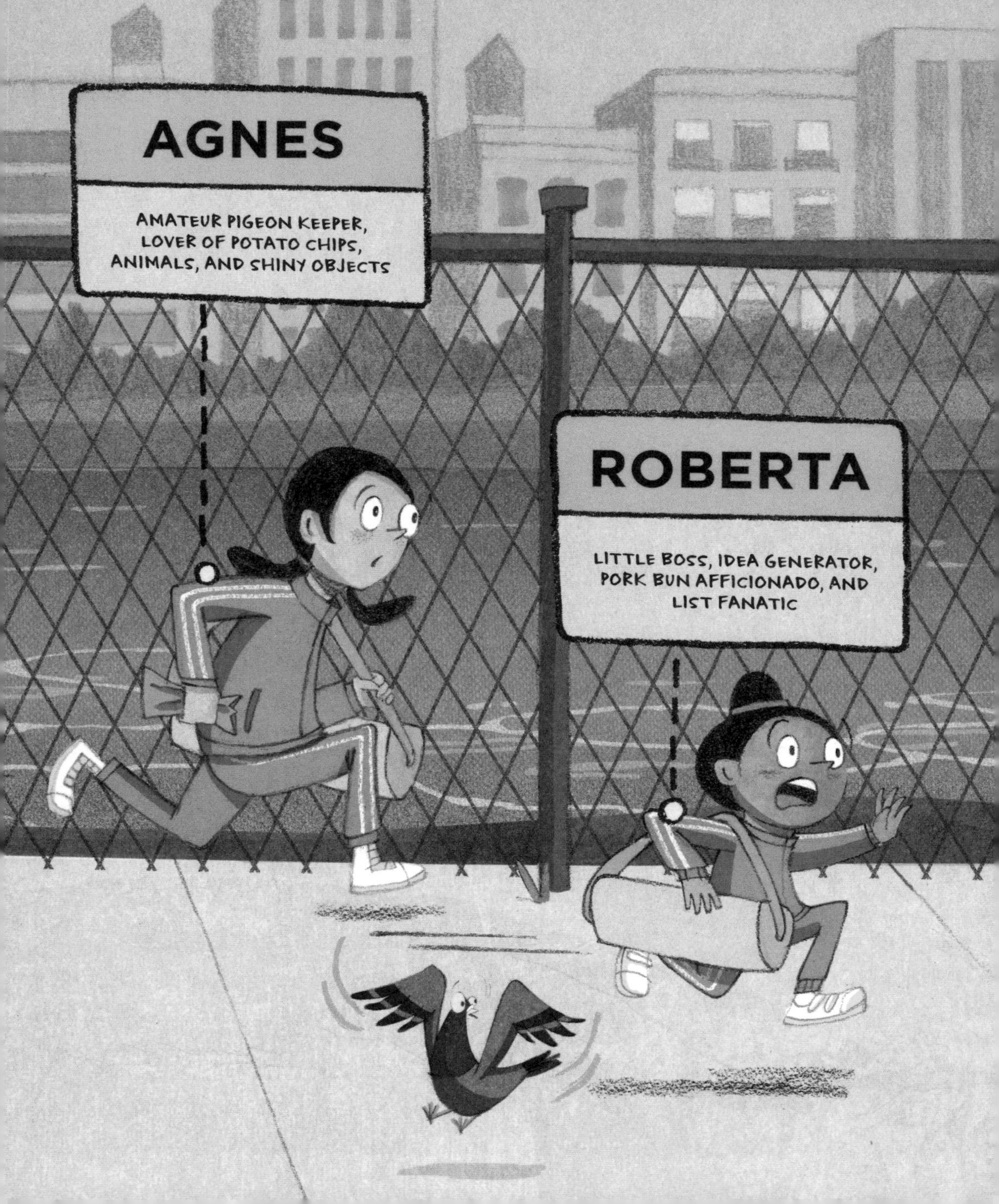
AGNES
AMATEUR PIGEON KEEPER, LOVER OF POTATO CHIPS, ANIMALS, AND SHINY OBJECTS
ROBERTA
LITTLE BOSS, IDEA GENERATOR, PORK BUN AFFICIONADO, AND LIST FANATIC

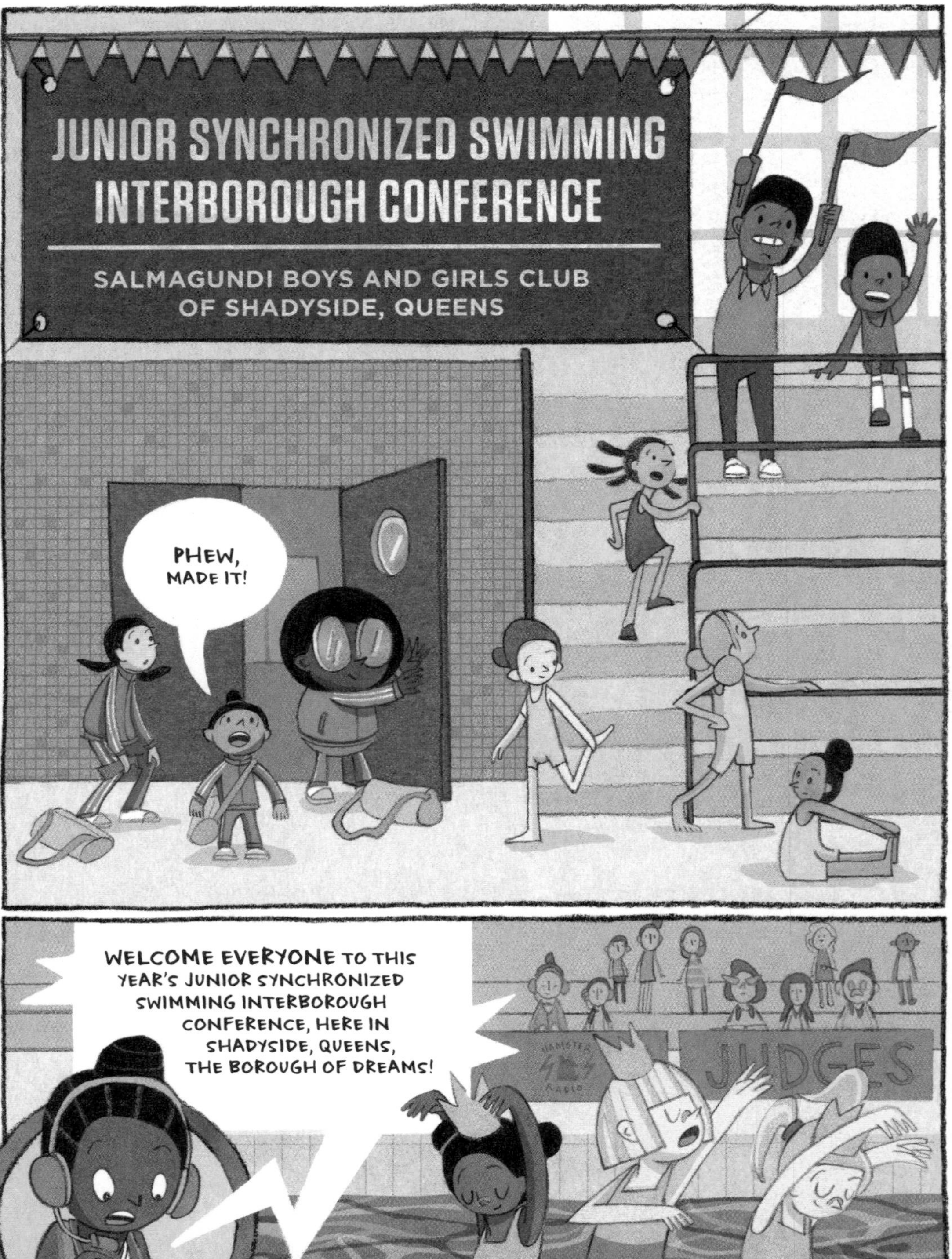
JUNIOR SYNCHRONIZED SWIMMING INTERBOROUGH CONFERENCE
SALMAGUNDI BOYS AND GIRLS CLUB OF SHADYSIDE, QUEENS
PHEW, MADE IT!
WELCOME EVERYONE TO THIS YEAR'S JUNIOR SYNCHRONIZED SWIMMING INTERBOROUGH CONFERENCE, HERE IN SHADYSIDE, QUEENS, THE BOROUGH OF DREAMS!

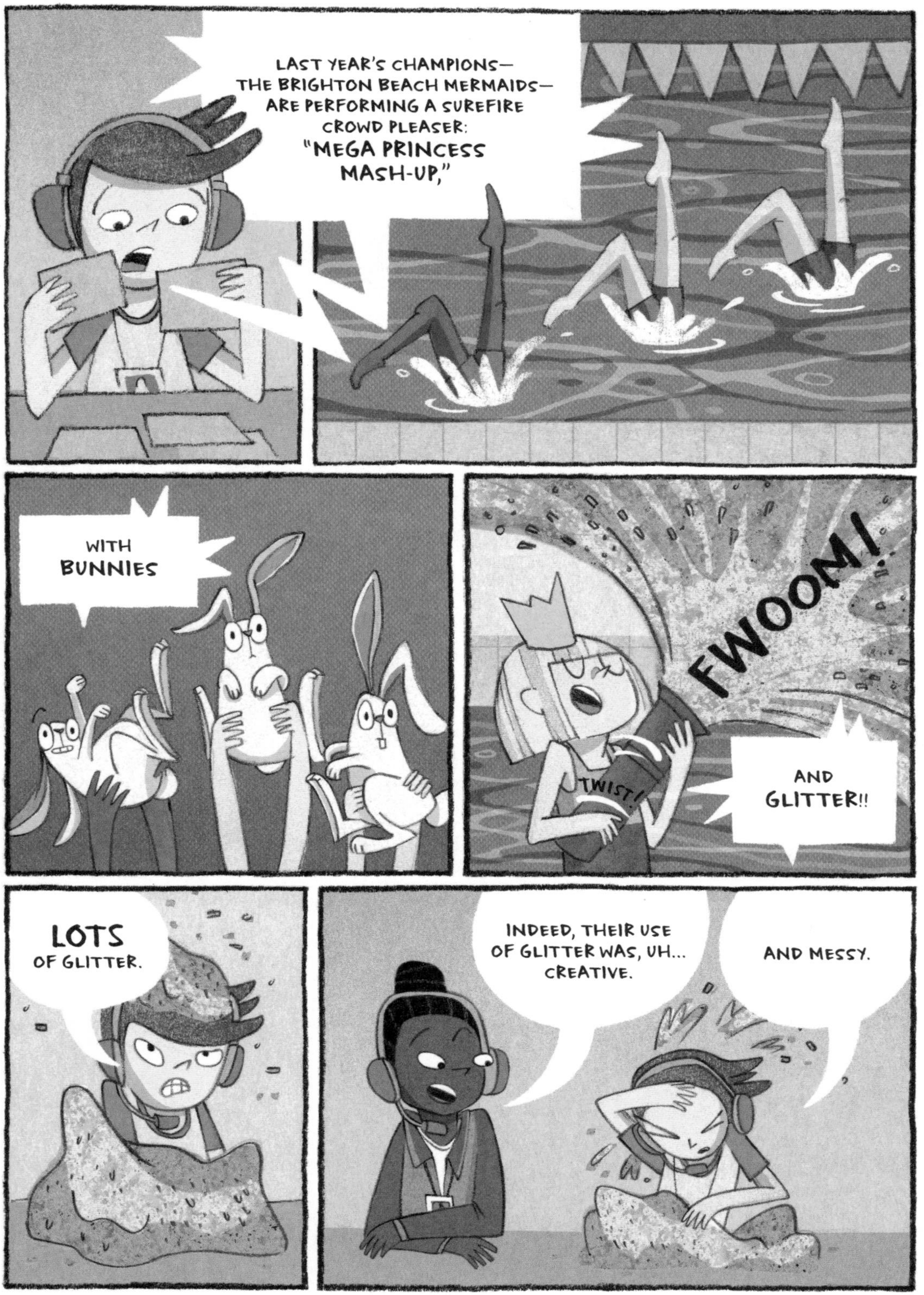
LAST YEAR'S CHAMPIONS— THE BRIGHTON BEACH MERMAIDS— ARE PERFORMING A SUREFIRE CROWD PLEASER: "MEGA PRINCESS MASH-UP,"
WITH BUNNIES
FWOOM!
TWIST!
AND GLITTER!!
LOTS OF GLITTER.
INDEED, THEIR USE OF GLITTER WAS, UH... CREATIVE.
AND MESSY.

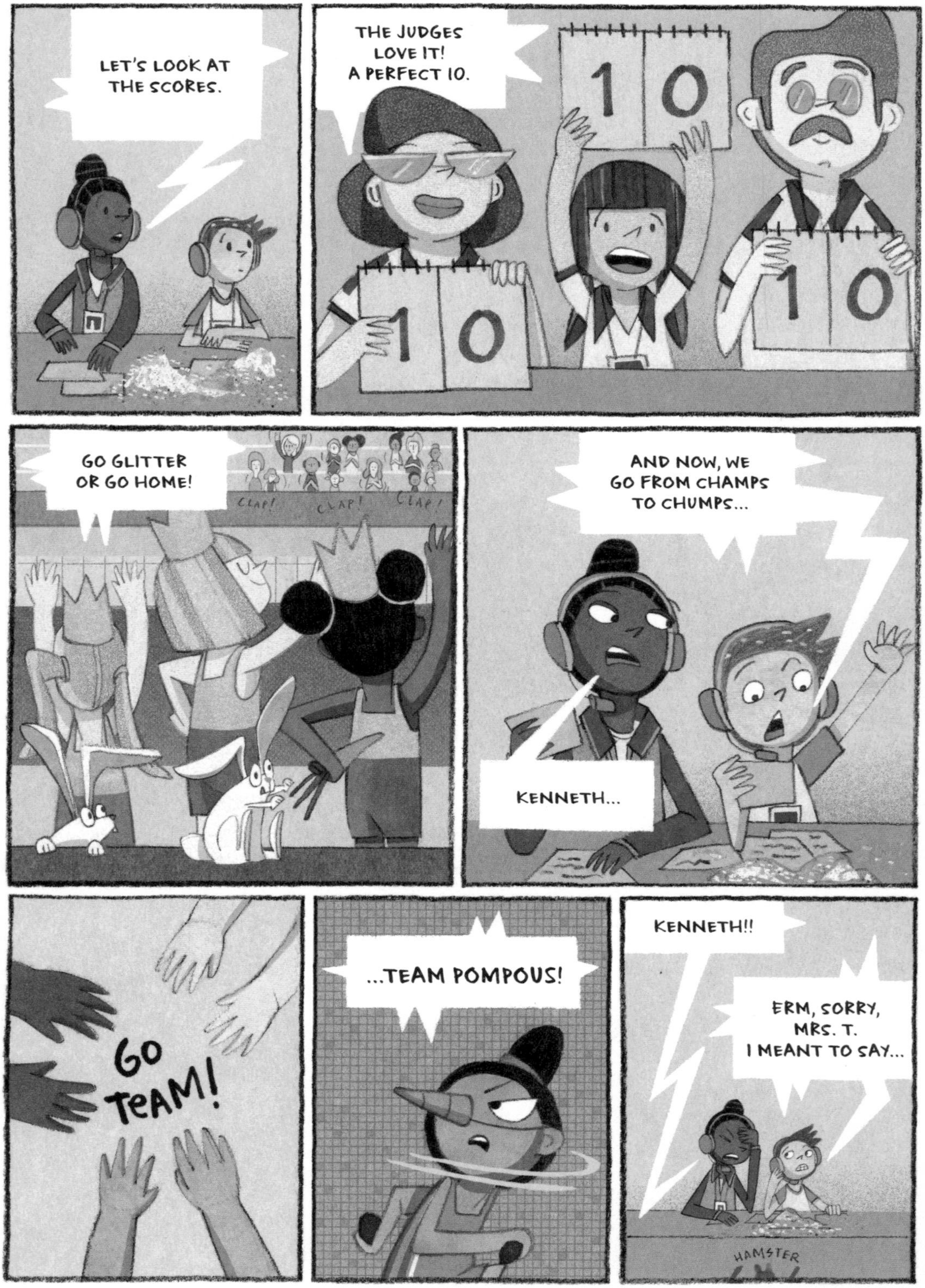
LET'S LOOK AT THE SCORES.
THE JUDGES LOVE IT! A PERFECT 10.
10
10
10
GO GLITTER OR GO HOME!
CLAP! CLAP! CLAP!
AND NOW, WE GO FROM CHAMPS TO CHUMPS...
KENNETH...
GO TEAM!
...TEAM POMPOUS!
KENNETH!!
ERM, SORRY, MRS. T. I MEANT TO SAY...
HAMSTER

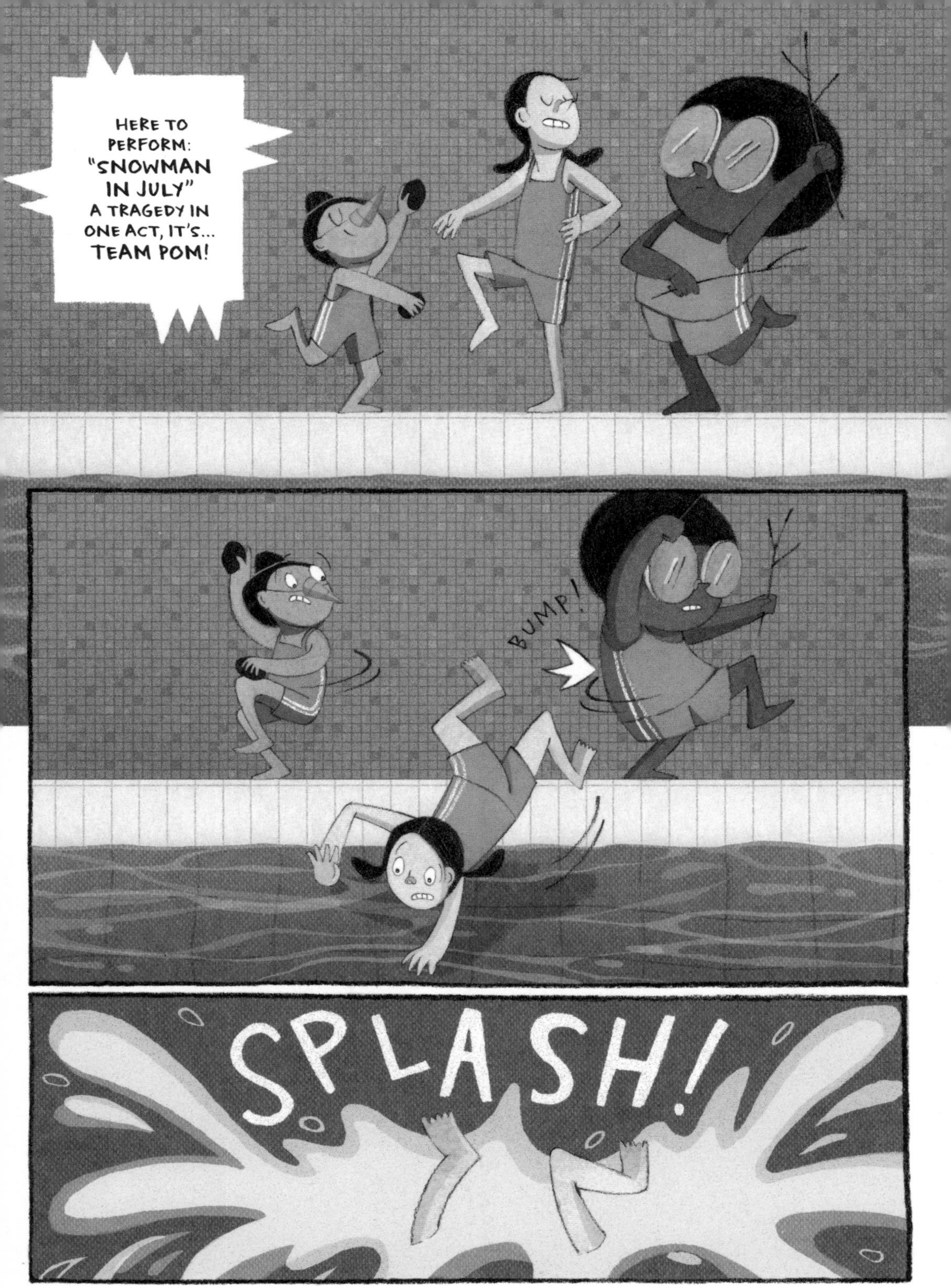
HERE TO PERFORM: "SNOWMAN IN JULY" A TRAGEDY IN ONE ACT, IT'S... TEAM POM!
BUMP!
SPLASH!

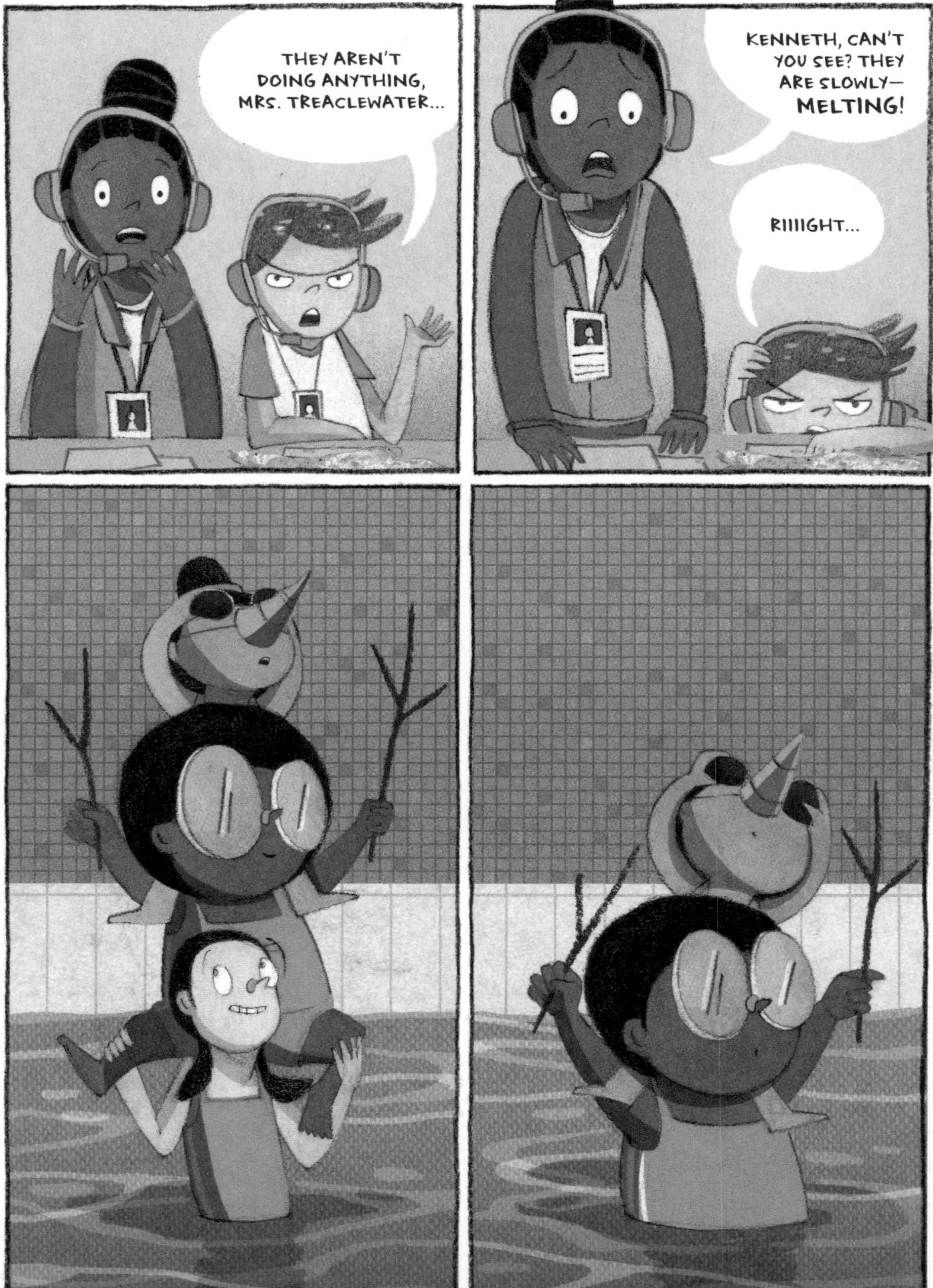
THEY AREN'T DOING ANYTHING, MRS. TREACLEWATER...
KENNETH, CAN'T YOU SEE? THEY ARE SLOWLY— MELTING!
RIIIIGHT...

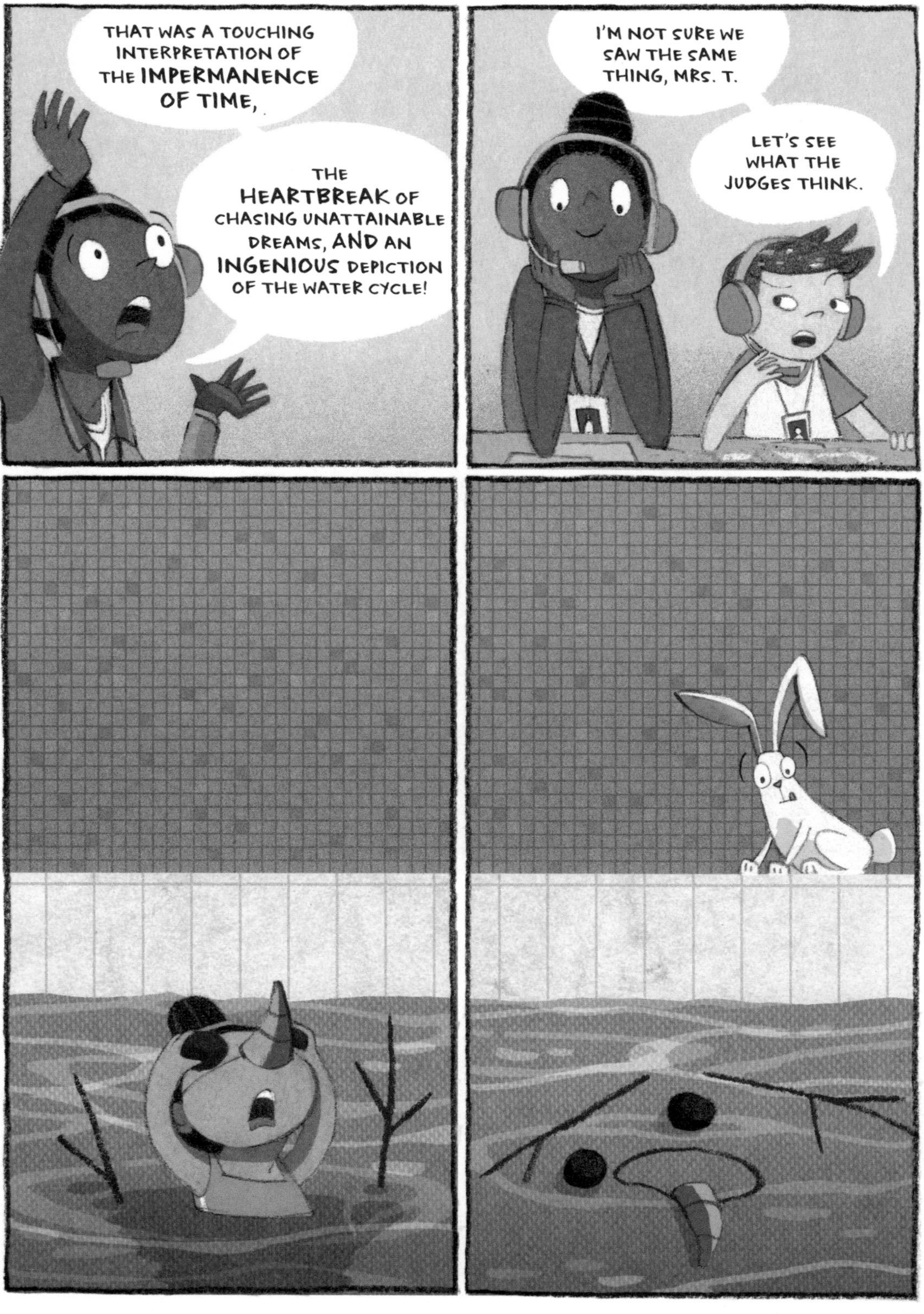
THAT WAS A TOUCHING INTERPRETATION OF THE IMPERMANENCE OF TIME,
THE HEARTBREAK OF CHASING UNATTAINABLE DREAMS, AND AN INGENIOUS DEPICTION OF THE WATER CYCLE!
I'M NOT SURE WE SAW THE SAME THING, MRS. T.
LET'S SEE WHAT THE JUDGES THINK.

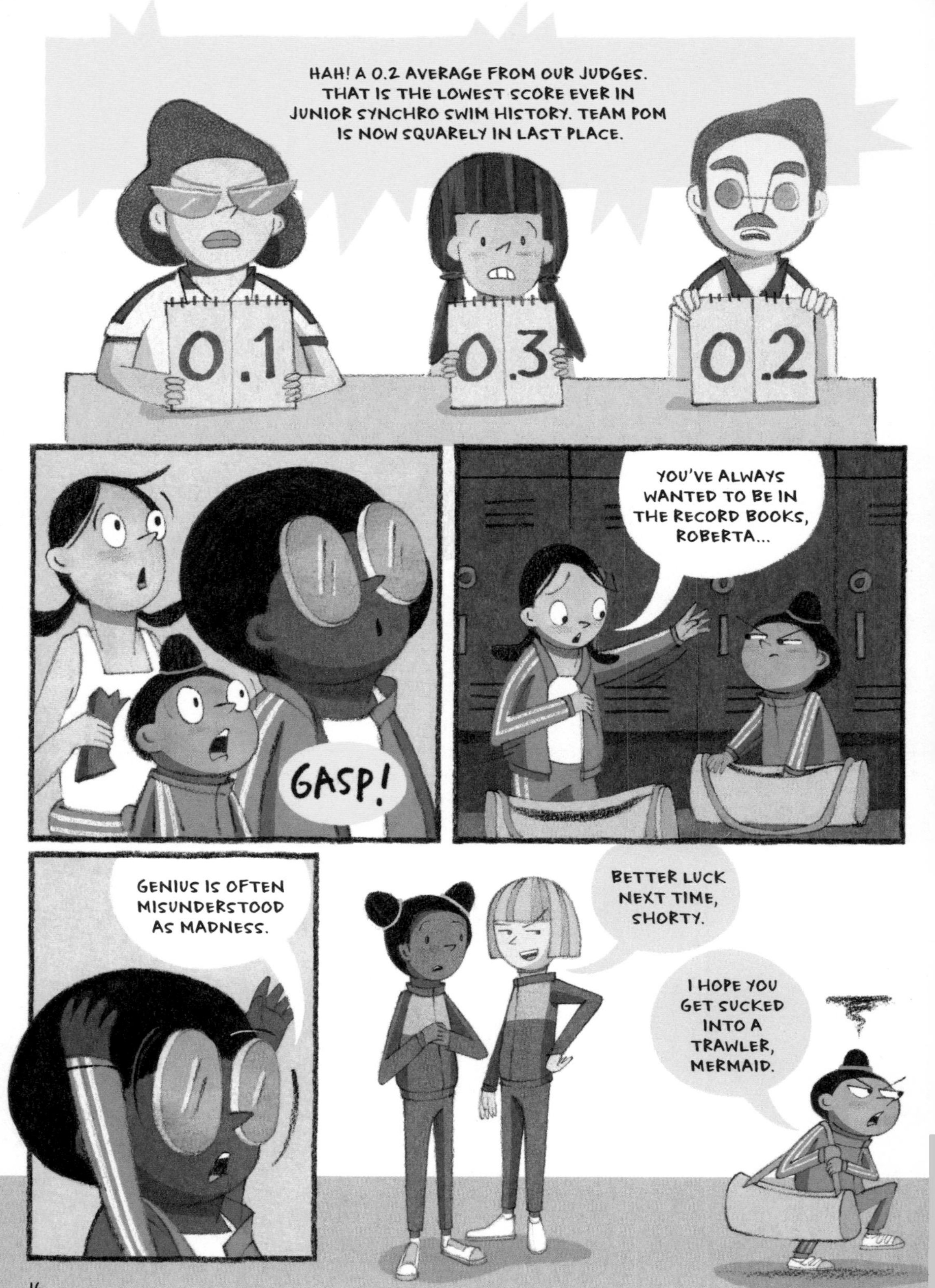

HAH! A 0.2 AVERAGE FROM OUR JUDGES. THAT IS THE LOWEST SCORE EVER IN JUNIOR SYNCHRO SWIM HISTORY. TEAM POM IS NOW SQUARELY IN LAST PLACE.
0.1
0.3
0.2
GASP!
YOU'VE ALWAYS WANTED TO BE IN THE RECORD BOOKS, ROBERTA...
GENIUS IS OFTEN MISUNDERSTOOD AS MADNESS.
BETTER LUCK NEXT TIME, SHORTY.
I HOPE YOU GET SUCKED INTO A TRAWLER, MERMAID.

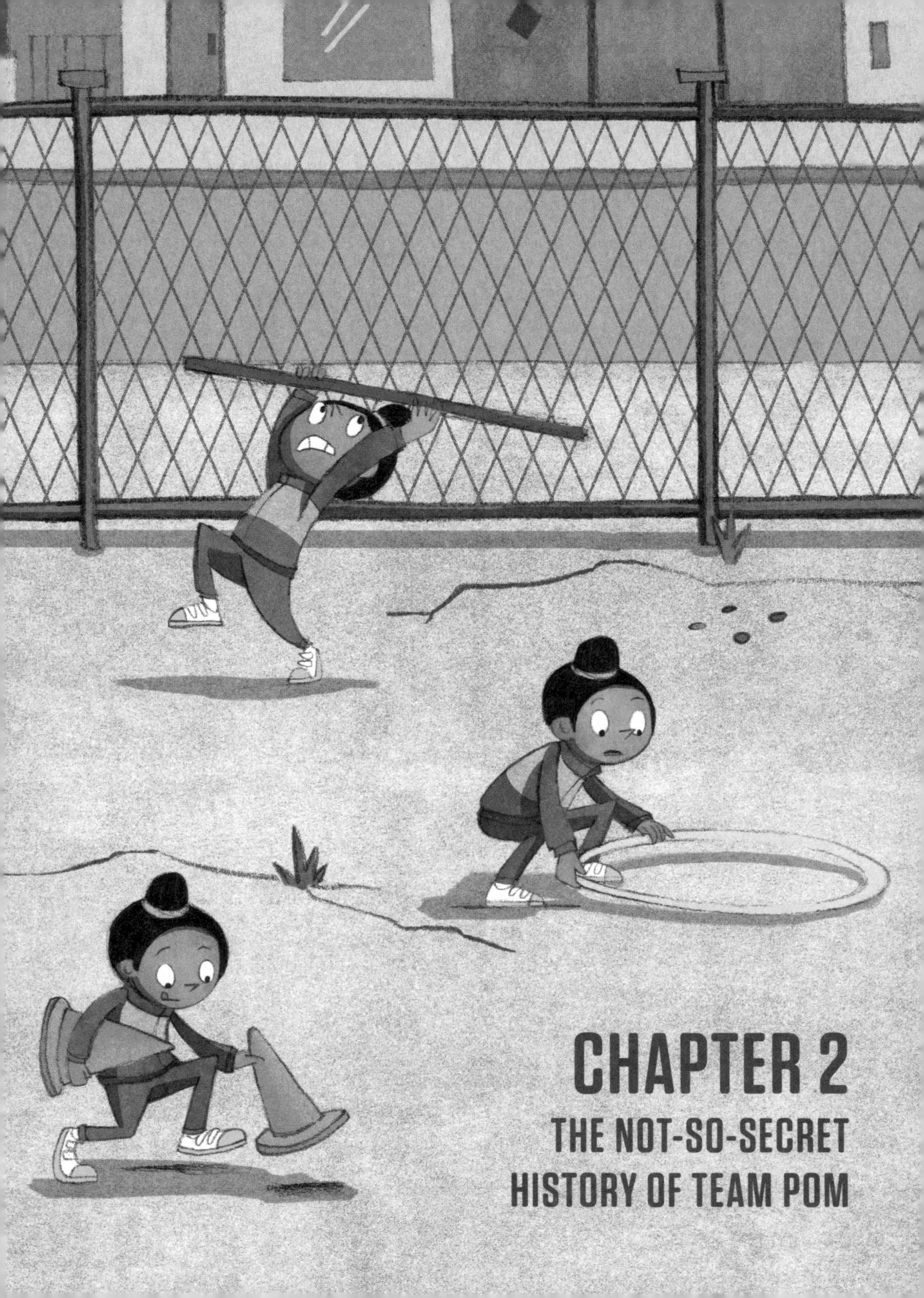

CHAPTER 2

THE NOT-SO-SECRET HISTORY OF TEAM POM

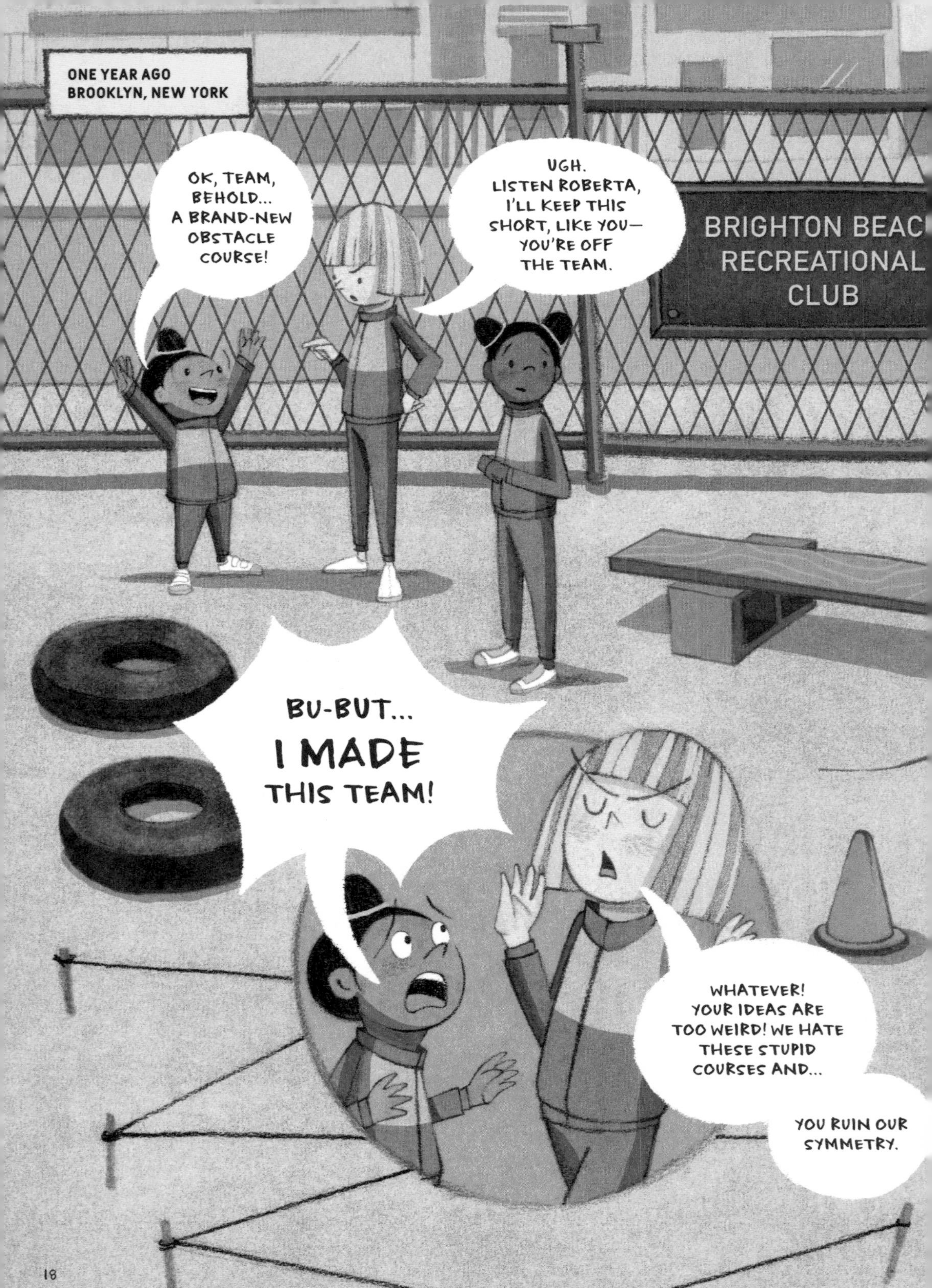
ONE YEAR AGO BROOKLYN, NEW YORK
OK, TEAM, BEHOLD... A BRAND-NEW OBSTACLE COURSE!
UGH. LISTEN ROBERTA, I'LL KEEP THIS SHORT, LIKE YOU— YOU'RE OFF THE TEAM.
BRIGHTON BEAC RECREATIONAL CLUB
BU-BUT... I MADE THIS TEAM!
WHATEVER! YOUR IDEAS ARE TOO WEIRD! WE HATE THESE STUPID COURSES AND...
YOU RUIN OUR SYMMETRY.

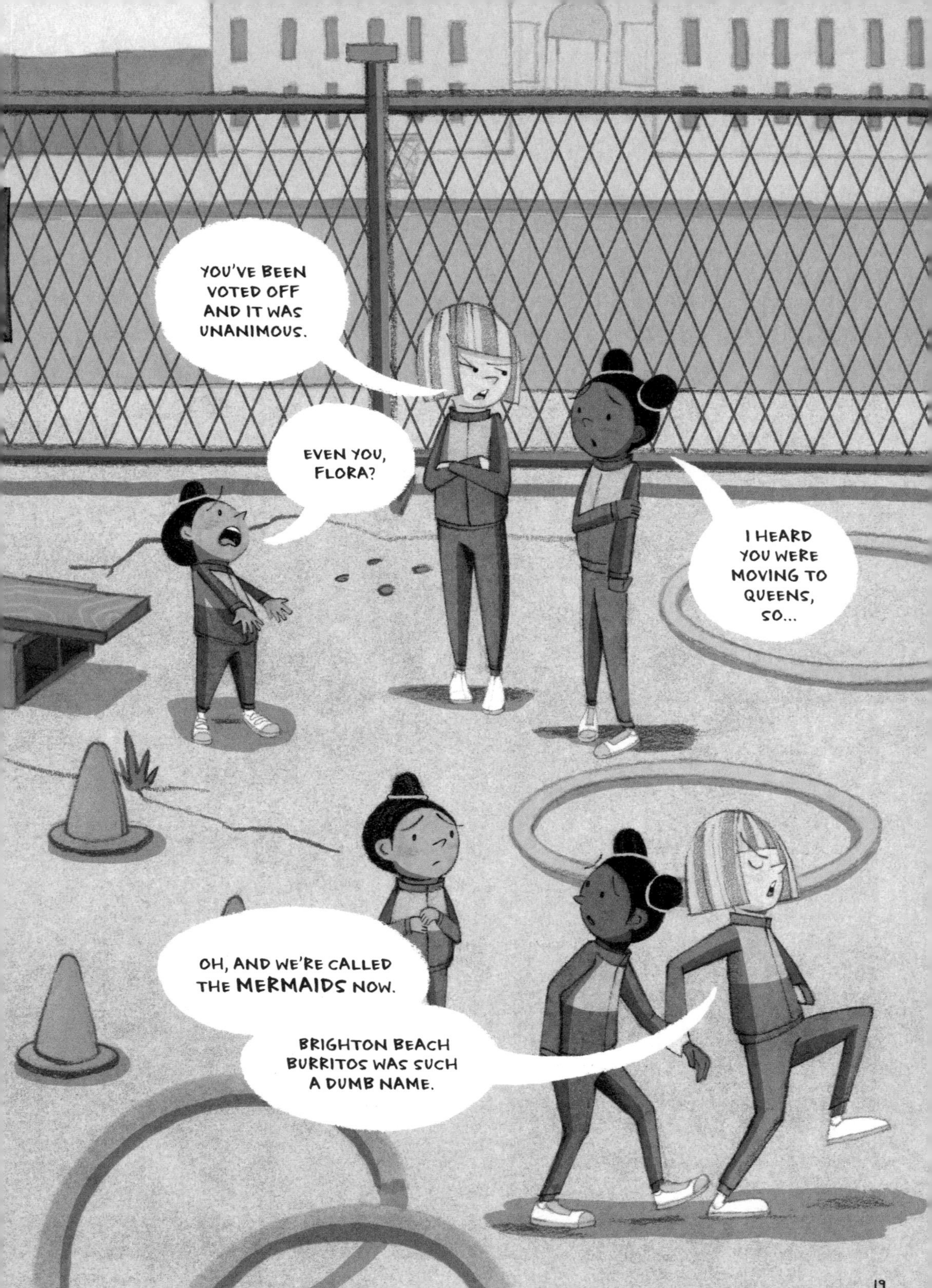
YOU'VE BEEN VOTED OFF AND IT WAS UNANIMOUS.
EVEN YOU, FLORA?
I HEARD YOU WERE MOVING TO QUEENS, SO...
OH, AND WE'RE CALLED THE **MERMAIDS** NOW.
BRIGHTON BEACH BURRITOS WAS SUCH A DUMB NAME.

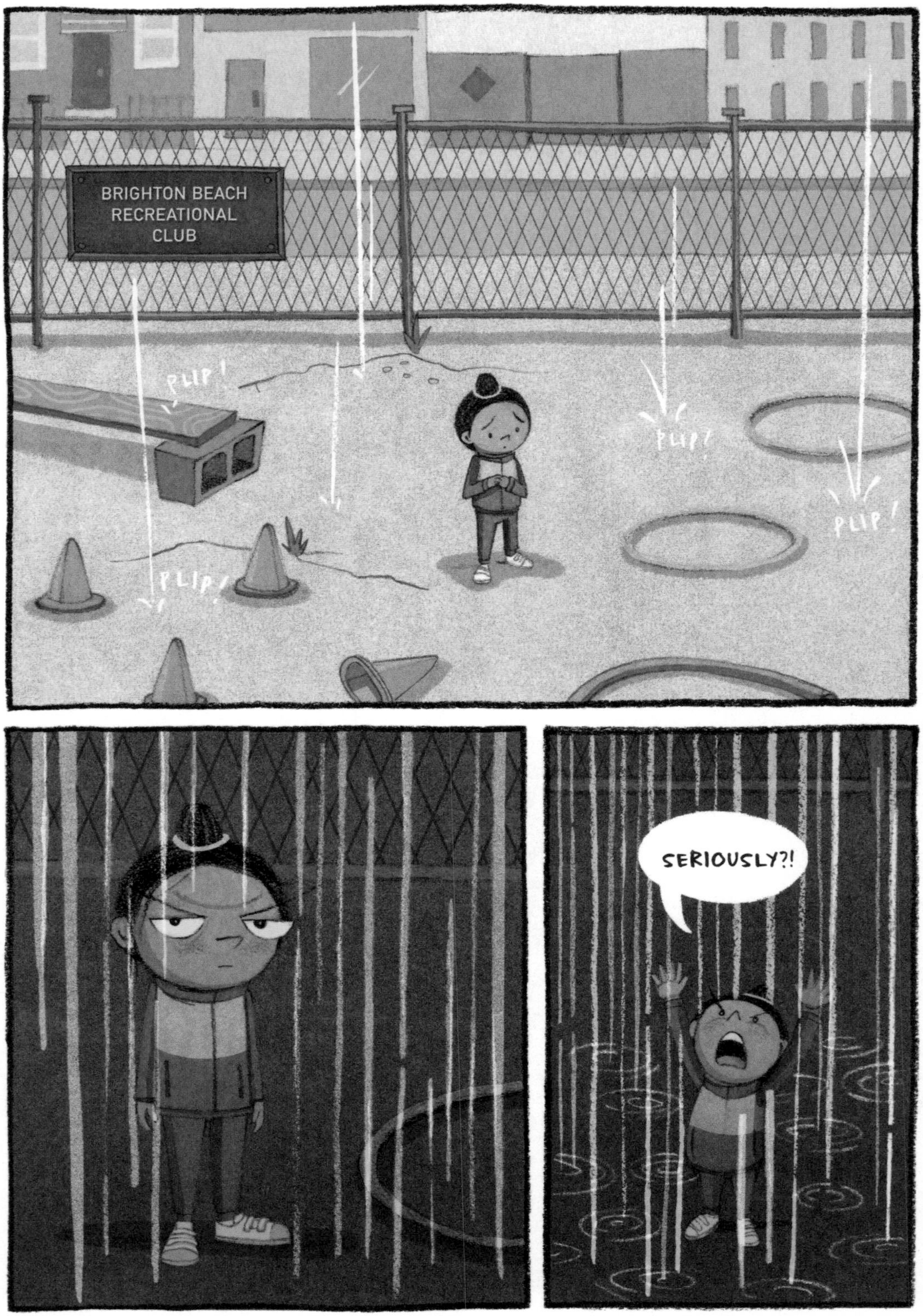
BRIGHTON BEACH
RECREATIONAL
CLUB
PLIP!
PLIP!
PLIP!
PLIP!
SERIOUSLY?!

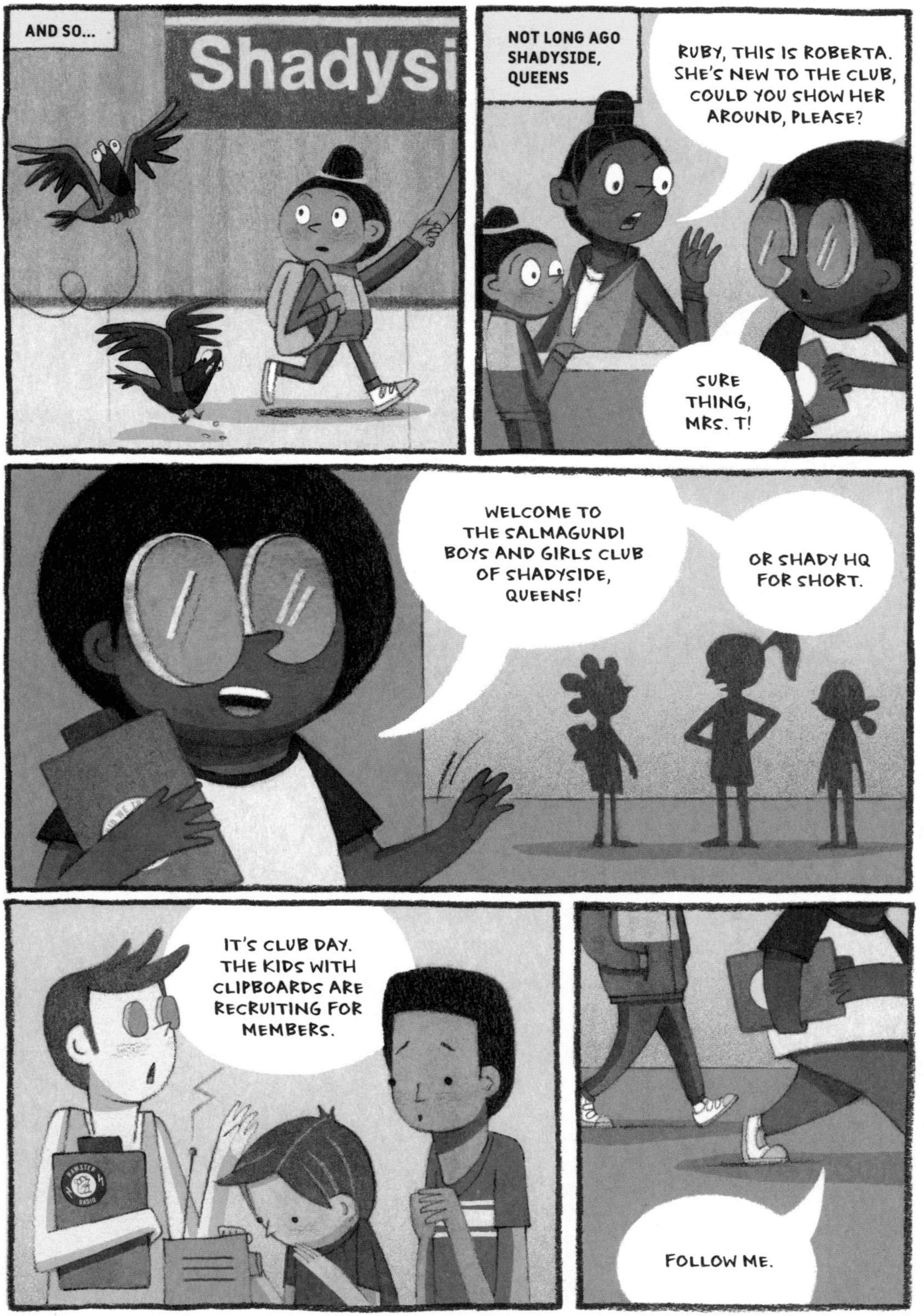
AND SO...
Shadysi
NOT LONG AGO SHADYSIDE, QUEENS
RUBY, THIS IS ROBERTA. SHE'S NEW TO THE CLUB, COULD YOU SHOW HER AROUND, PLEASE?
SURE THING, MRS. T!
WELCOME TO THE SALMAGUNDI BOYS AND GIRLS CLUB OF SHADYSIDE, QUEENS!
OR SHADY HQ FOR SHORT.
IT'S CLUB DAY. THE KIDS WITH CLIPBOARDS ARE RECRUITING FOR MEMBERS.
FOLLOW ME.

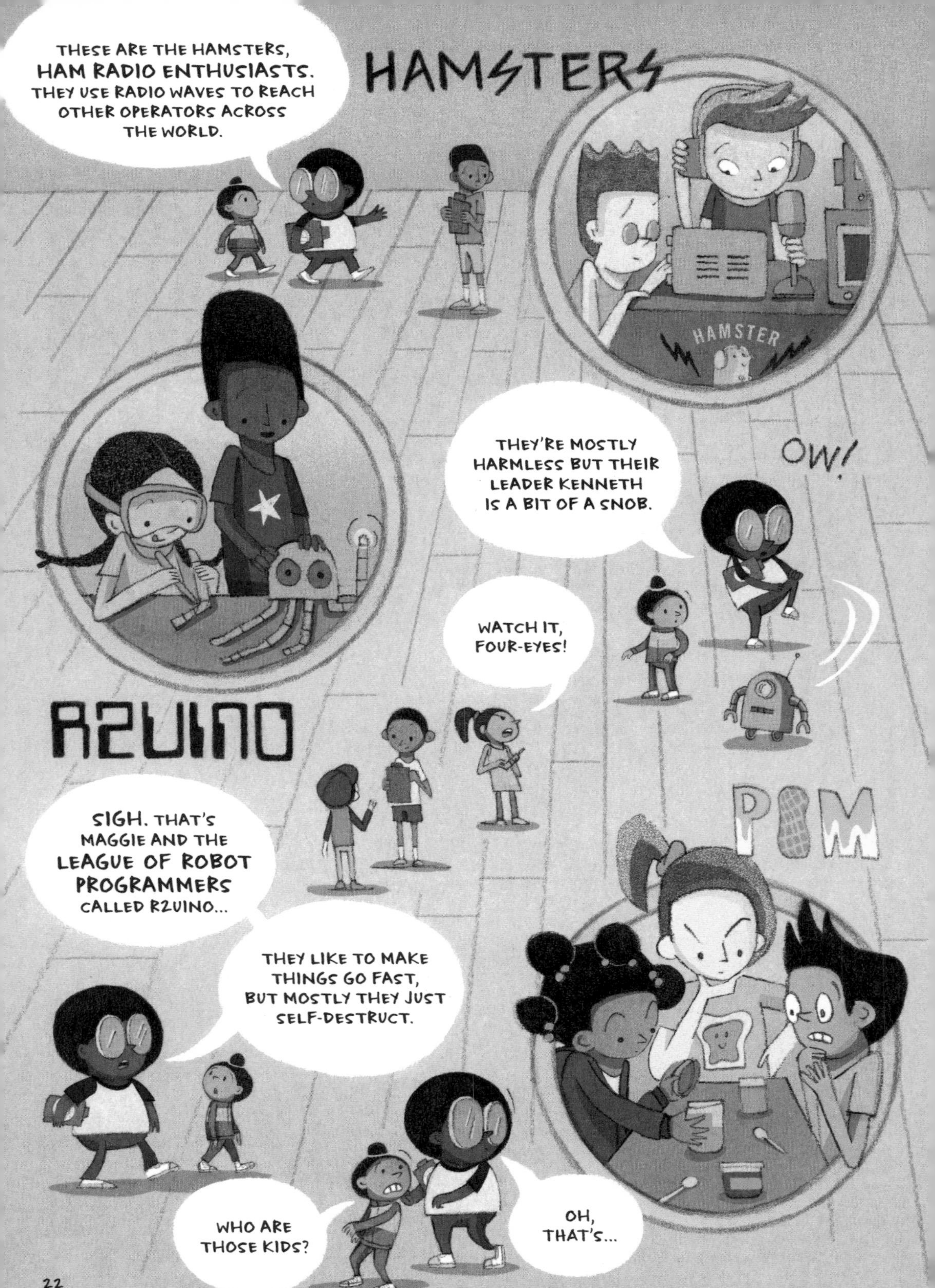
THESE ARE THE HAMSTERS, HAM RADIO ENTHUSIASTS. THEY USE RADIO WAVES TO REACH OTHER OPERATORS ACROSS THE WORLD.
HAMSTERS
HAMSTER
THEY'RE MOSTLY HARMLESS BUT THEIR LEADER KENNETH IS A BIT OF A SNOB.
OW!
WATCH IT, FOUR-EYES!
R2UINO
SIGH. THAT'S MAGGIE AND THE LEAGUE OF ROBOT PROGRAMMERS CALLED R2UINO...
THEY LIKE TO MAKE THINGS GO FAST, BUT MOSTLY THEY JUST SELF-DESTRUCT.
PBM
WHO ARE THOSE KIDS?
OH, THAT'S...

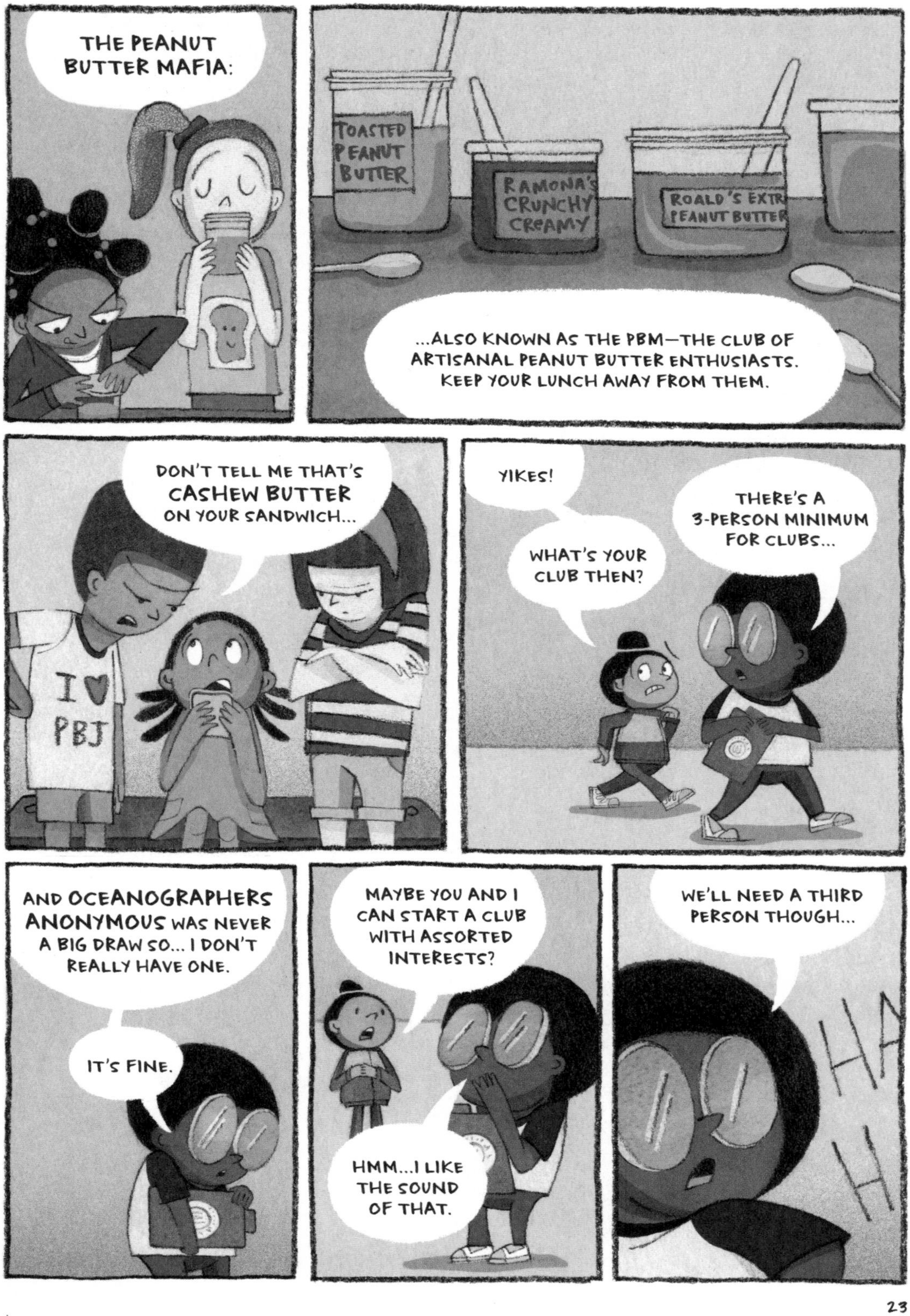
THE PEANUT BUTTER MAFIA:
TOASTED PEANUT BUTTER
RAMONA'S CRUNCHY CREAMY
ROALD'S EXTR PEANUT BUTTER
...ALSO KNOWN AS THE PBM—THE CLUB OF ARTISANAL PEANUT BUTTER ENTHUSIASTS. KEEP YOUR LUNCH AWAY FROM THEM.
DON'T TELL ME THAT'S CASHEW BUTTER ON YOUR SANDWICH...
I ♥ PBJ
YIKES!
WHAT'S YOUR CLUB THEN?
THERE'S A 3-PERSON MINIMUM FOR CLUBS...
AND OCEANOGRAPHERS ANONYMOUS WAS NEVER A BIG DRAW SO... I DON'T REALLY HAVE ONE.
IT'S FINE.
MAYBE YOU AND I CAN START A CLUB WITH ASSORTED INTERESTS?
HMM...I LIKE THE SOUND OF THAT.
WE'LL NEED A THIRD PERSON THOUGH...
HA
H

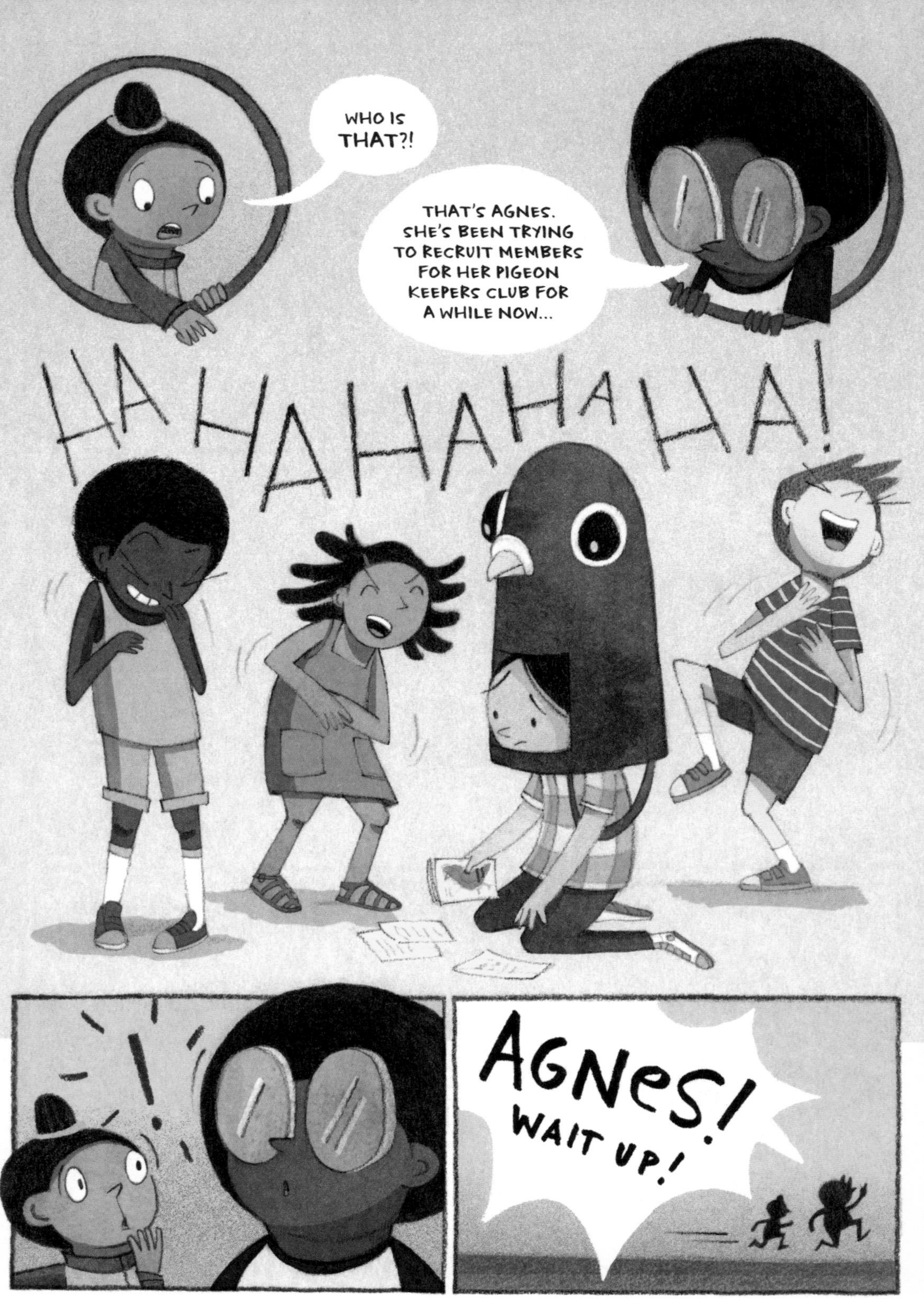
WHO IS THAT?!
THAT'S AGNES. SHE'S BEEN TRYING TO RECRUIT MEMBERS FOR HER PIGEON KEEPERS CLUB FOR A WHILE NOW...
HA HA HA HA HA HA!
!
AGNES! WAIT UP!

CHAPTER 3
THE DIVING DIVAS

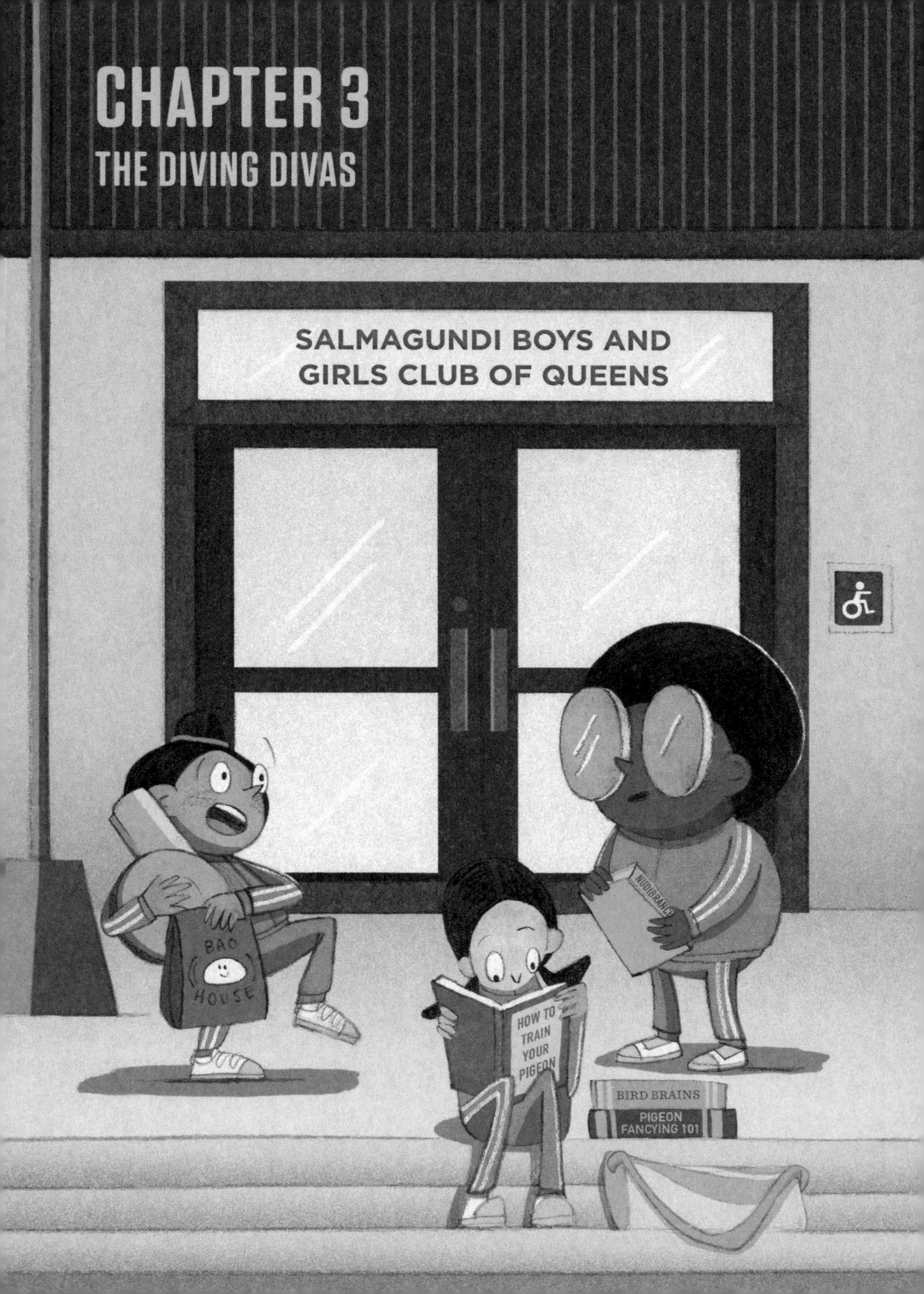
SALMAGUNDI BOYS AND GIRLS CLUB OF QUEENS
BAO HOUSE
HOW TO TRAIN YOUR PIGEON
BIRD BRAINS
PIGEON FANCYING 101

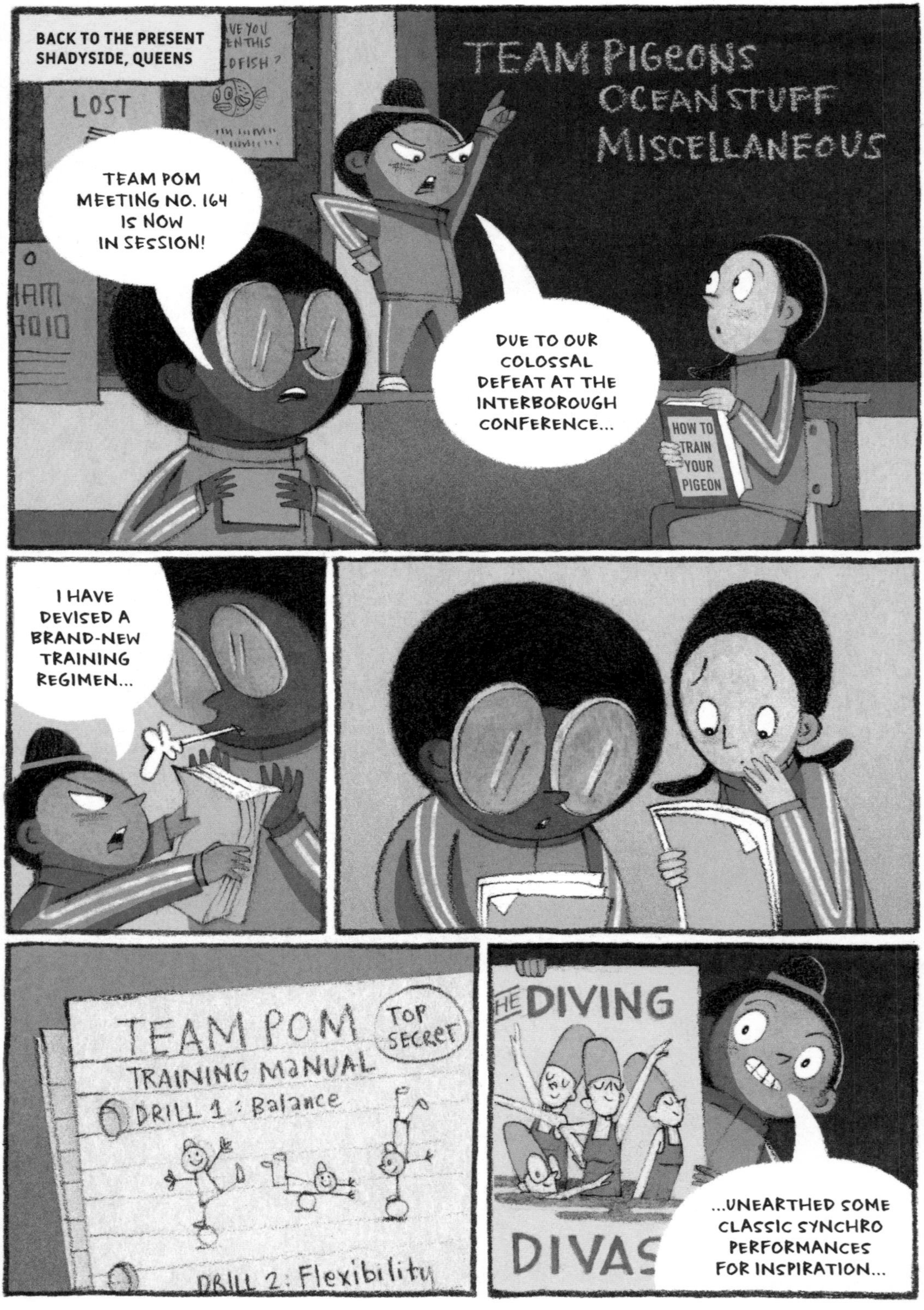
BACK TO THE PRESENT
SHADYSIDE, QUEENS
LOST
TEAM PIGEONS
OCEAN STUFF
MISCELLANEOUS
TEAM POM MEETING NO. 164 IS NOW IN SESSION!
DUE TO OUR COLOSSAL DEFEAT AT THE INTERBOROUGH CONFERENCE...
HOW TO TRAIN YOUR PIGEON
I HAVE DEVISED A BRAND-NEW TRAINING REGIMEN...
TEAM POM
Top Secret
TRAINING MANUAL
DRILL 1: Balance
DRILL 2: Flexibility
DIVING
DIVAS
...UNEARTHED SOME CLASSIC SYNCHRO PERFORMANCES FOR INSPIRATION...

...AND BROUGHT A SELECTION OF MY UNCLE'S SPECIAL BAOS FOR IMPROVED MOTIVATION.

BAO HOUSE

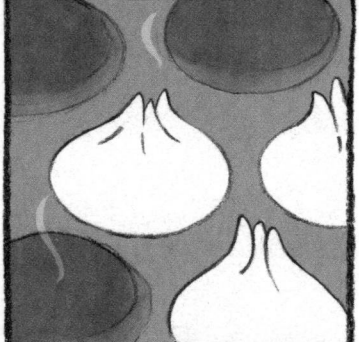

*BAO OR BAOZI ARE SOFT BUNS (STEAMED OR BAKED) WITH DELICIOUS FILLINGS THAT ARE SWEET OR SAVORY

I'LL GET THE PROJECTOR READY!

I'LL GET THE SCREEN!

HAVE YOU SEEN THIS GOLDFISH?

LOST
PEANUT BUTTER

THE DIVING DIVAS

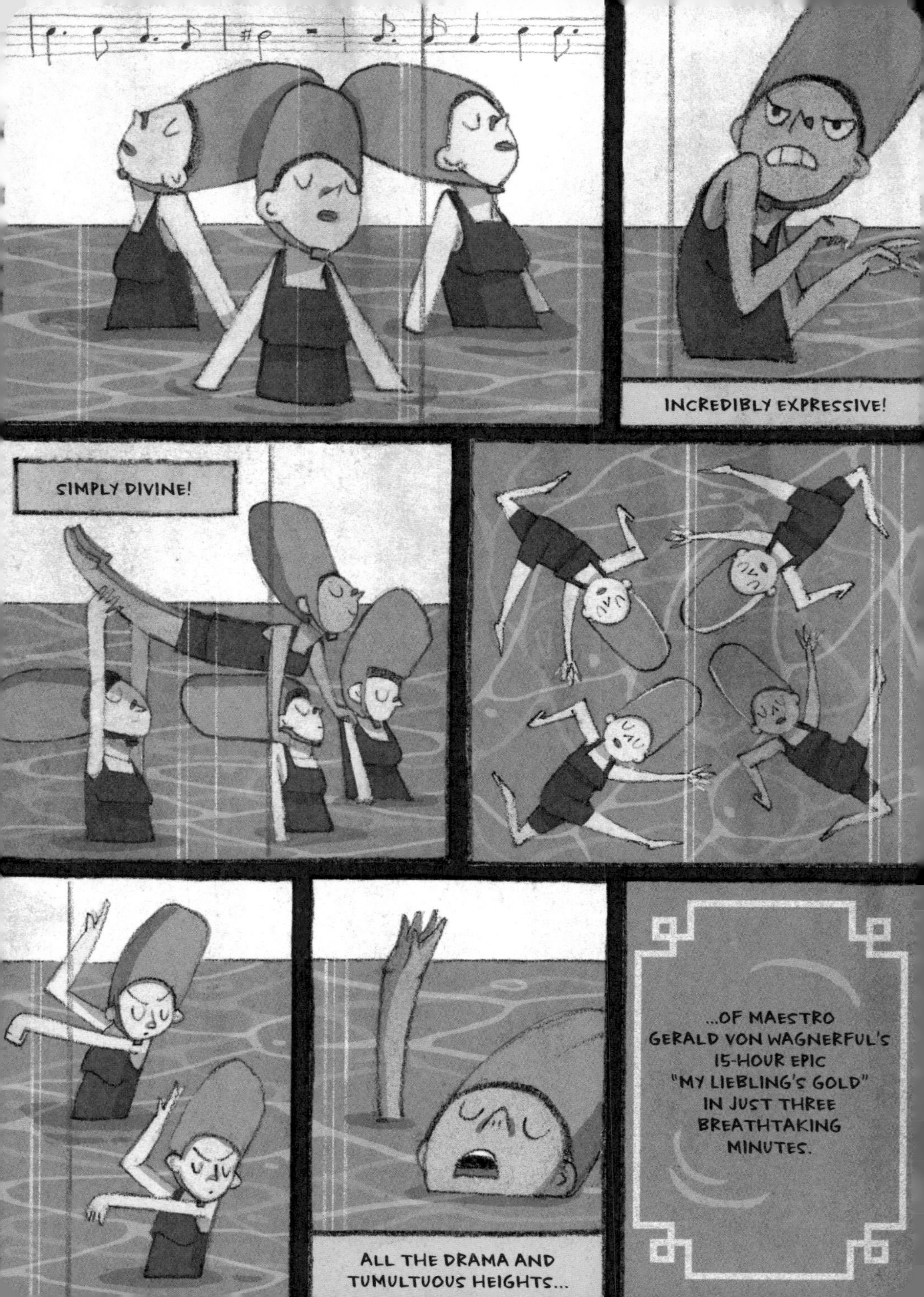
INCREDIBLY EXPRESSIVE!
SIMPLY DIVINE!
ALL THE DRAMA AND TUMULTUOUS HEIGHTS...
...OF MAESTRO GERALD VON WAGNERFUL'S 15-HOUR EPIC "MY LIEBLING'S GOLD" IN JUST THREE BREATHTAKING MINUTES.

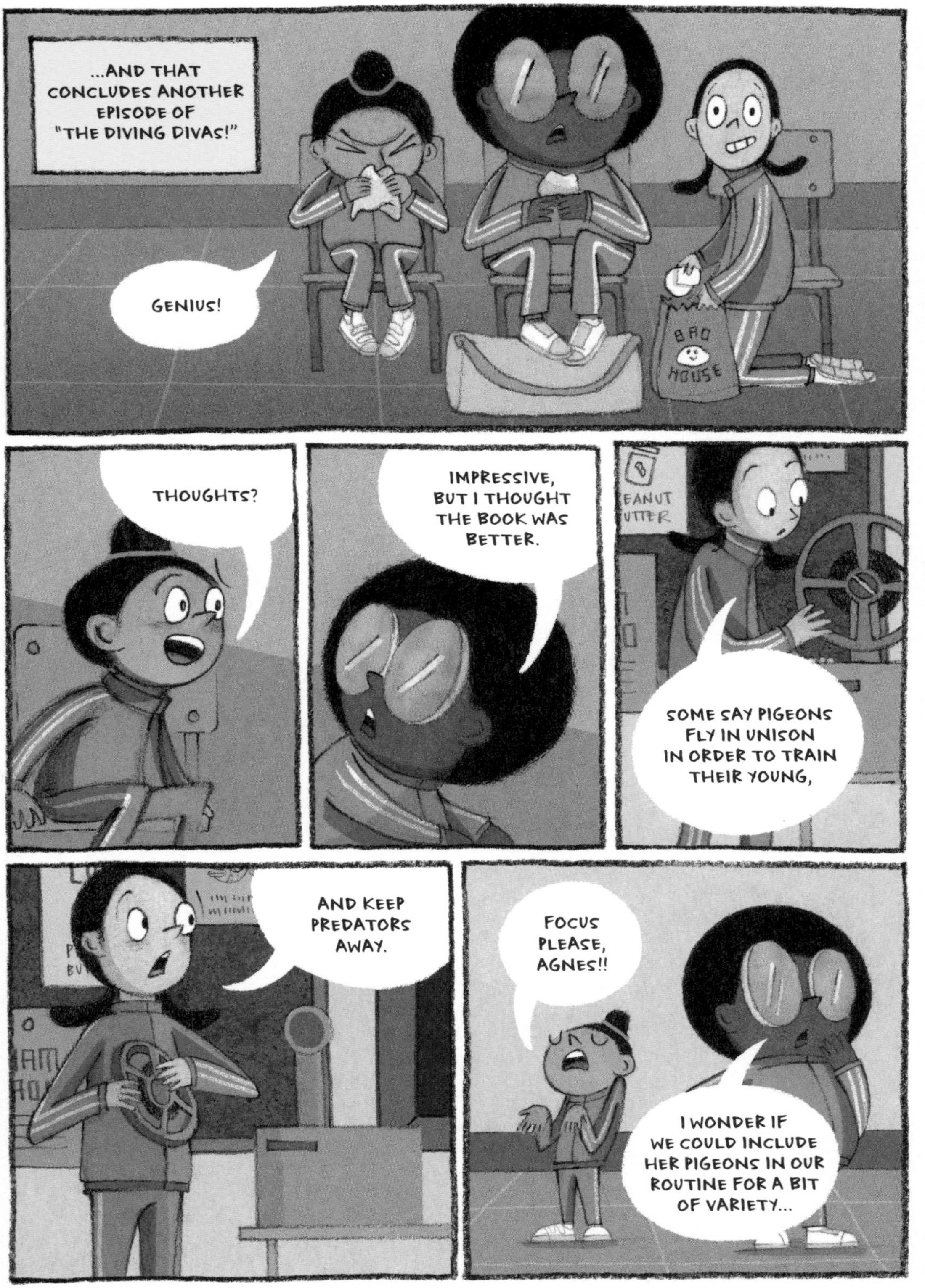
...AND THAT CONCLUDES ANOTHER EPISODE OF "THE DIVING DIVAS!"
GENIUS!
BAO HOUSE
THOUGHTS?
IMPRESSIVE, BUT I THOUGHT THE BOOK WAS BETTER.
SOME SAY PIGEONS FLY IN UNISON IN ORDER TO TRAIN THEIR YOUNG,
AND KEEP PREDATORS AWAY.
FOCUS PLEASE, AGNES!!
I WONDER IF WE COULD INCLUDE HER PIGEONS IN OUR ROUTINE FOR A BIT OF VARIETY...

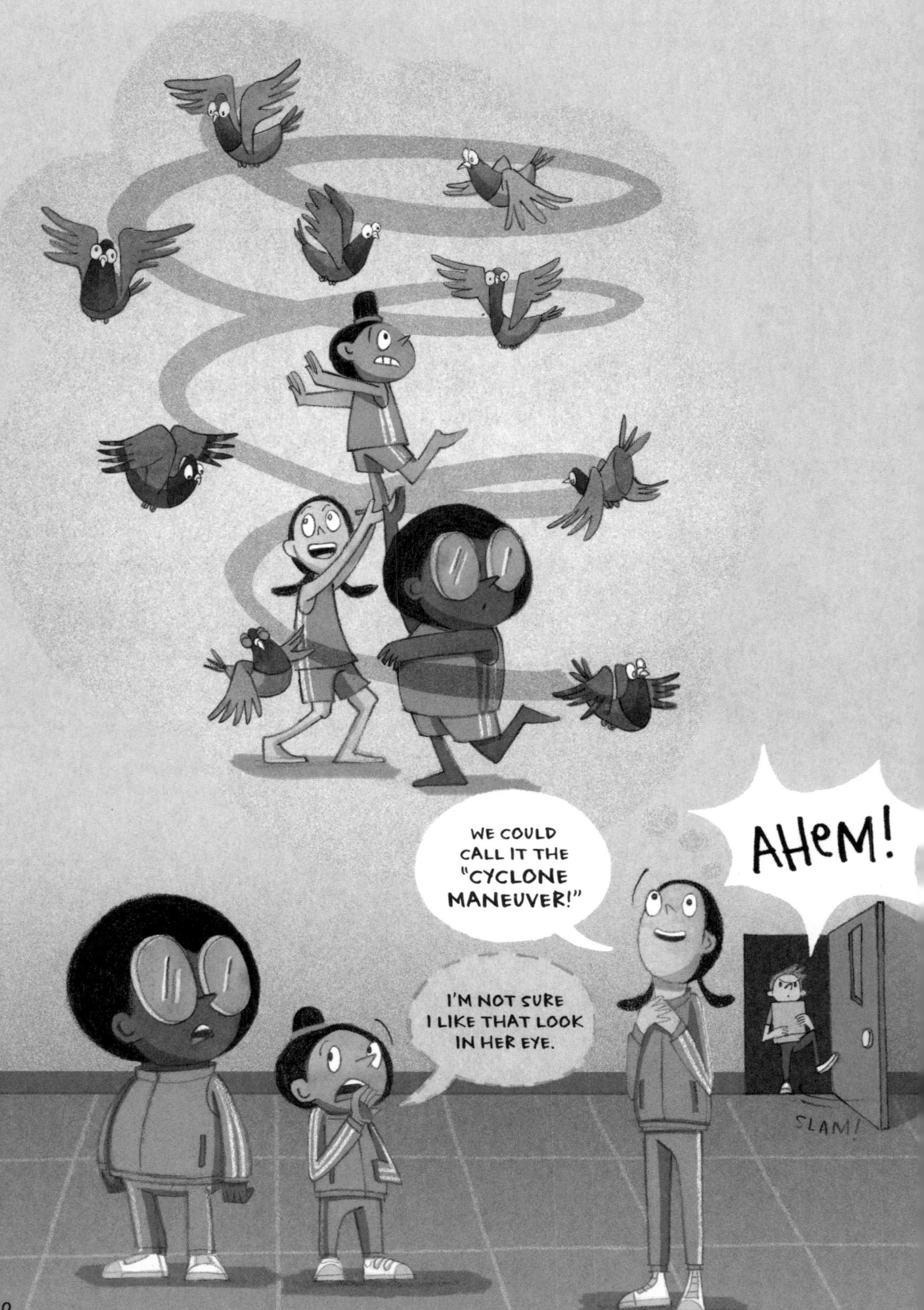
WE COULD CALL IT THE "CYCLONE MANEUVER!"
AHeM!
I'M NOT SURE I LIKE THAT LOOK IN HER EYE.
SLAM!

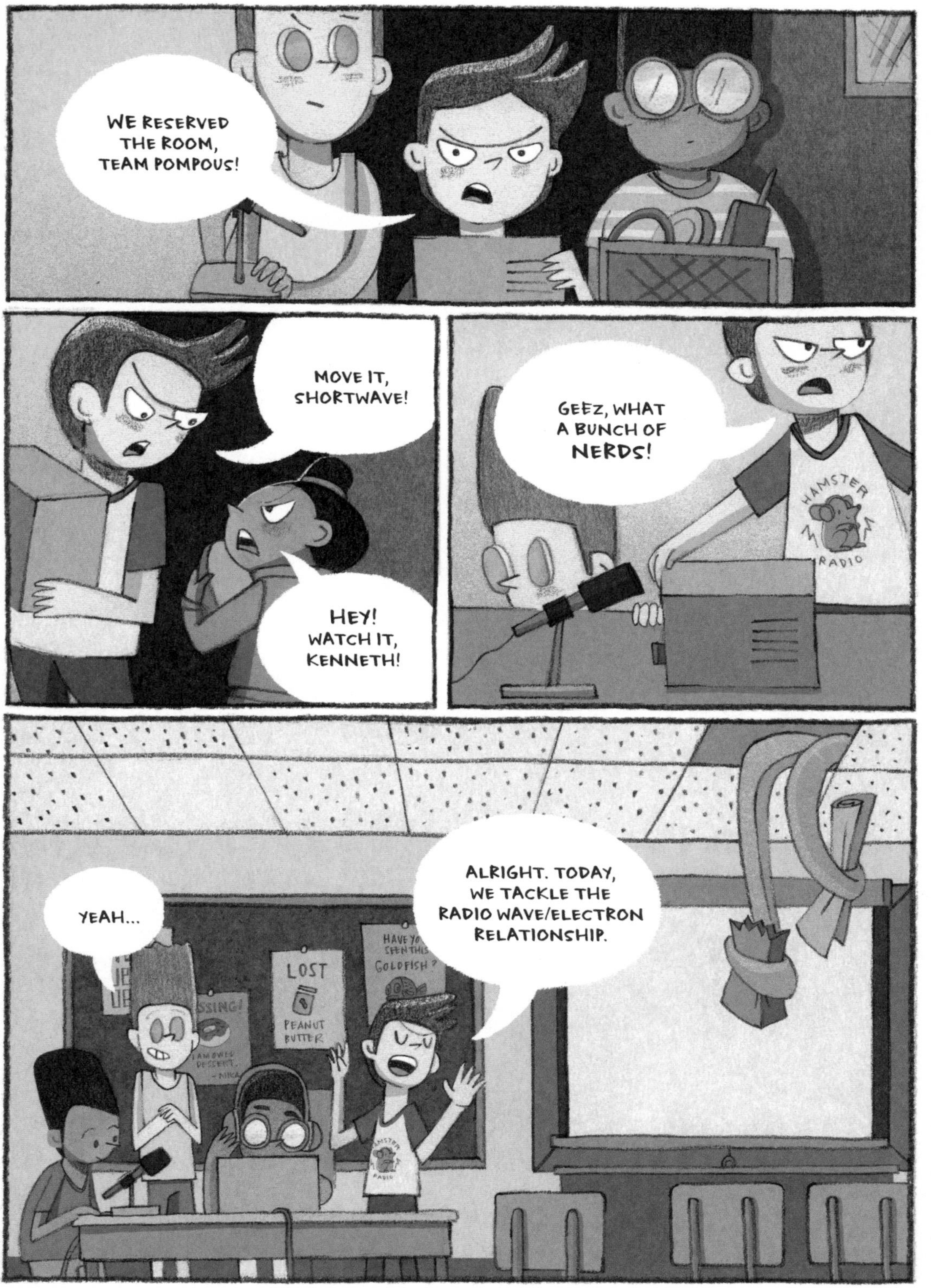
WE RESERVED THE ROOM, TEAM POMPOUS!
MOVE IT, SHORTWAVE!
HEY! WATCH IT, KENNETH!
GEEZ, WHAT A BUNCH OF NERDS!
HAMSTER RADIO
YEAH...
ALRIGHT. TODAY, WE TACKLE THE RADIO WAVE/ELECTRON RELATIONSHIP.
LOST
PEANUT BUTTER

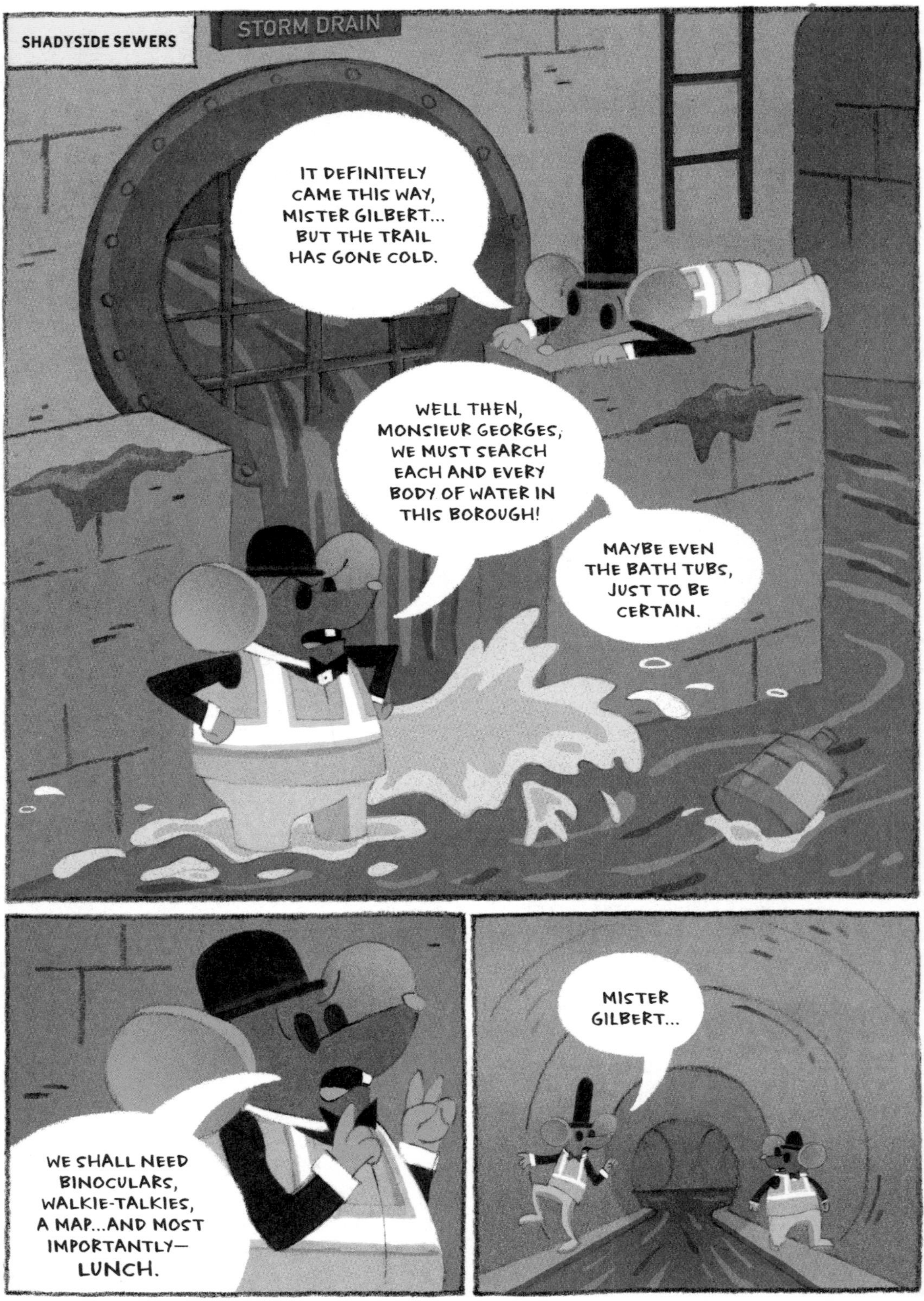
SHADYSIDE SEWERS
STORM DRAIN
IT DEFINITELY CAME THIS WAY, MISTER GILBERT... BUT THE TRAIL HAS GONE COLD.
WELL THEN, MONSIEUR GEORGES, WE MUST SEARCH EACH AND EVERY BODY OF WATER IN THIS BOROUGH!
MAYBE EVEN THE BATH TUBS, JUST TO BE CERTAIN.
WE SHALL NEED BINOCULARS, WALKIE-TALKIES, A MAP...AND MOST IMPORTANTLY—LUNCH.
MISTER GILBERT...

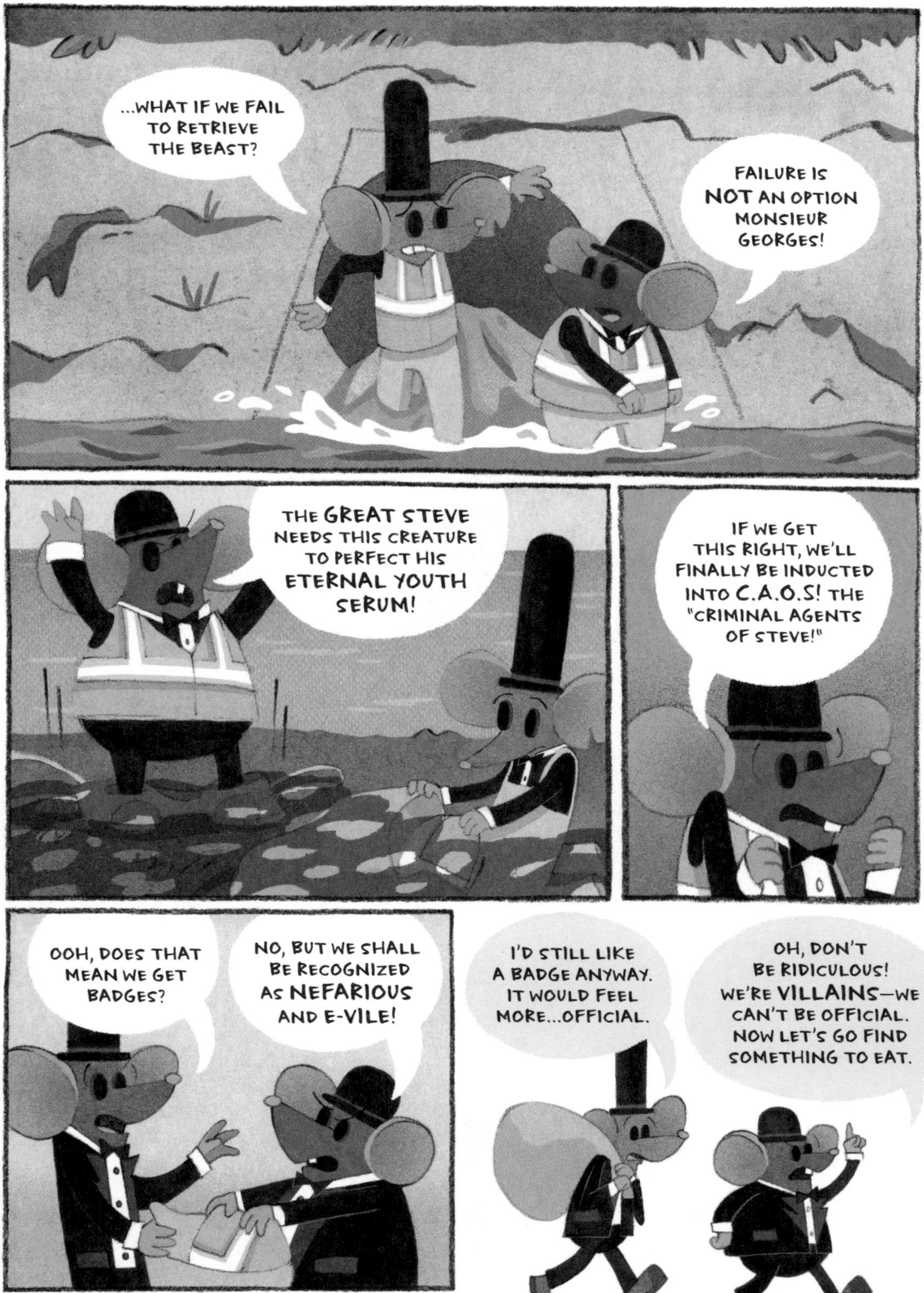
...WHAT IF WE FAIL TO RETRIEVE THE BEAST?
FAILURE IS NOT AN OPTION MONSIEUR GEORGES!
THE GREAT STEVE NEEDS THIS CREATURE TO PERFECT HIS ETERNAL YOUTH SERUM!
IF WE GET THIS RIGHT, WE'LL FINALLY BE INDUCTED INTO C.A.O.S! THE "CRIMINAL AGENTS OF STEVE!"
OOH, DOES THAT MEAN WE GET BADGES?
NO, BUT WE SHALL BE RECOGNIZED AS NEFARIOUS AND E-VILE!
I'D STILL LIKE A BADGE ANYWAY. IT WOULD FEEL MORE...OFFICIAL.
OH, DON'T BE RIDICULOUS! WE'RE VILLAINS—WE CAN'T BE OFFICIAL. NOW LET'S GO FIND SOMETHING TO EAT.

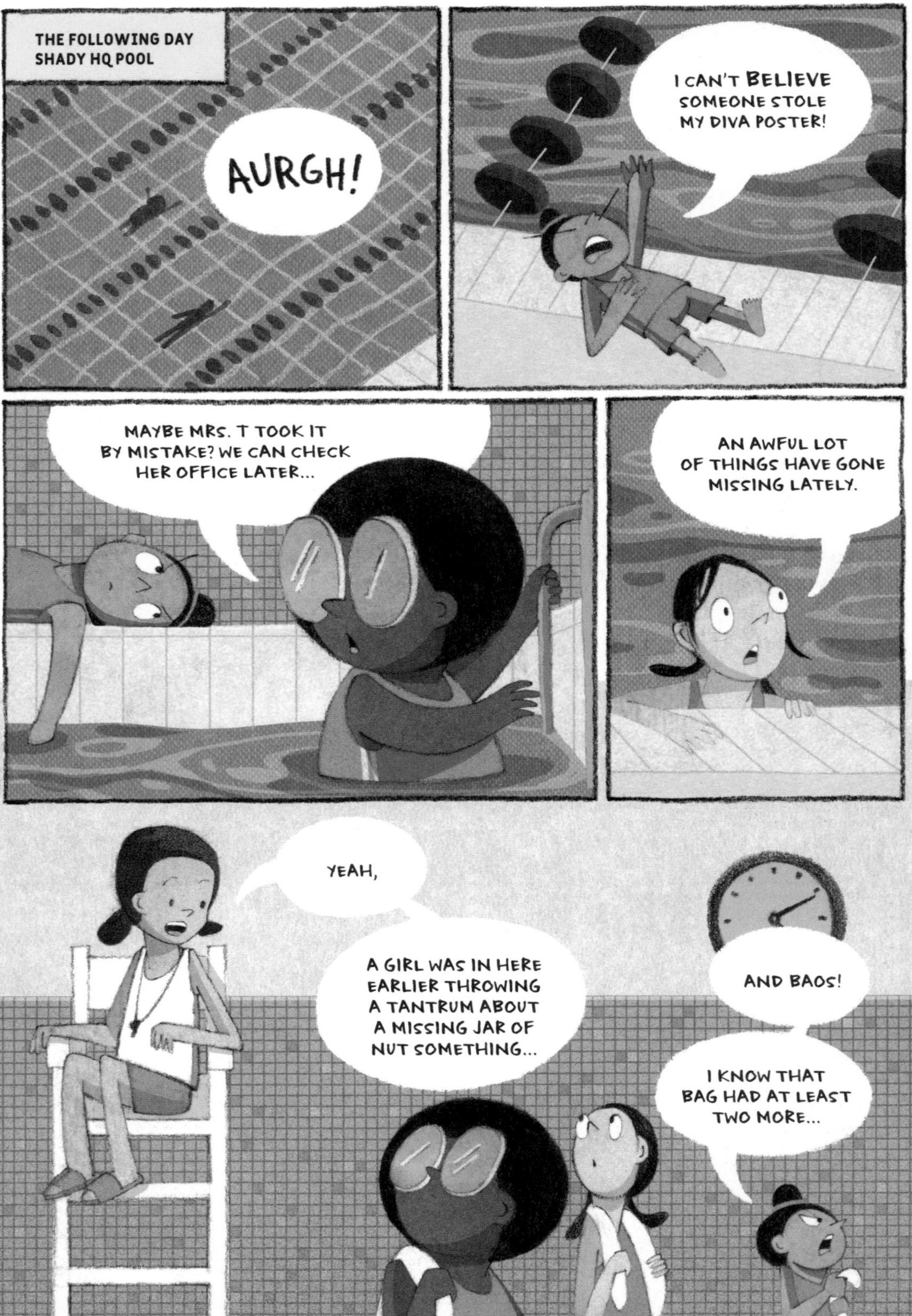
THE FOLLOWING DAY
SHADY HQ POOL
AURGH!
I CAN'T BELIEVE SOMEONE STOLE MY DIVA POSTER!
MAYBE MRS. T TOOK IT BY MISTAKE? WE CAN CHECK HER OFFICE LATER...
AN AWFUL LOT OF THINGS HAVE GONE MISSING LATELY.
YEAH,
A GIRL WAS IN HERE EARLIER THROWING A TANTRUM ABOUT A MISSING JAR OF NUT SOMETHING...
AND BAOS!
I KNOW THAT BAG HAD AT LEAST TWO MORE...

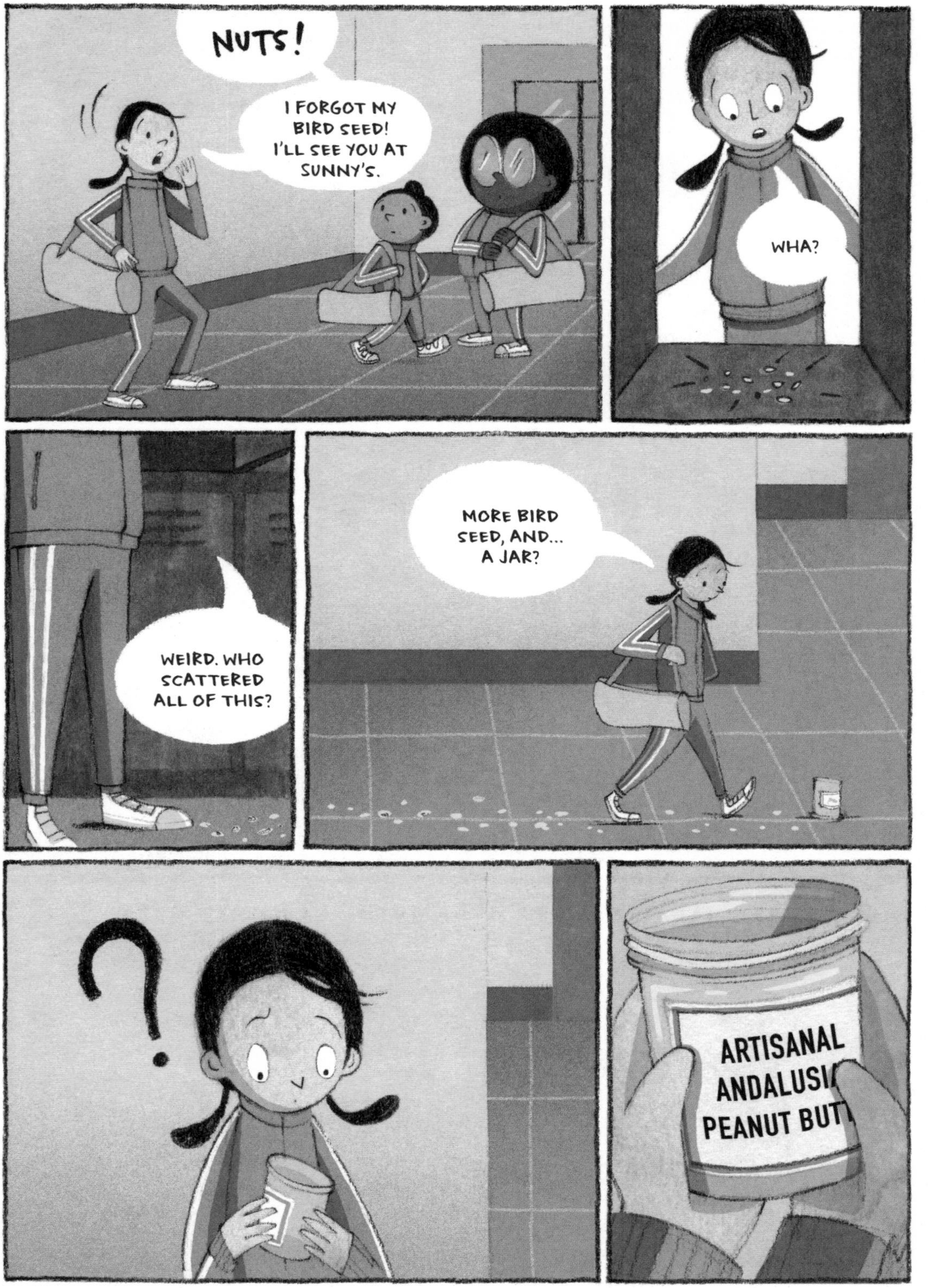
NUTS!
I FORGOT MY BIRD SEED! I'LL SEE YOU AT SUNNY'S.
WHA?
WEIRD. WHO SCATTERED ALL OF THIS?
MORE BIRD SEED, AND... A JAR?
?
ARTISANAL ANDALUSIA PEANUT BUTT

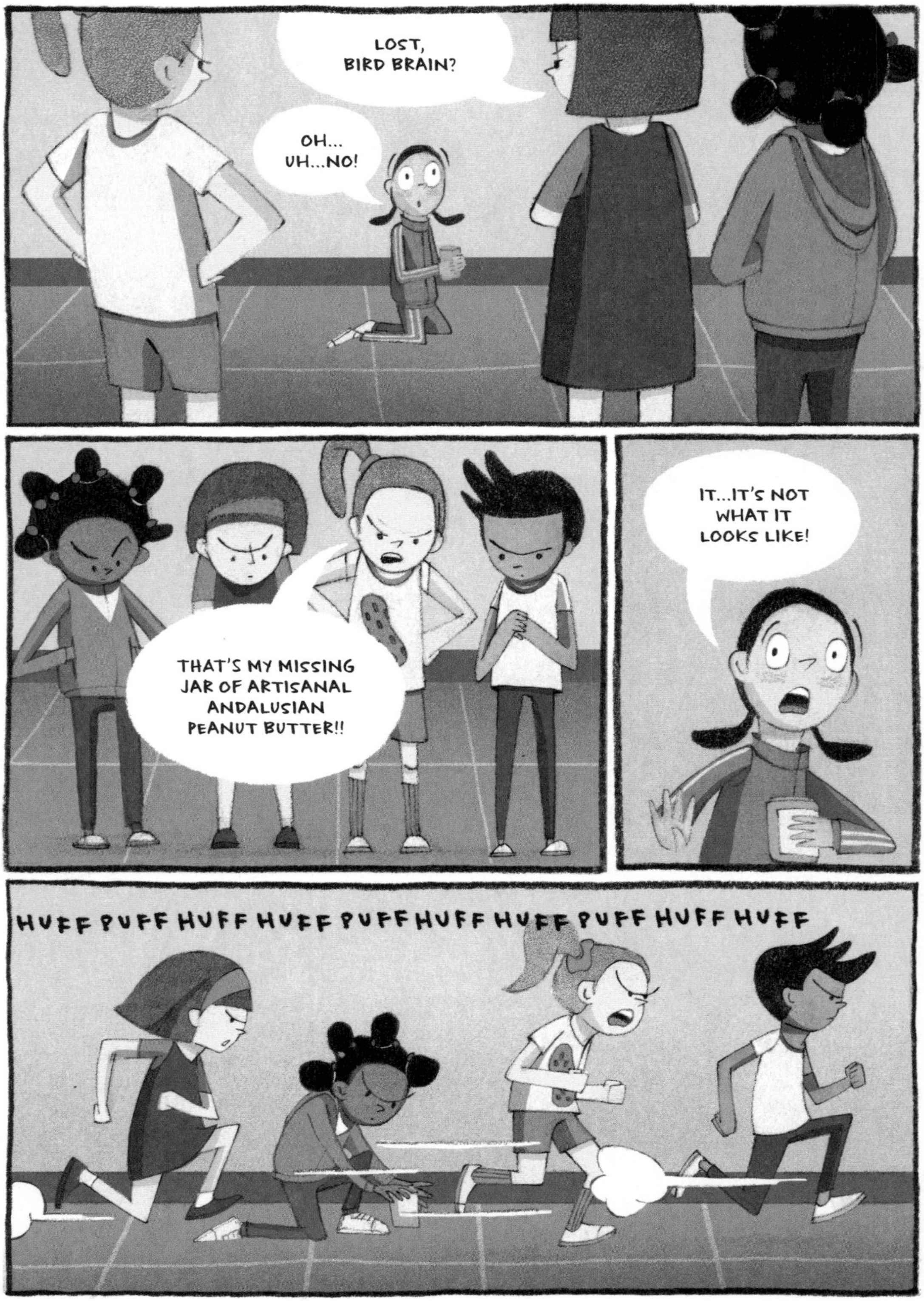
LOST, BIRD BRAIN?
OH... UH...NO!
THAT'S MY MISSING JAR OF ARTISANAL ANDALUSIAN PEANUT BUTTER!!
IT...IT'S NOT WHAT IT LOOKS LIKE!
HUFF PUFF HUFF HUFF PUFF HUFF HUFF PUFF HUFF HUFF

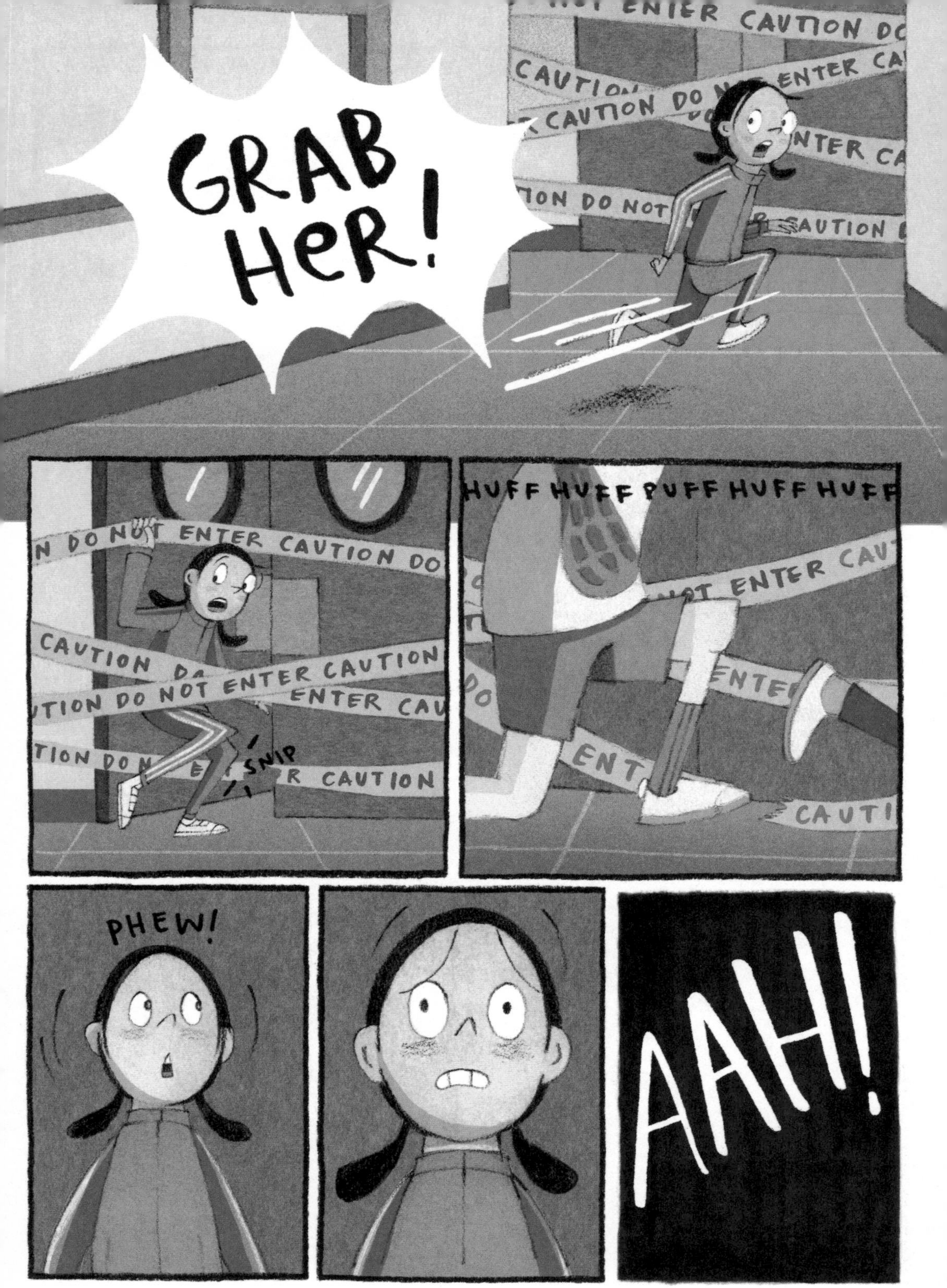
GRAB HER!
SNIP
HUFF HUFF PUFF HUFF HUFF
PHEW!
AAH!

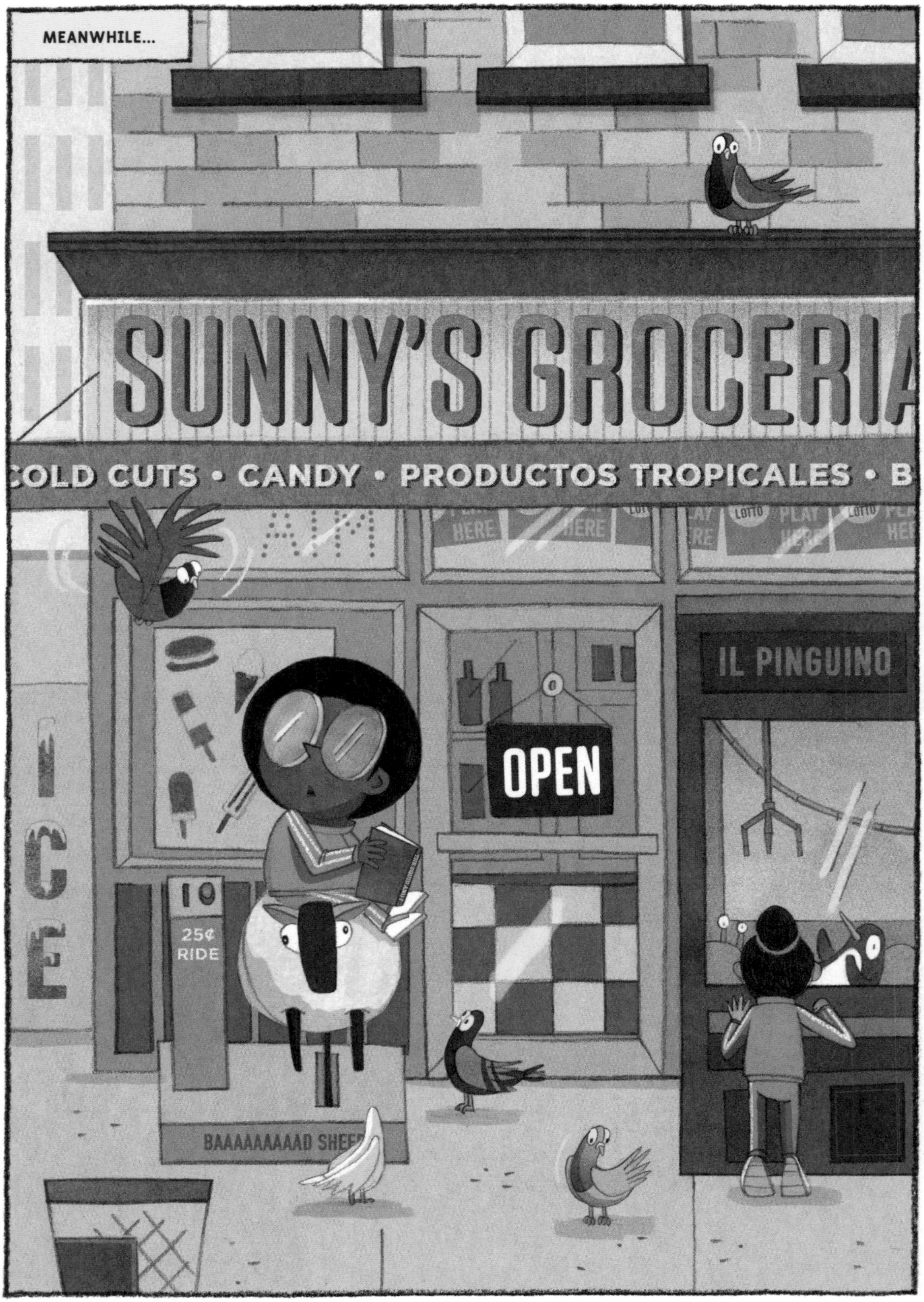
MEANWHILE...
SUNNY'S GROCERIA
COLD CUTS • CANDY • PRODUCTOS TROPICALES • B
LOTTO
PLAY HERE
IL PINGUINO
OPEN
ICE
25¢
RIDE
BAAAAAAAAAD SHEEP

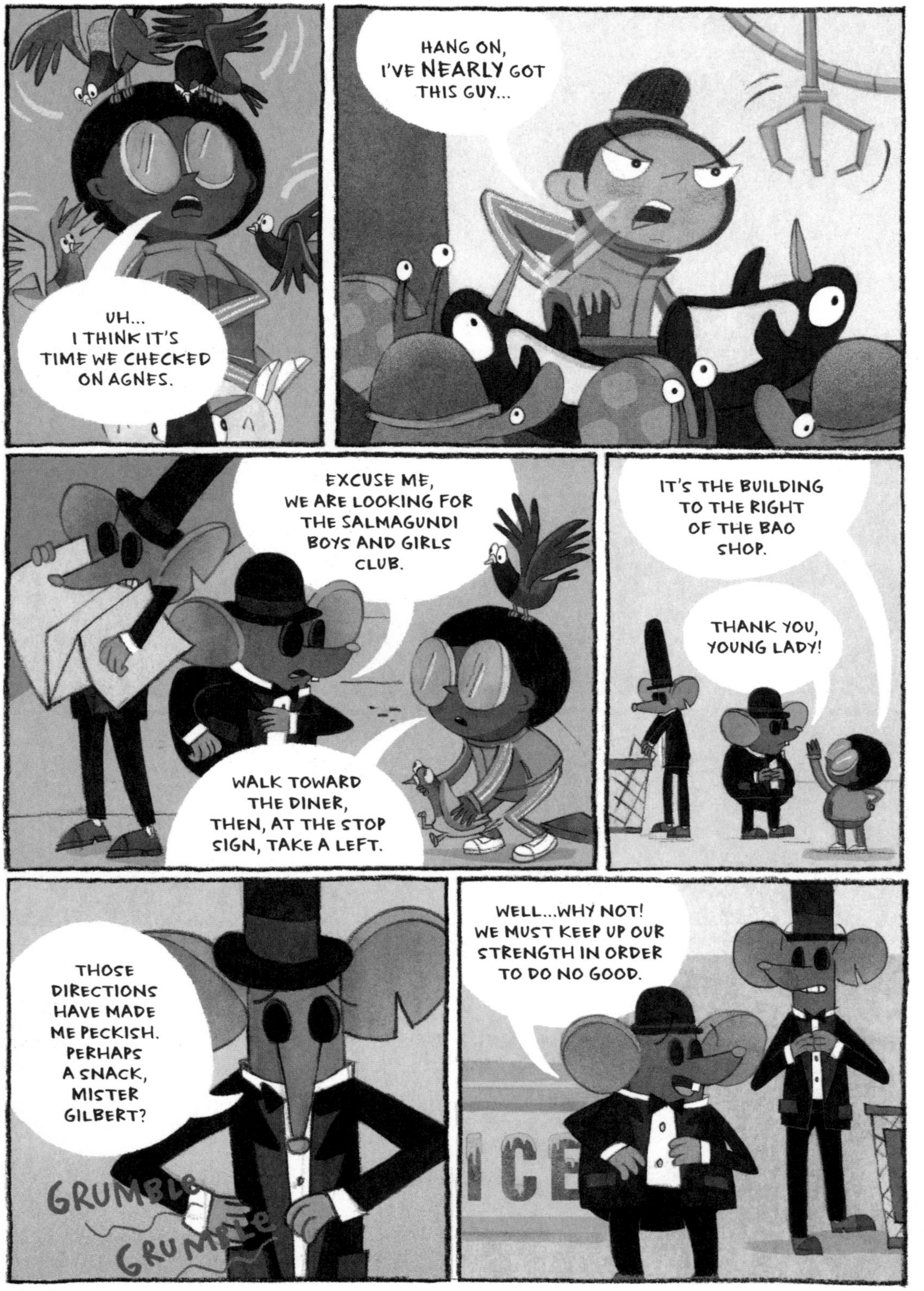
UH... I THINK IT'S TIME WE CHECKED ON AGNES.
HANG ON, I'VE NEARLY GOT THIS GUY...
EXCUSE ME, WE ARE LOOKING FOR THE SALMAGUNDI BOYS AND GIRLS CLUB.
WALK TOWARD THE DINER, THEN, AT THE STOP SIGN, TAKE A LEFT.
IT'S THE BUILDING TO THE RIGHT OF THE BAO SHOP.
THANK YOU, YOUNG LADY!
THOSE DIRECTIONS HAVE MADE ME PECKISH. PERHAPS A SNACK, MISTER GILBERT?
GRUMBLE
GRUMBLE
WELL...WHY NOT! WE MUST KEEP UP OUR STRENGTH IN ORDER TO DO NO GOOD.
ICE

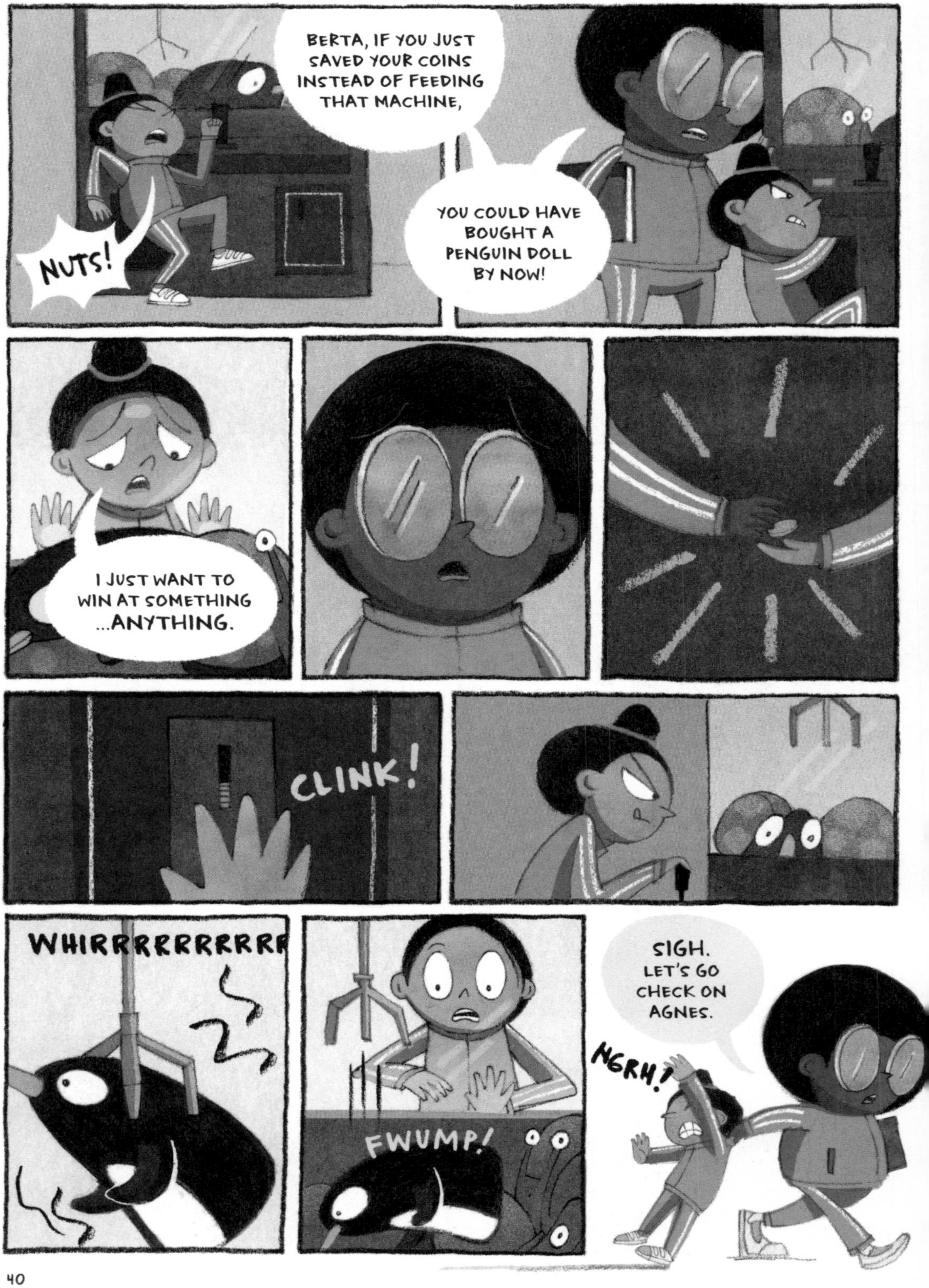
BERTA, IF YOU JUST SAVED YOUR COINS INSTEAD OF FEEDING THAT MACHINE,
NUTS!
YOU COULD HAVE BOUGHT A PENGUIN DOLL BY NOW!
I JUST WANT TO WIN AT SOMETHING ...ANYTHING.
CLINK!
WHIRRRRRRRRRR
FWUMP!
SIGH. LET'S GO CHECK ON AGNES.
NGRH!

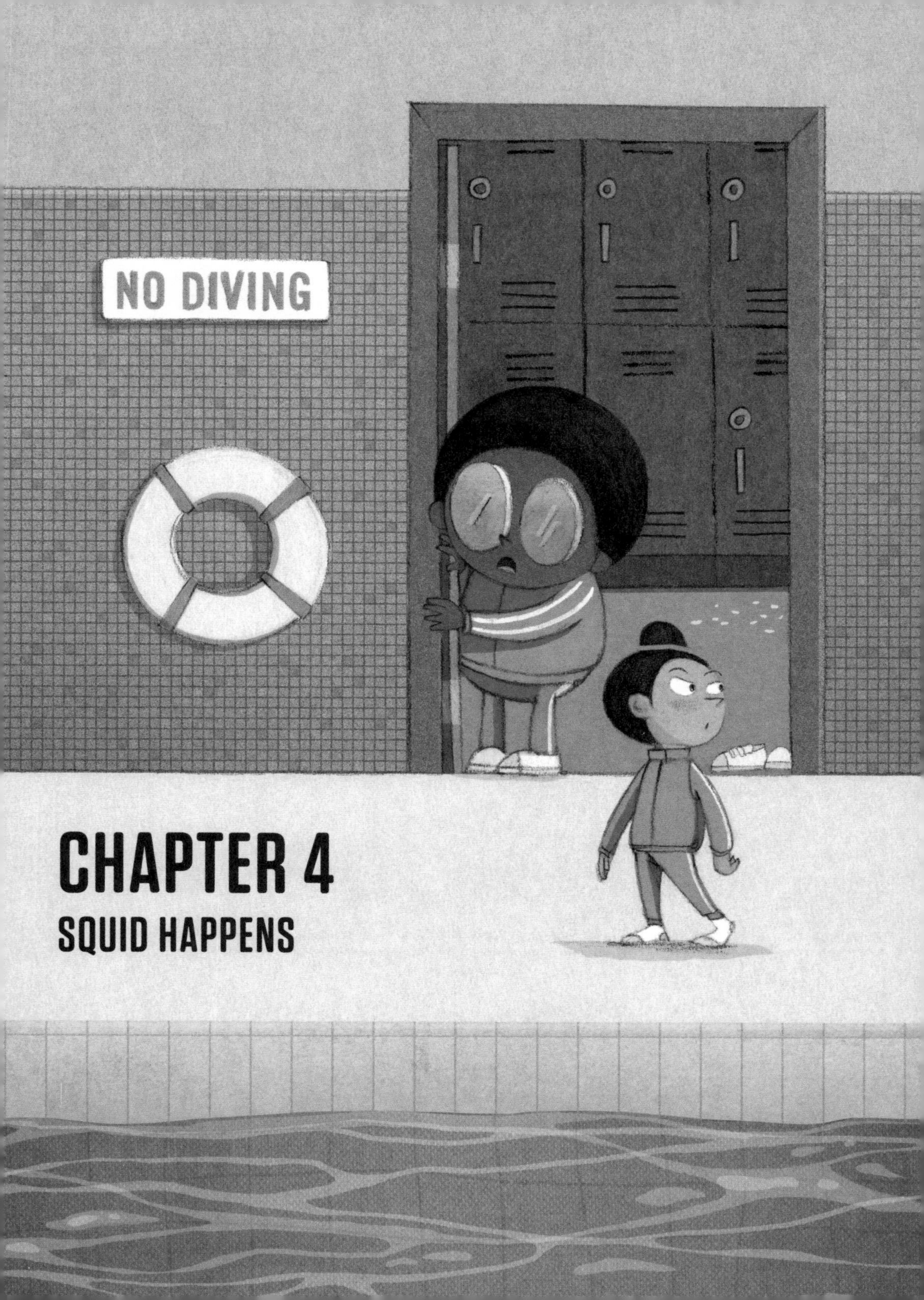
NO DIVING

CHAPTER 4

SQUID HAPPENS

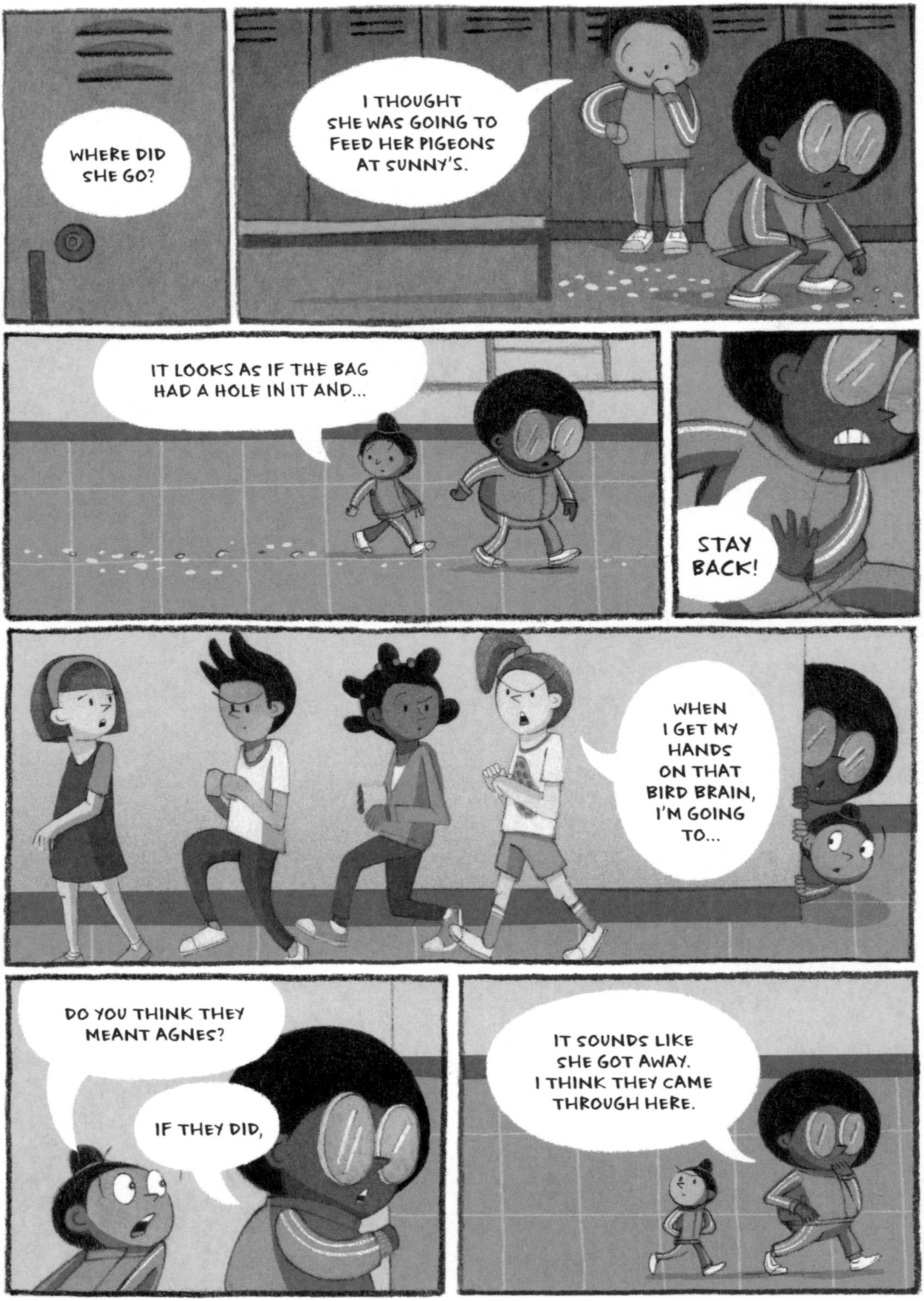
WHERE DID SHE GO?
I THOUGHT SHE WAS GOING TO FEED HER PIGEONS AT SUNNY'S.
IT LOOKS AS IF THE BAG HAD A HOLE IN IT AND...
STAY BACK!
WHEN I GET MY HANDS ON THAT BIRD BRAIN, I'M GOING TO...
DO YOU THINK THEY MEANT AGNES?
IF THEY DID,
IT SOUNDS LIKE SHE GOT AWAY. I THINK THEY CAME THROUGH HERE.

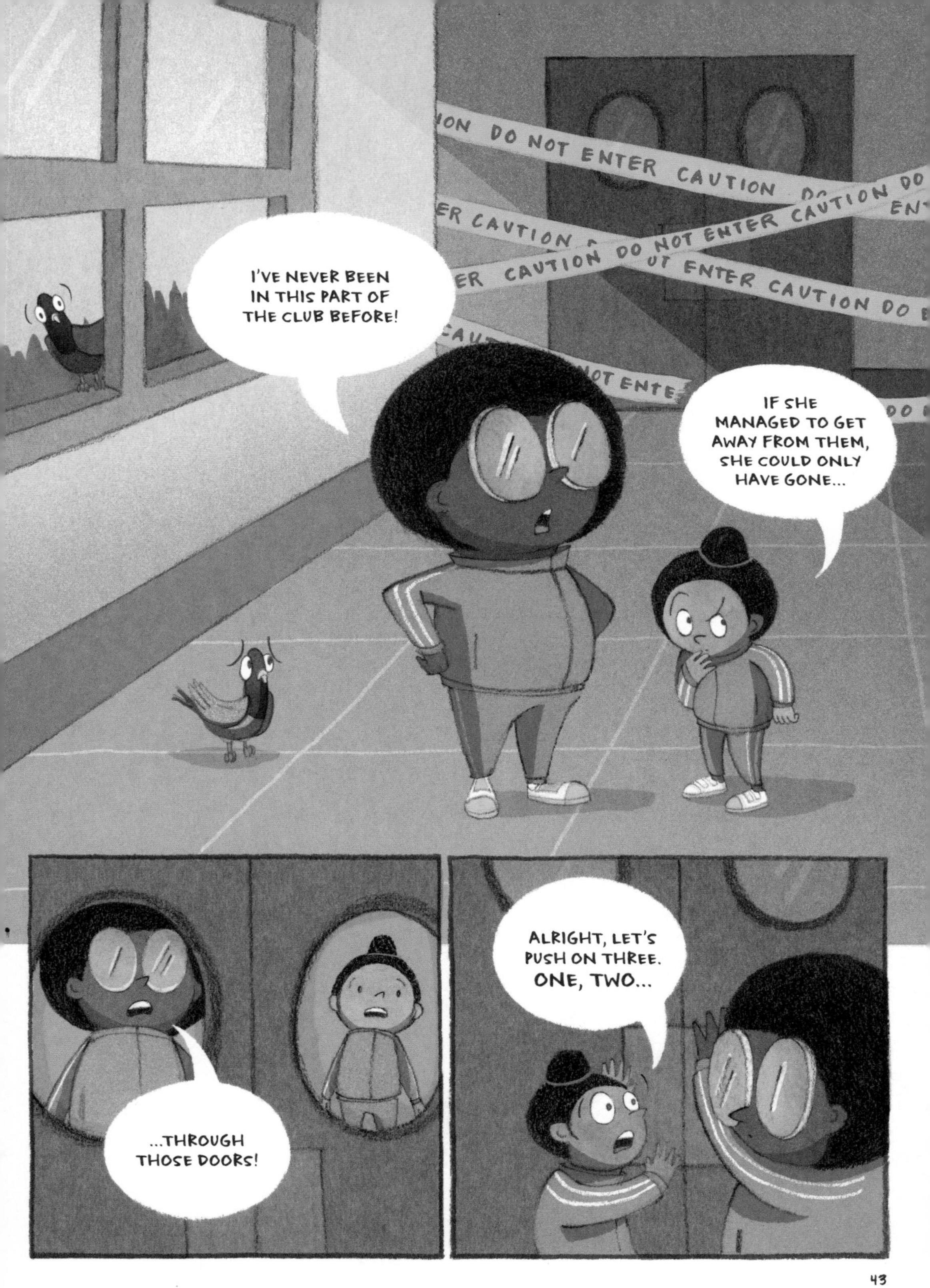
DO NOT ENTER CAUTION
I'VE NEVER BEEN IN THIS PART OF THE CLUB BEFORE!
IF SHE MANAGED TO GET AWAY FROM THEM, SHE COULD ONLY HAVE GONE...
...THROUGH THOSE DOORS!
ALRIGHT, LET'S PUSH ON THREE. ONE, TWO...

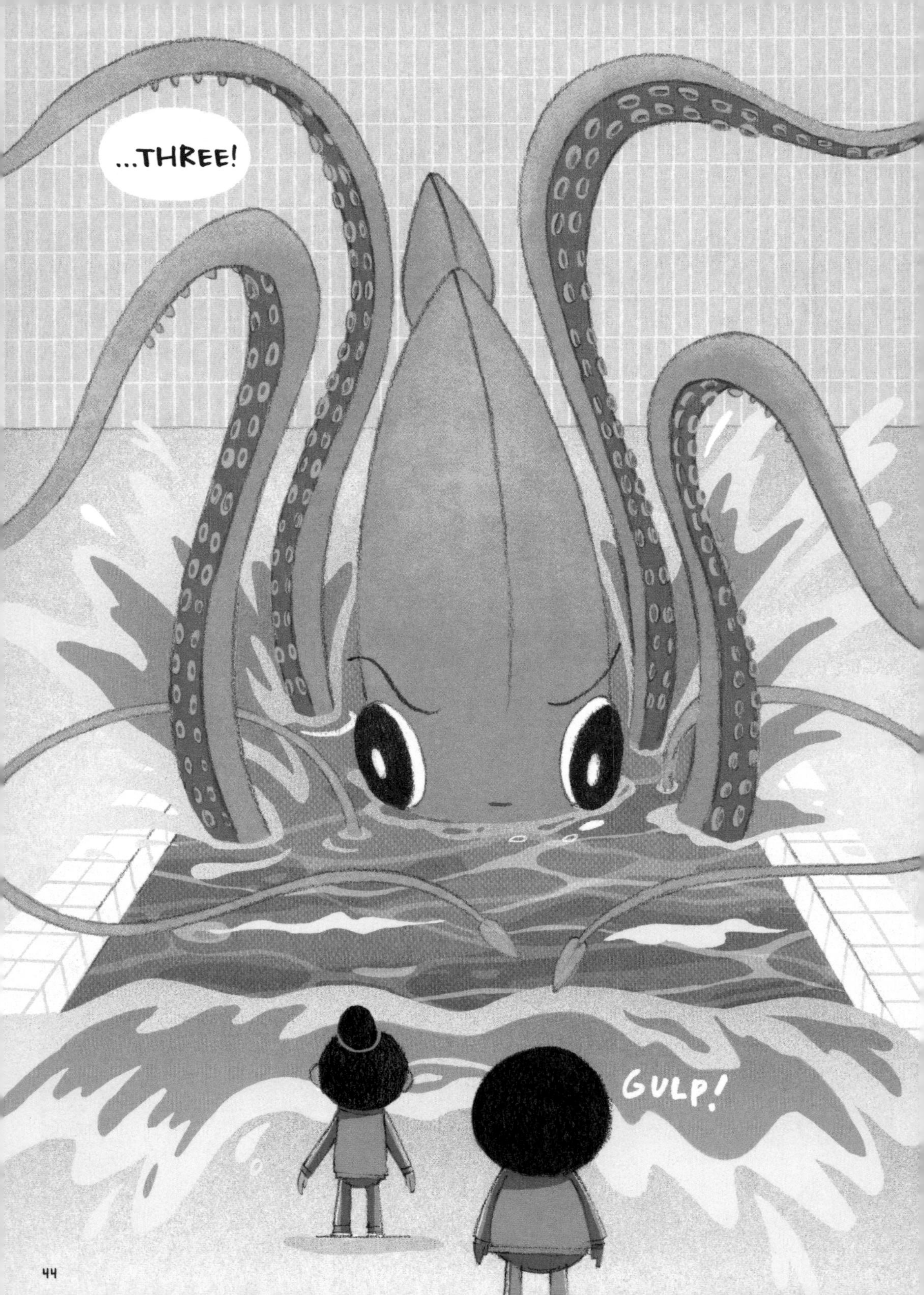
...THREE!
GULP!

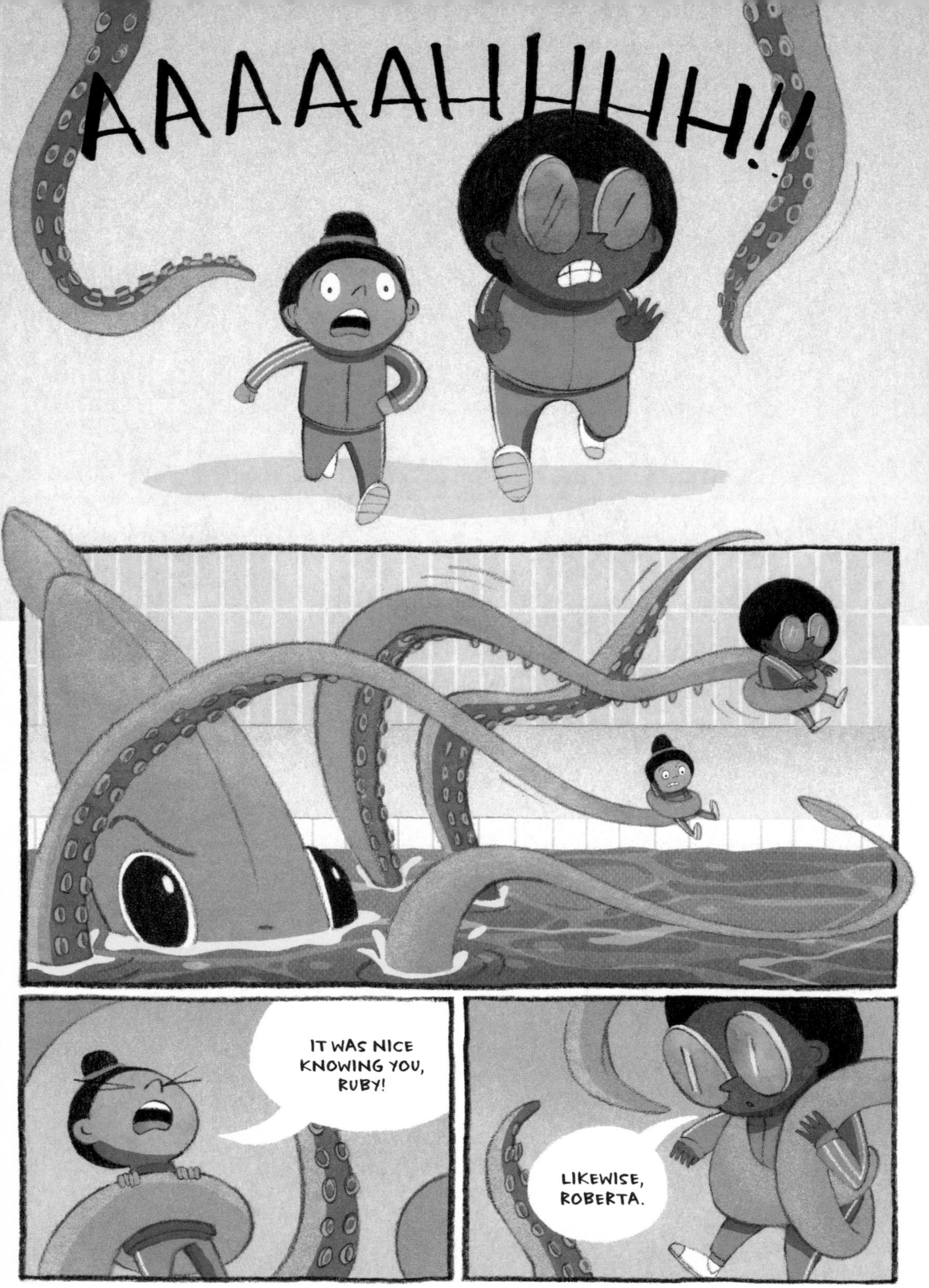
AAAAAHHHHH!!
IT WAS NICE KNOWING YOU, RUBY!
LIKEWISE, ROBERTA.

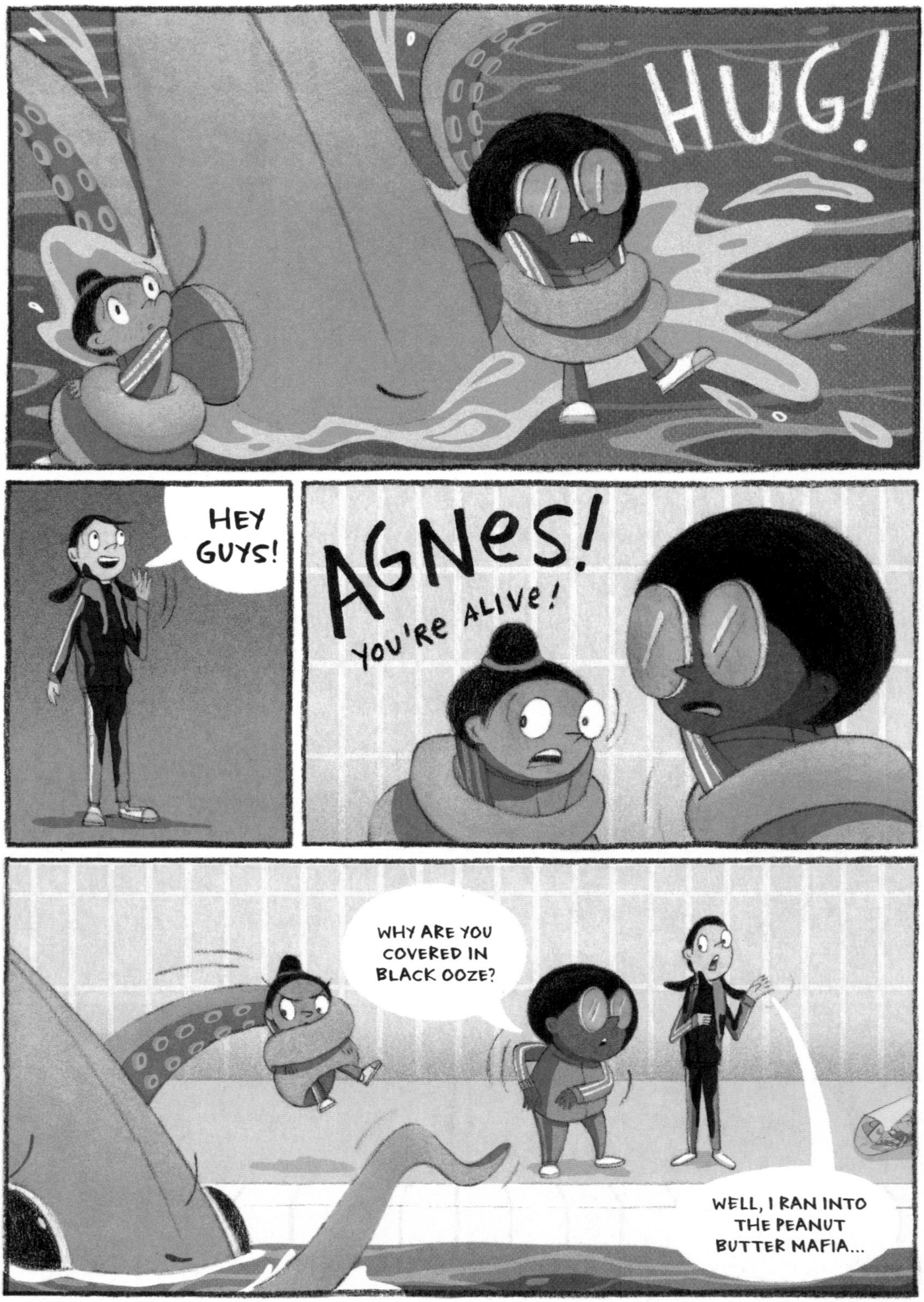
HUG!
HEY GUYS!
AGNES!
YOU'RE ALIVE!
WHY ARE YOU COVERED IN BLACK OOZE?
WELL, I RAN INTO THE PEANUT BUTTER MAFIA...

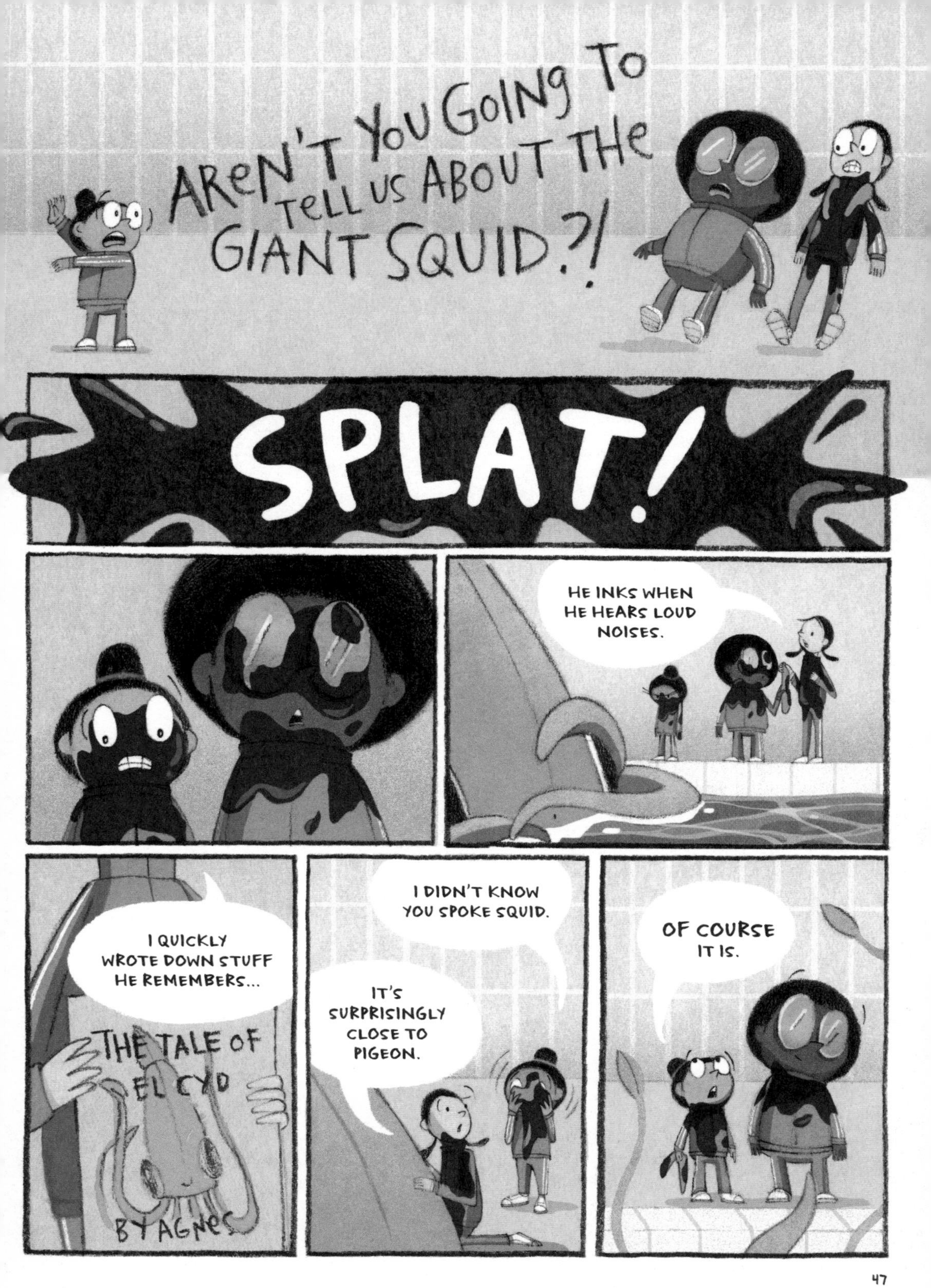
AREN'T YOU GOING TO TELL US ABOUT THE GIANT SQUID?!
SPLAT!
HE INKS WHEN HE HEARS LOUD NOISES.
I QUICKLY WROTE DOWN STUFF HE REMEMBERS...
THE TALE OF EL CYD
BY AGNES
I DIDN'T KNOW YOU SPOKE SQUID.
IT'S SURPRISINGLY CLOSE TO PIGEON.
OF COURSE IT IS.

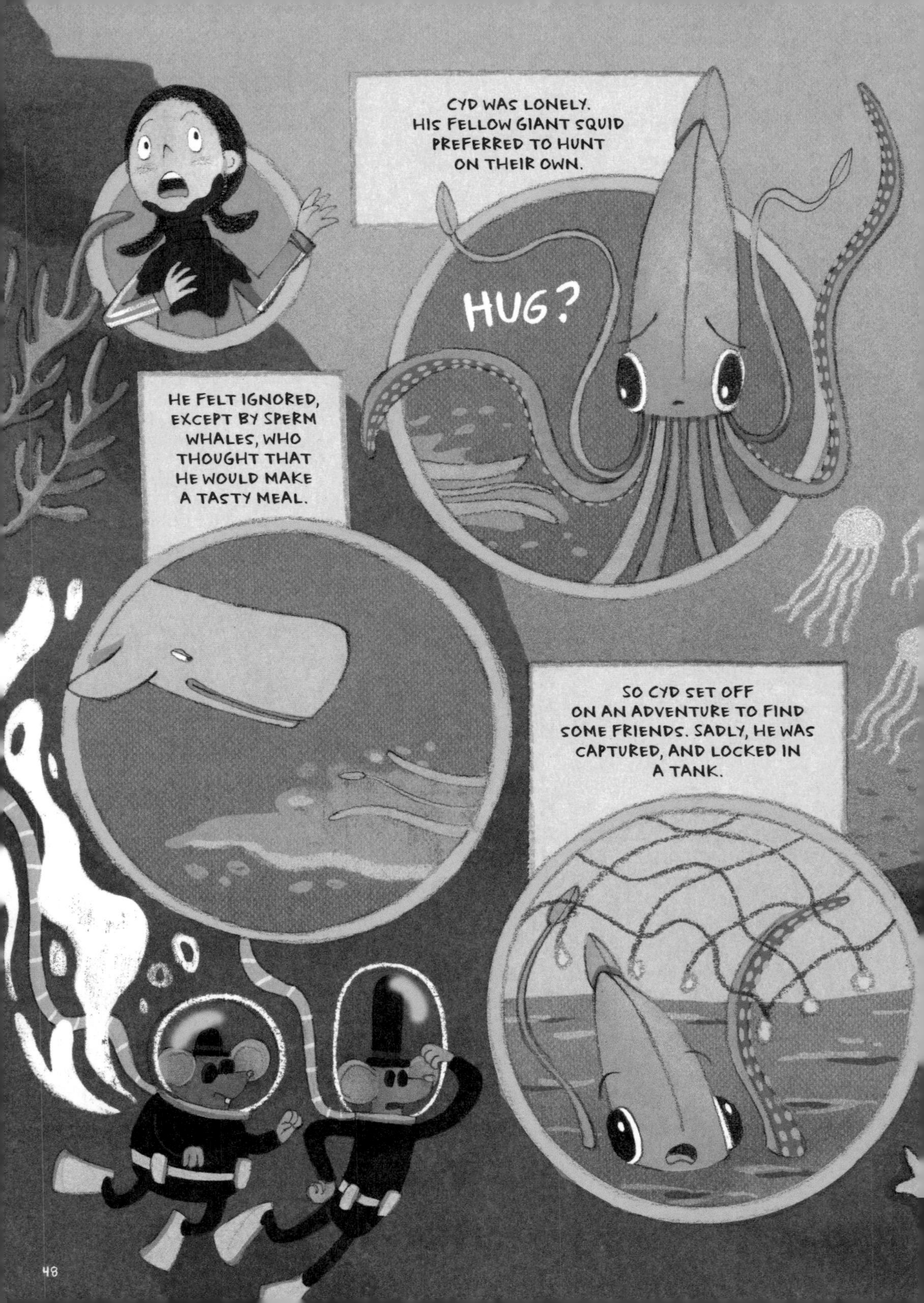

CYD WAS LONELY. HIS FELLOW GIANT SQUID PREFERRED TO HUNT ON THEIR OWN.
HUG?
HE FELT IGNORED, EXCEPT BY SPERM WHALES, WHO THOUGHT THAT HE WOULD MAKE A TASTY MEAL.
SO CYD SET OFF ON AN ADVENTURE TO FIND SOME FRIENDS. SADLY, HE WAS CAPTURED, AND LOCKED IN A TANK.

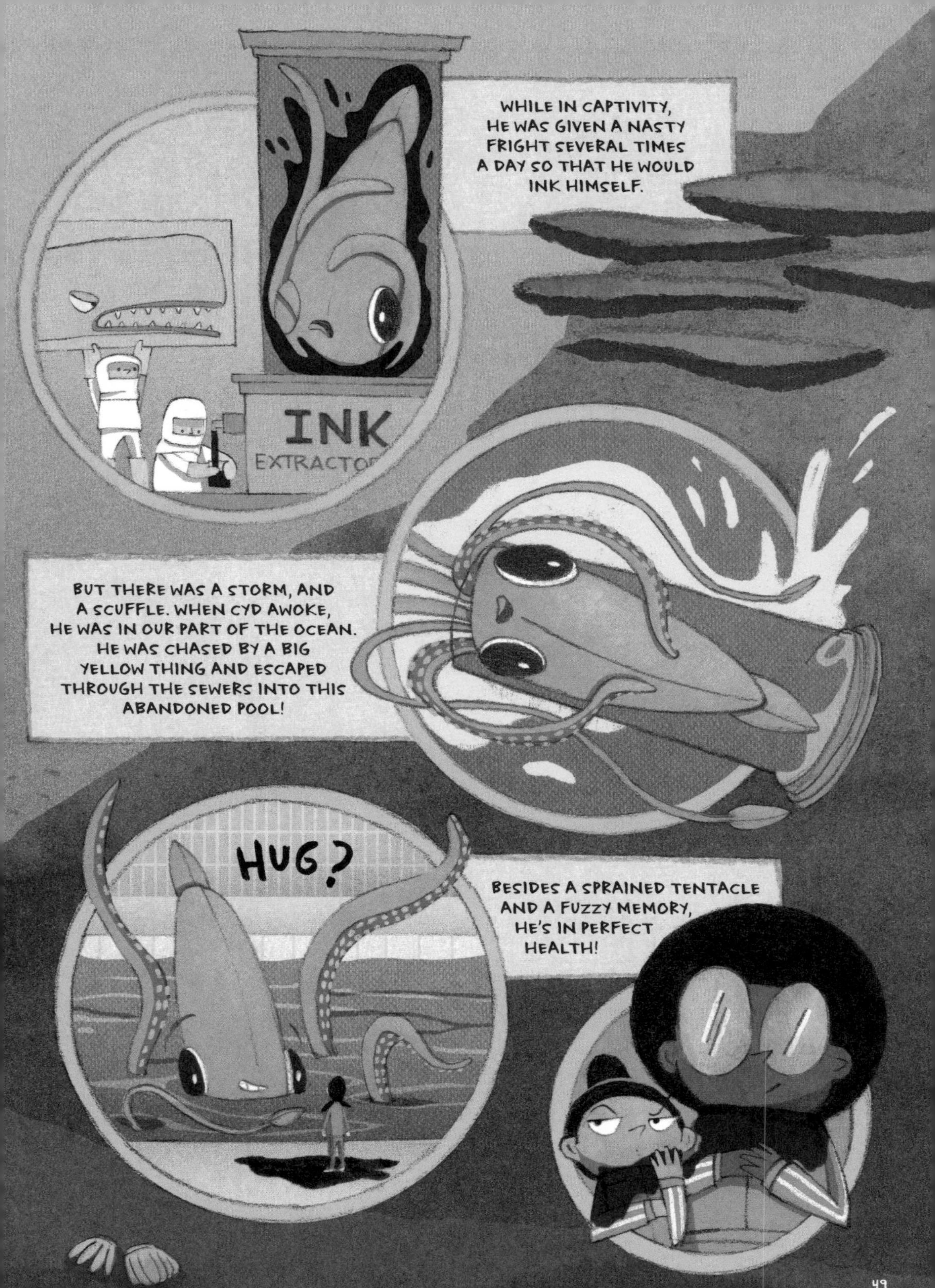
WHILE IN CAPTIVITY, HE WAS GIVEN A NASTY FRIGHT SEVERAL TIMES A DAY SO THAT HE WOULD INK HIMSELF.
INK EXTRACTOR
BUT THERE WAS A STORM, AND A SCUFFLE. WHEN CYD AWOKE, HE WAS IN OUR PART OF THE OCEAN. HE WAS CHASED BY A BIG YELLOW THING AND ESCAPED THROUGH THE SEWERS INTO THIS ABANDONED POOL!
HUG?
BESIDES A SPRAINED TENTACLE AND A FUZZY MEMORY, HE'S IN PERFECT HEALTH!

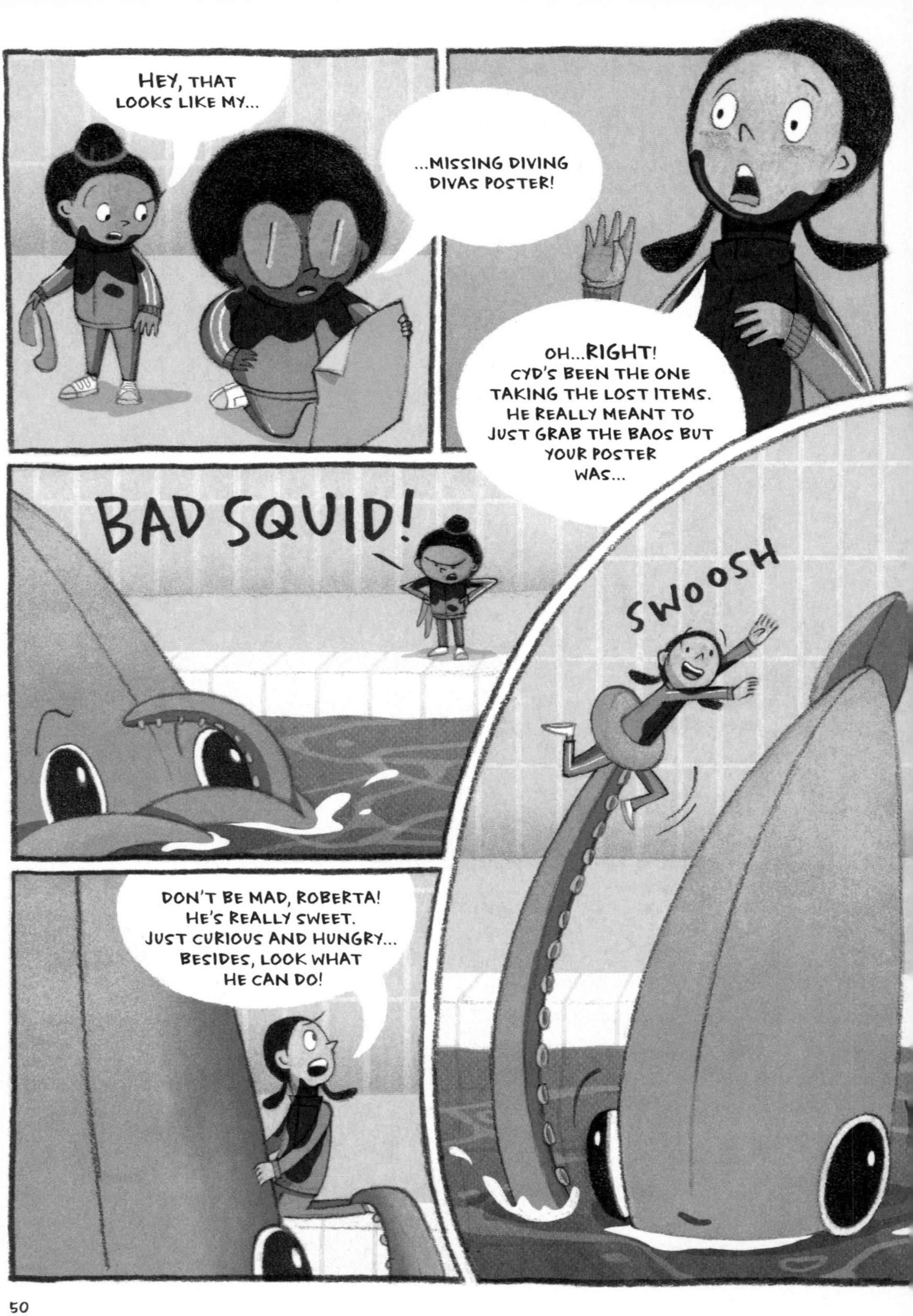
HEY, THAT LOOKS LIKE MY...
...MISSING DIVING DIVAS POSTER!
OH...RIGHT! CYD'S BEEN THE ONE TAKING THE LOST ITEMS. HE REALLY MEANT TO JUST GRAB THE BAOS BUT YOUR POSTER WAS...
BAD SQUID!
SWOOSH
DON'T BE MAD, ROBERTA! HE'S REALLY SWEET. JUST CURIOUS AND HUNGRY... BESIDES, LOOK WHAT HE CAN DO!

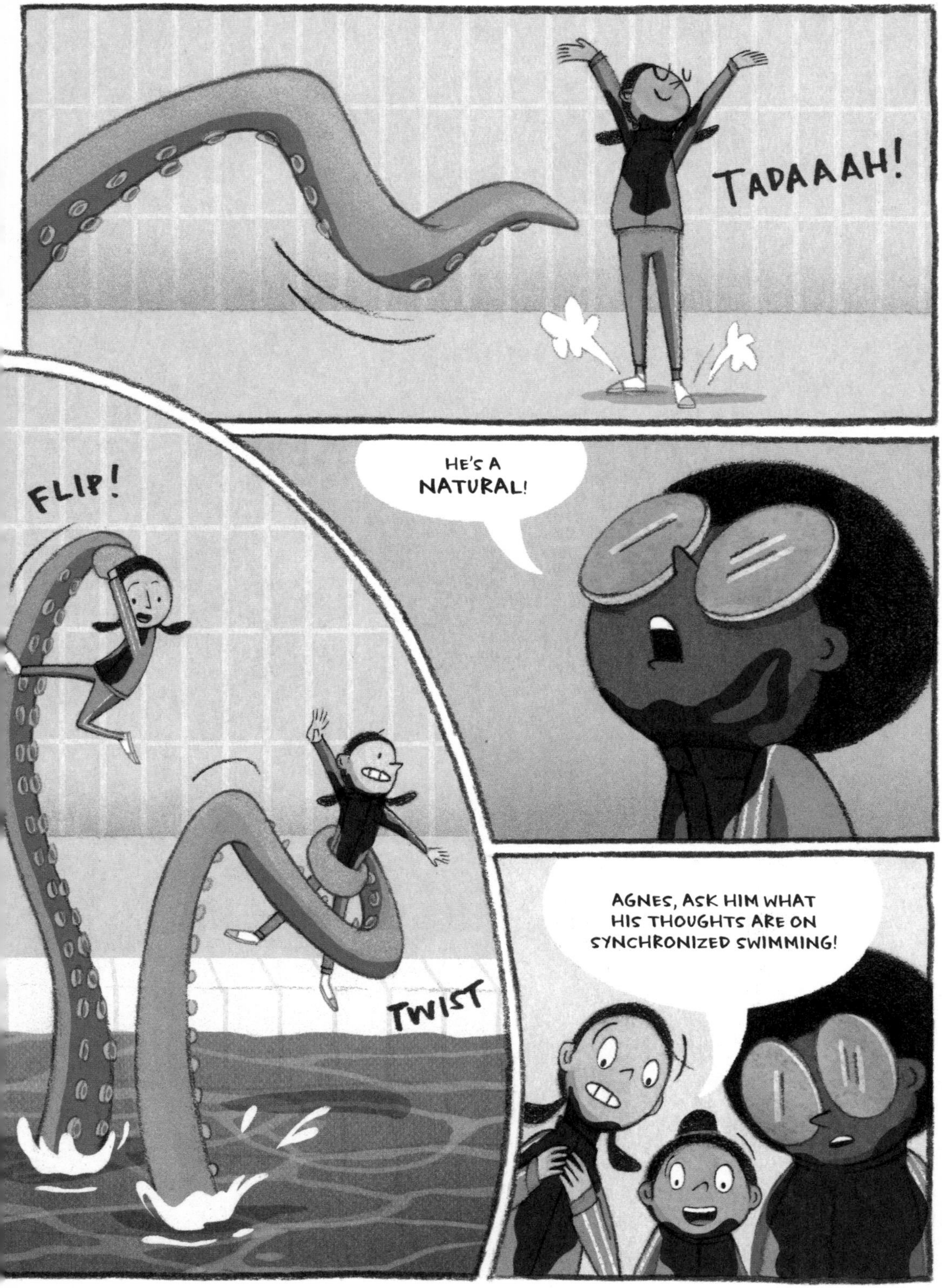
TADAAAH!
FLIP!
TWIST
HE'S A NATURAL!
AGNES, ASK HIM WHAT HIS THOUGHTS ARE ON SYNCHRONIZED SWIMMING!

LATER, AT THE SALMAGUNDI BOYS AND GIRLS CLUB

BOYS AND GIRLS CLUB

I CAN SENSE THAT SQUID'S PRESENCE.

WHAT'S THE PLAN, MISTER GILBERT?

I'LL SEARCH THE BUILDING,

YOU GET UP ON THAT ROOFTOP AND BE ON THE ALERT FOR UNUSUAL ACTIVITY.

UNUSUAL ACTIVITY. OKIE DOKIE.

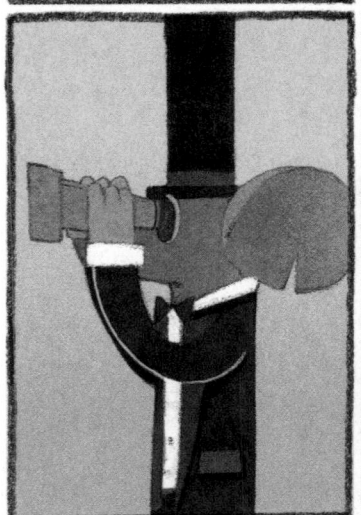

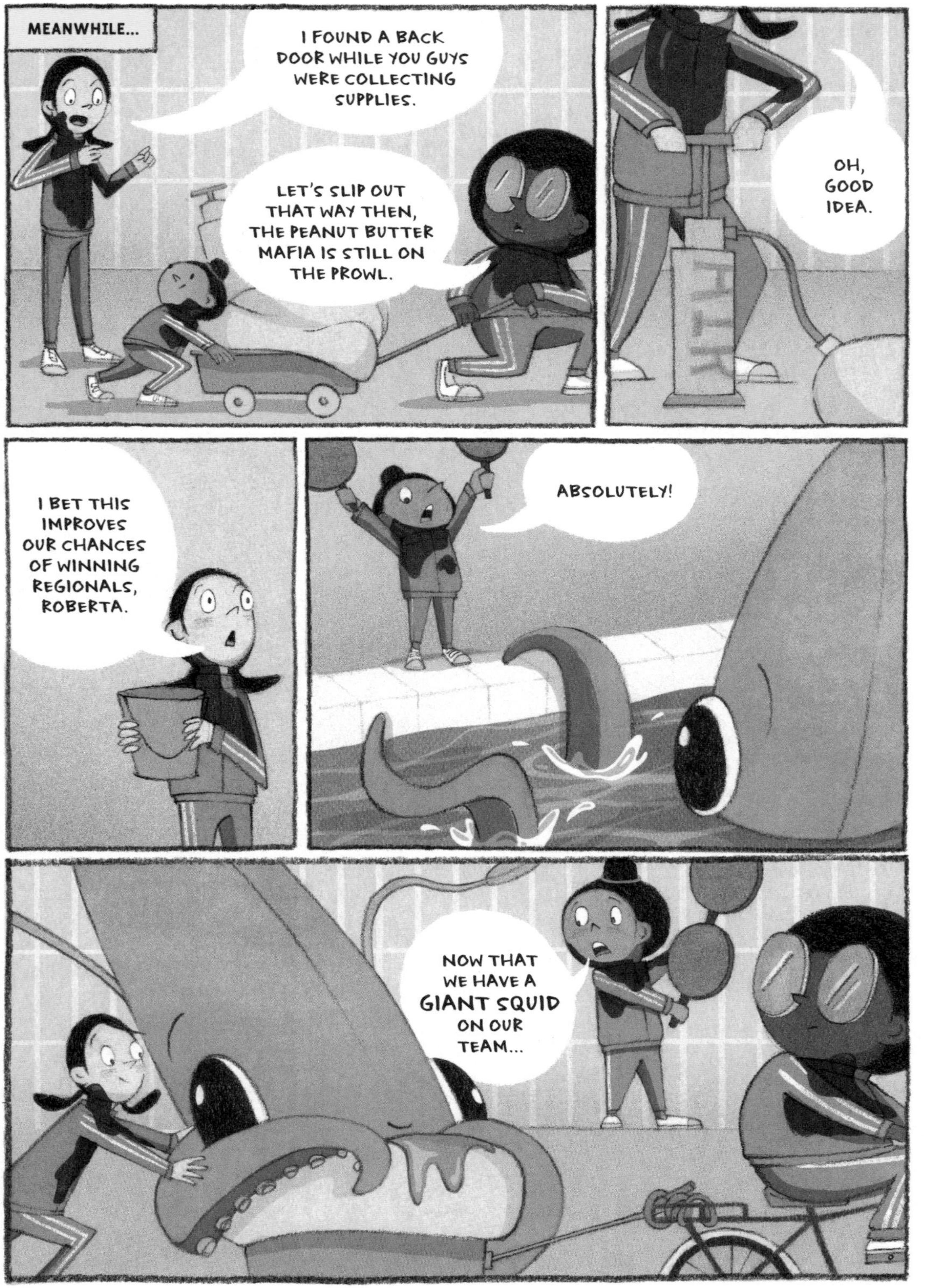
MEANWHILE...
I FOUND A BACK DOOR WHILE YOU GUYS WERE COLLECTING SUPPLIES.
LET'S SLIP OUT THAT WAY THEN, THE PEANUT BUTTER MAFIA IS STILL ON THE PROWL.
OH, GOOD IDEA.
AIR
I BET THIS IMPROVES OUR CHANCES OF WINNING REGIONALS, ROBERTA.
ABSOLUTELY!
NOW THAT WE HAVE A GIANT SQUID ON OUR TEAM...

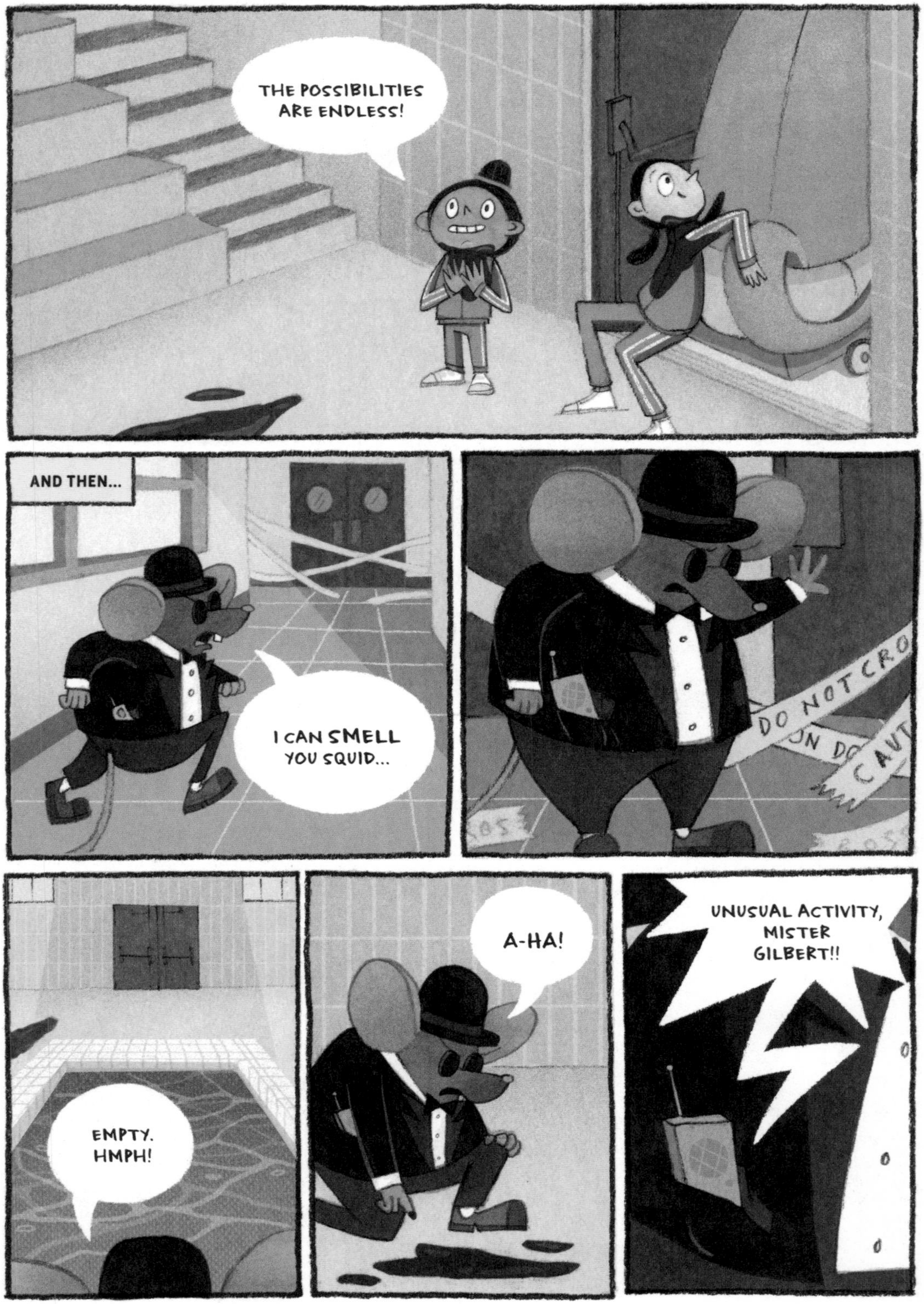
THE POSSIBILITIES ARE ENDLESS!
AND THEN...
I CAN SMELL YOU SQUID...
EMPTY. HMPH!
A-HA!
UNUSUAL ACTIVITY, MISTER GILBERT!!

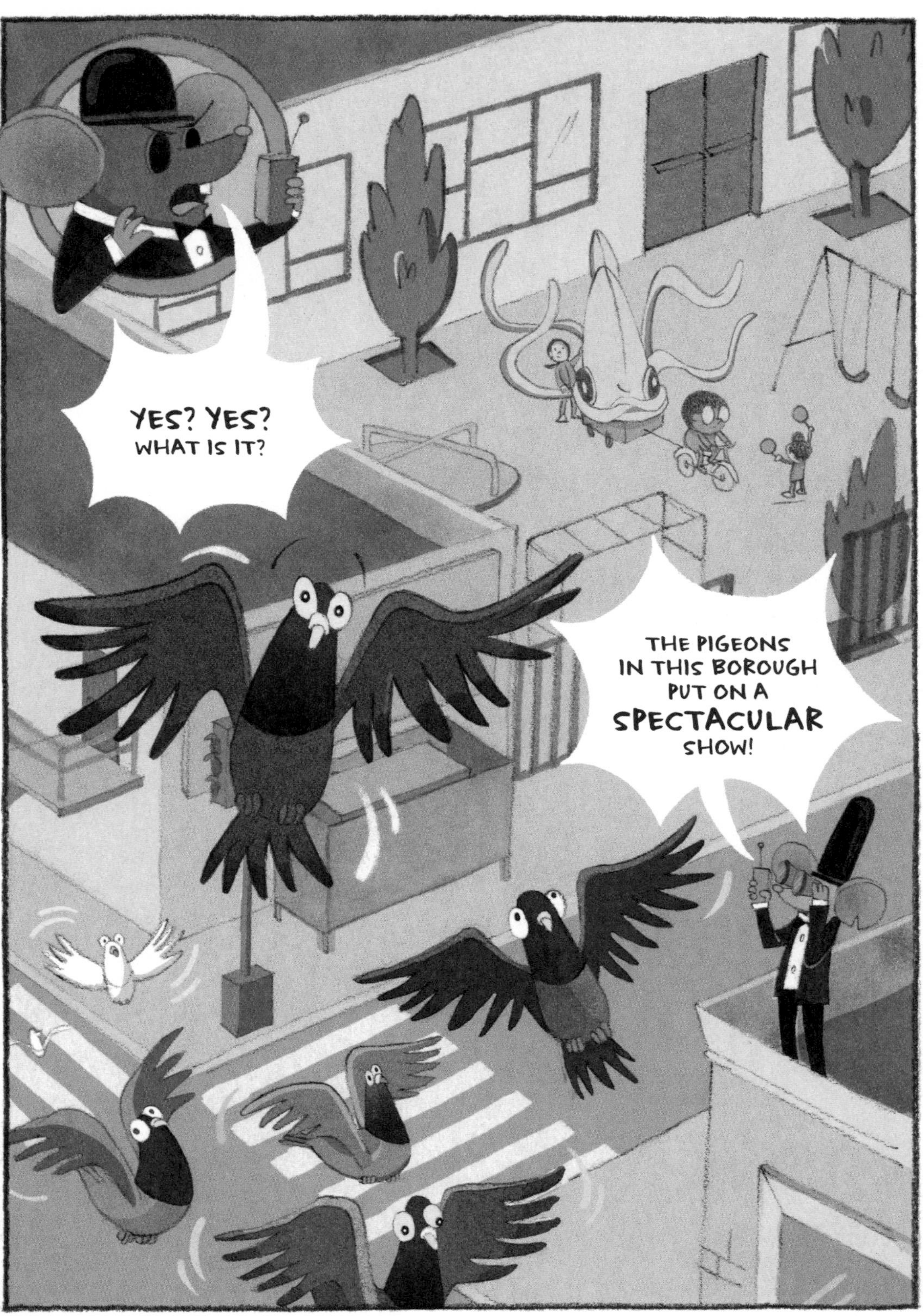
YES? YES? WHAT IS IT?
THE PIGEONS IN THIS BOROUGH PUT ON A SPECTACULAR SHOW!

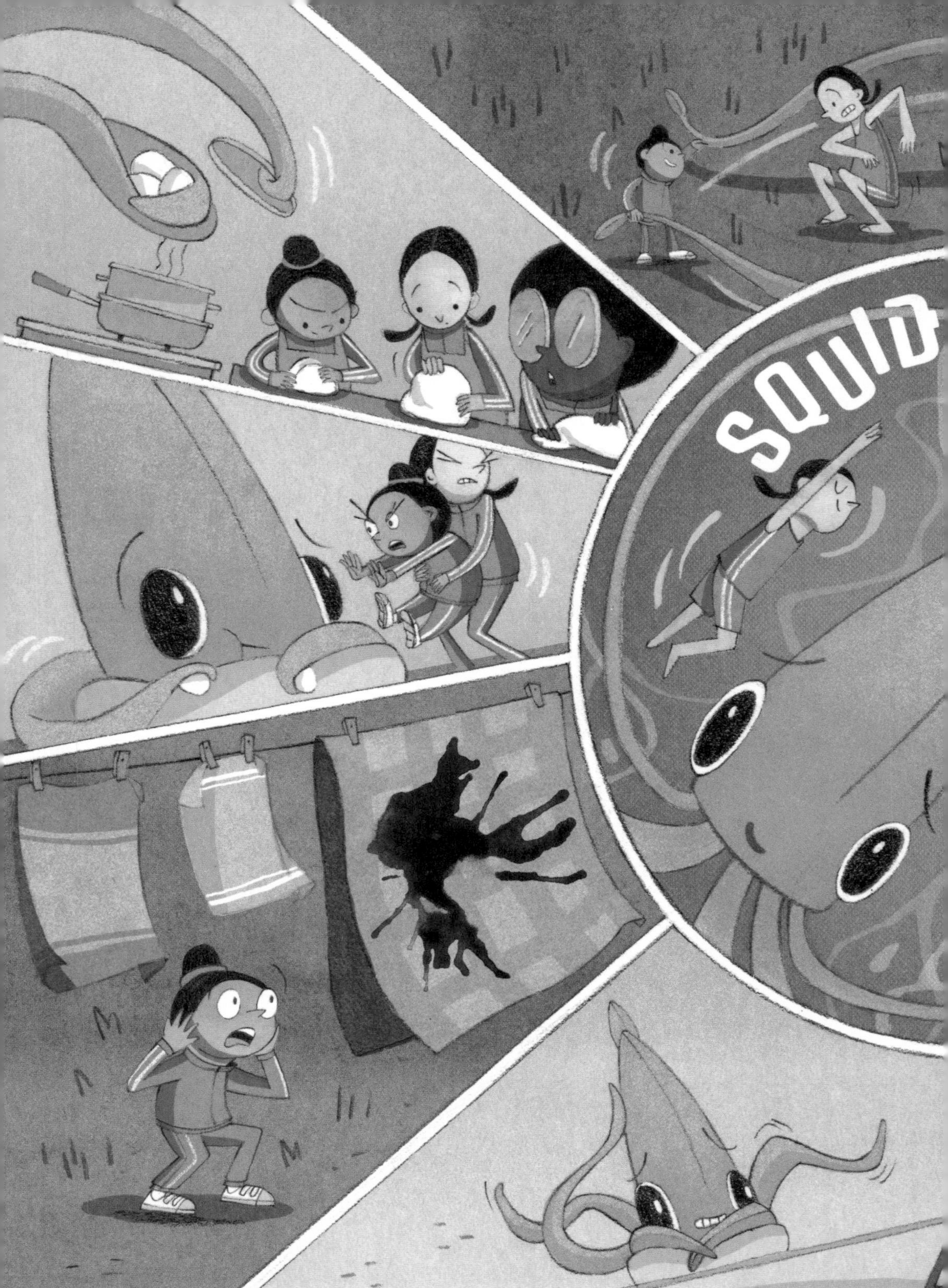
SQUID

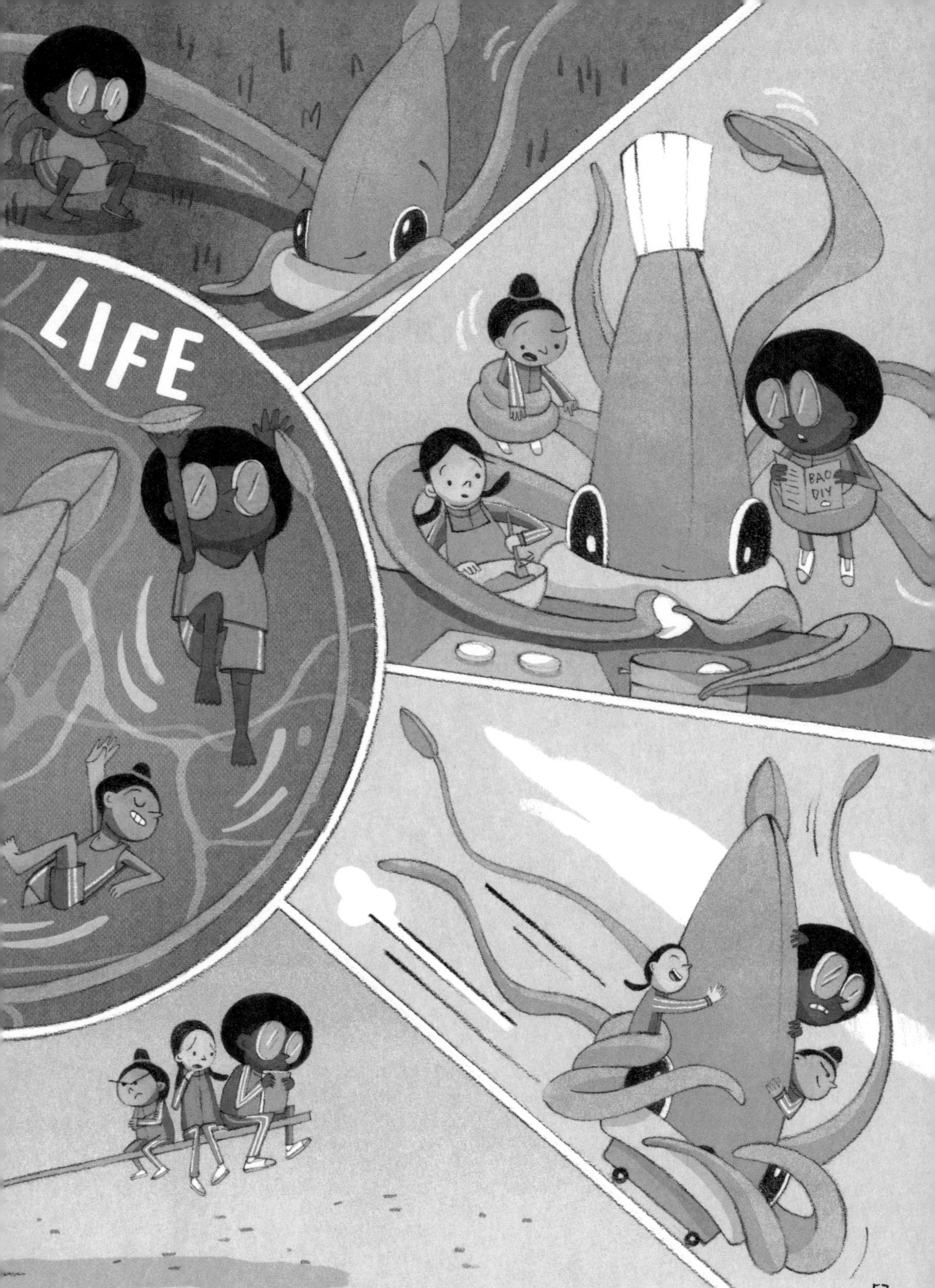
LIFE
BAD
DIY

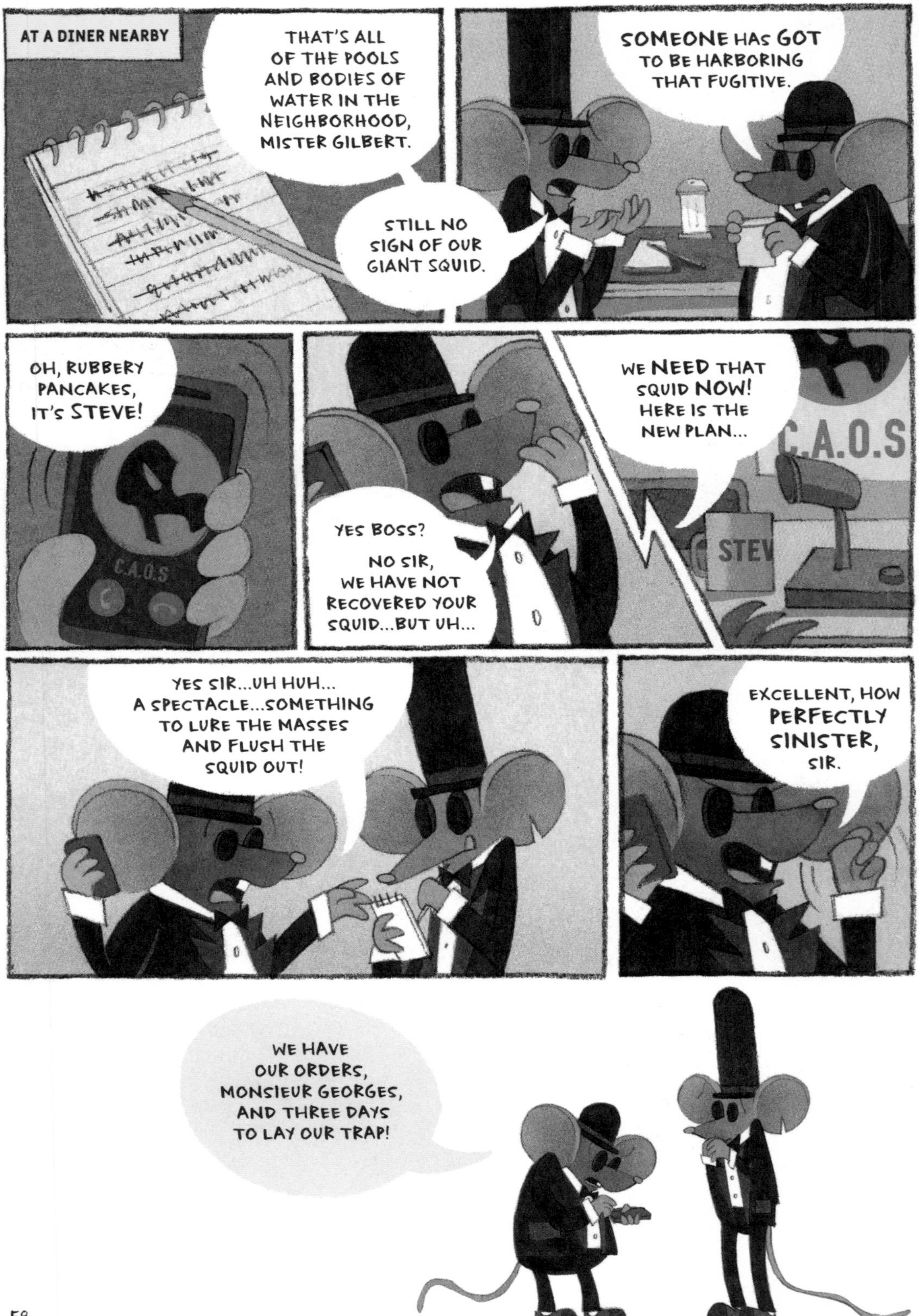
AT A DINER NEARBY
THAT'S ALL OF THE POOLS AND BODIES OF WATER IN THE NEIGHBORHOOD, MISTER GILBERT.
STILL NO SIGN OF OUR GIANT SQUID.
SOMEONE HAS GOT TO BE HARBORING THAT FUGITIVE.
OH, RUBBERY PANCAKES, IT'S STEVE!
C.A.O.S
YES BOSS?
NO SIR, WE HAVE NOT RECOVERED YOUR SQUID...BUT UH...
WE NEED THAT SQUID NOW! HERE IS THE NEW PLAN...
C.A.O.S
STEV
YES SIR...UH HUH... A SPECTACLE...SOMETHING TO LURE THE MASSES AND FLUSH THE SQUID OUT!
EXCELLENT, HOW PERFECTLY SINISTER, SIR.
WE HAVE OUR ORDERS, MONSIEUR GEORGES, AND THREE DAYS TO LAY OUR TRAP!

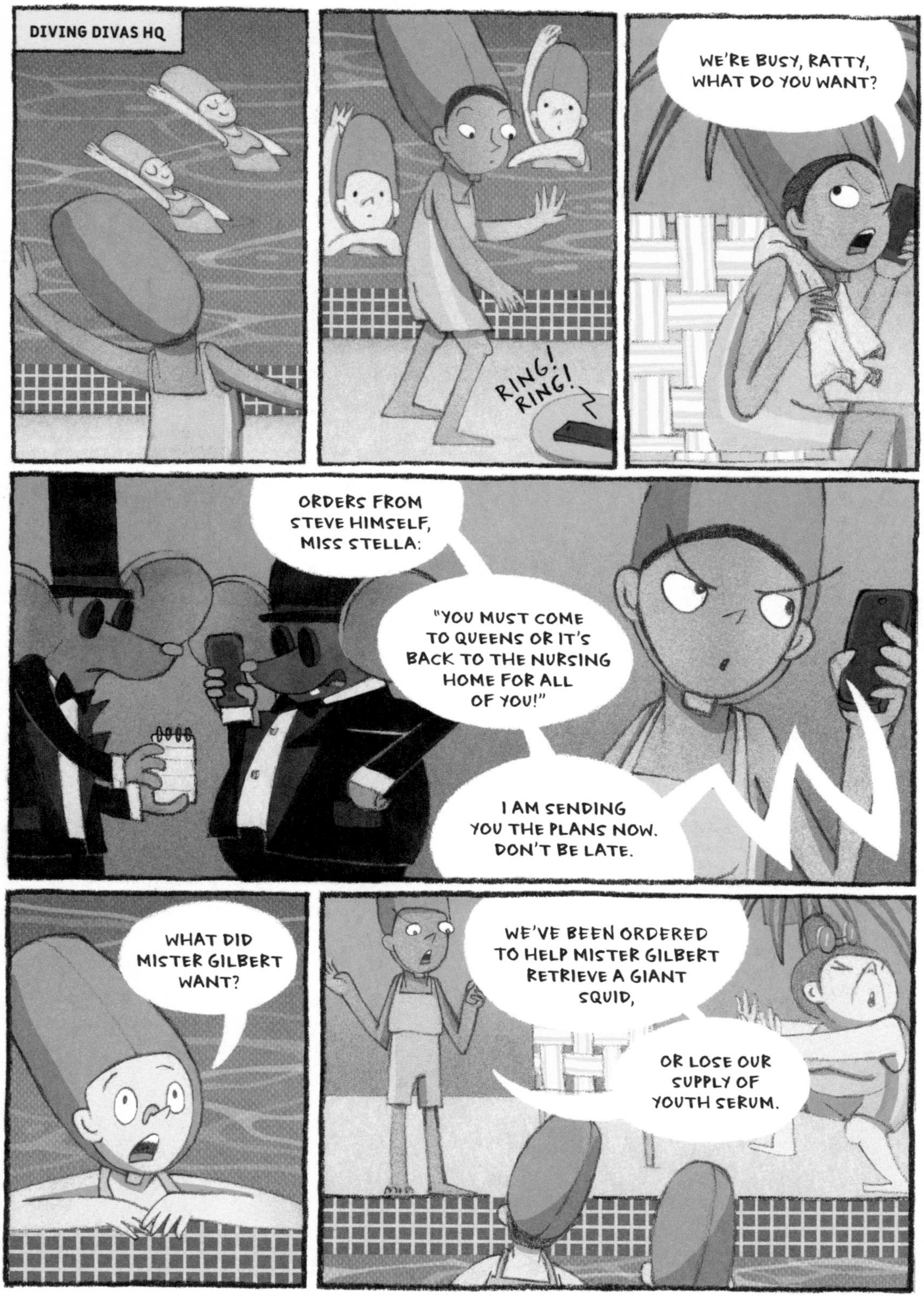
DIVING DIVAS HQ
RING! RING!
WE'RE BUSY, RATTY, WHAT DO YOU WANT?
ORDERS FROM STEVE HIMSELF, MISS STELLA:
"YOU MUST COME TO QUEENS OR IT'S BACK TO THE NURSING HOME FOR ALL OF YOU!"
I AM SENDING YOU THE PLANS NOW. DON'T BE LATE.
WHAT DID MISTER GILBERT WANT?
WE'VE BEEN ORDERED TO HELP MISTER GILBERT RETRIEVE A GIANT SQUID,
OR LOSE OUR SUPPLY OF YOUTH SERUM.

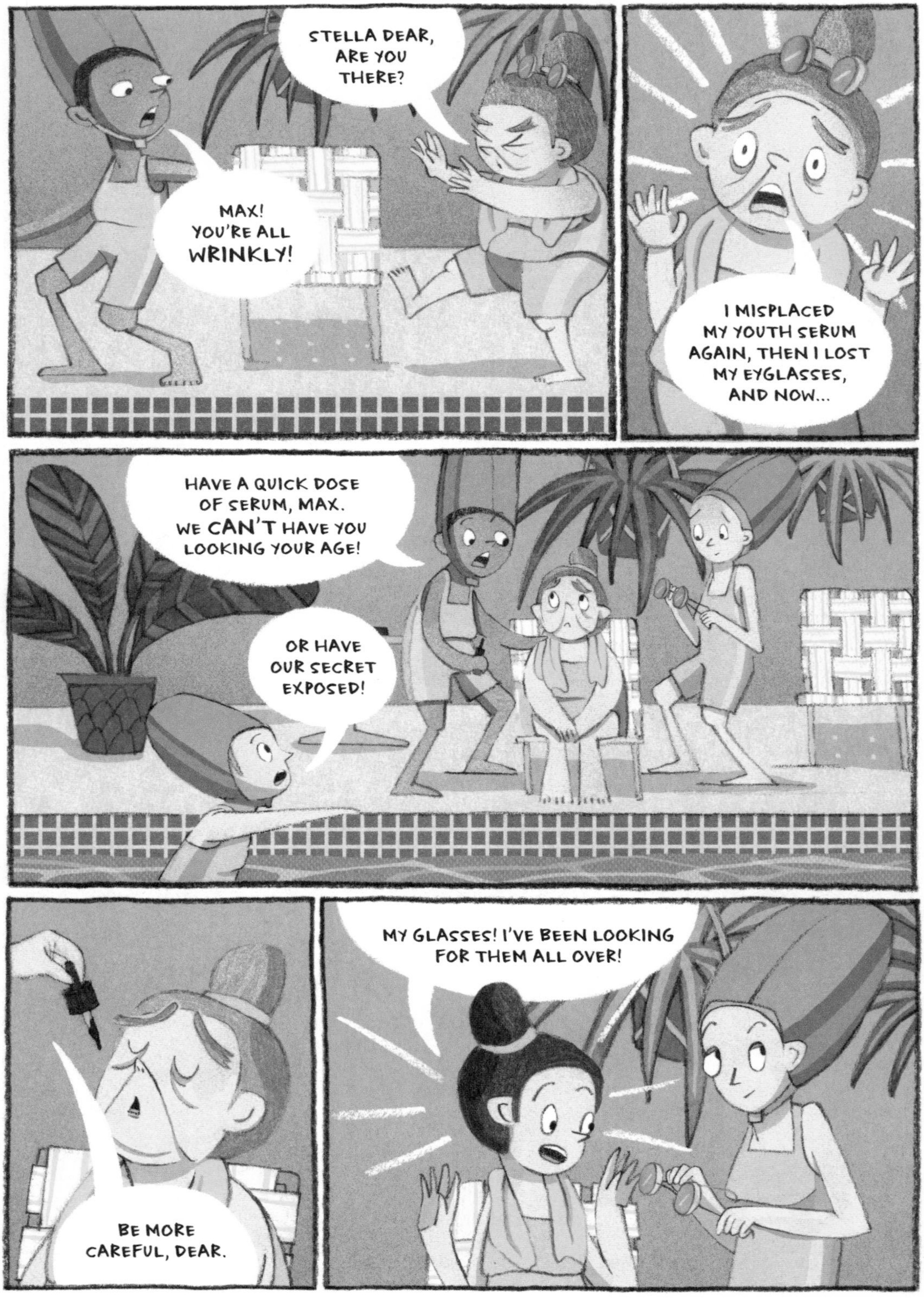

STELLA DEAR, ARE YOU THERE?
MAX! YOU'RE ALL **WRINKLY**!
I MISPLACED MY YOUTH SERUM AGAIN, THEN I LOST MY EYGLASSES, AND NOW...
HAVE A QUICK DOSE OF SERUM, MAX. WE **CAN'T** HAVE YOU LOOKING YOUR AGE!
OR HAVE OUR SECRET EXPOSED!
BE MORE CAREFUL, DEAR.
MY GLASSES! I'VE BEEN LOOKING FOR THEM ALL OVER!

CHAPTER 5
SYNCH OR SWIM

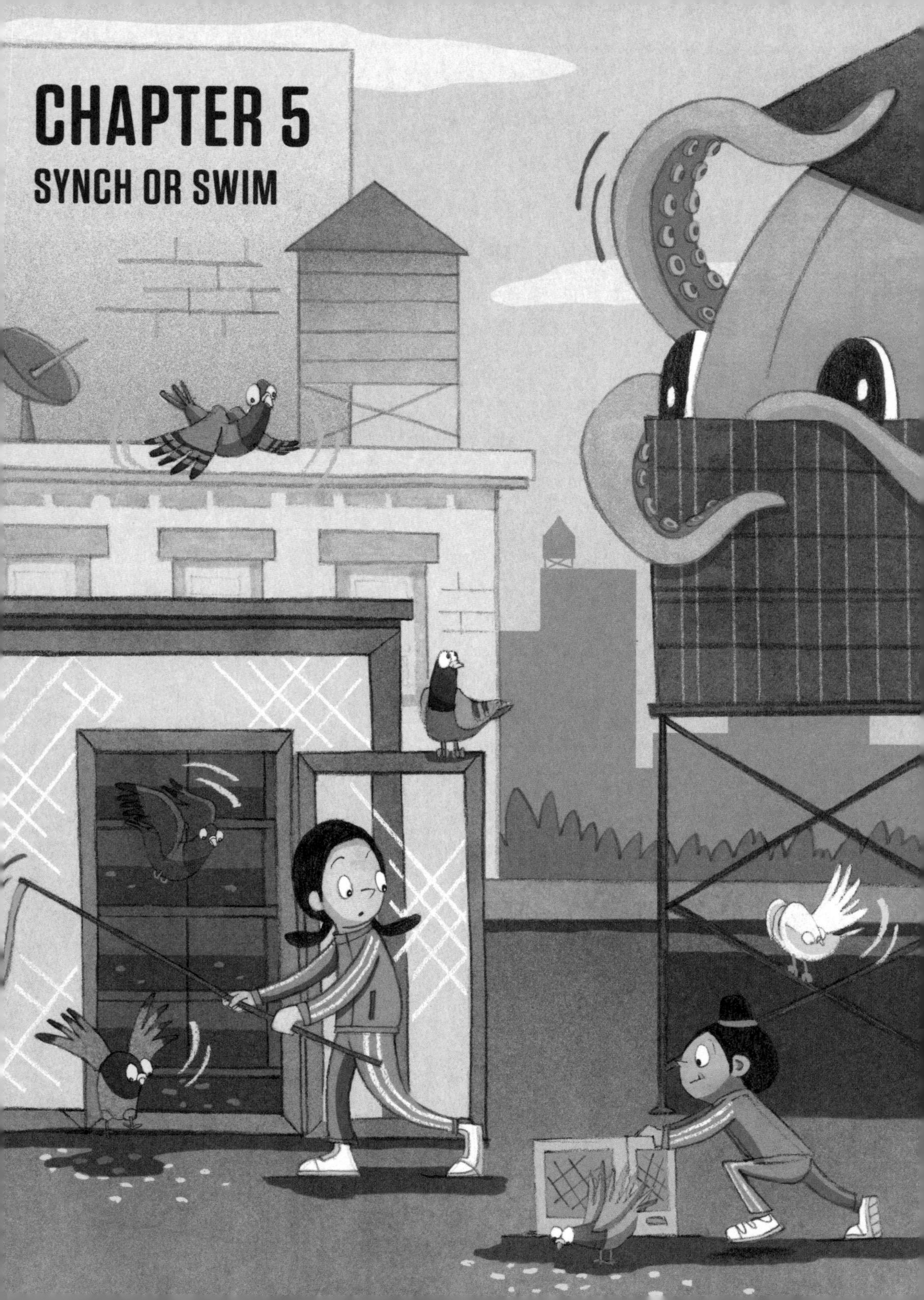

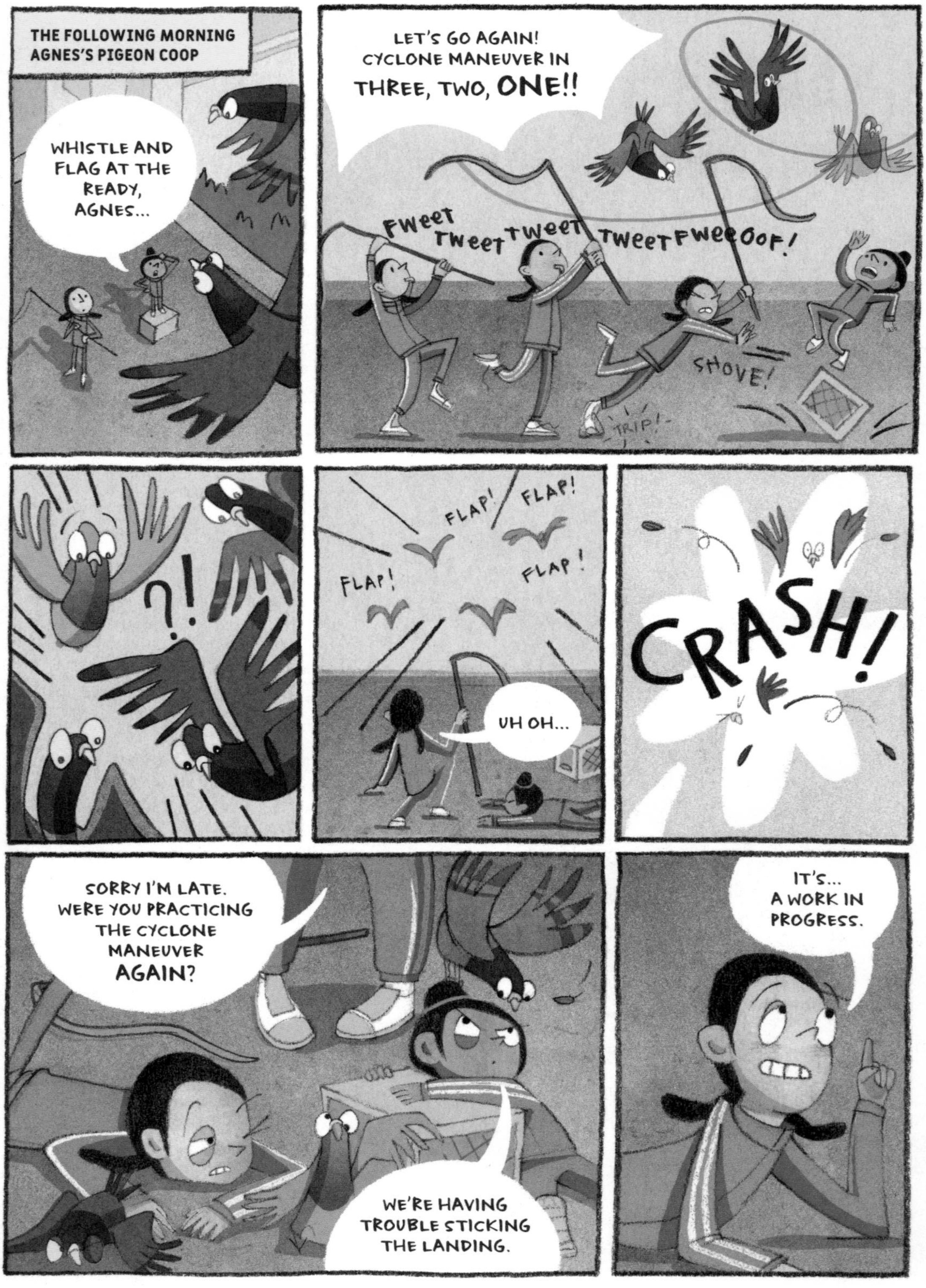
THE FOLLOWING MORNING
AGNES'S PIGEON COOP
WHISTLE AND FLAG AT THE READY, AGNES...
LET'S GO AGAIN! CYCLONE MANEUVER IN THREE, TWO, ONE!!
FWEET TWEET TWEET TWEET FWEEOOF!
SHOVE!
TRIP!
?!
FLAP! FLAP! FLAP! FLAP!
UH OH...
CRASH!
SORRY I'M LATE. WERE YOU PRACTICING THE CYCLONE MANEUVER AGAIN?
WE'RE HAVING TROUBLE STICKING THE LANDING.
IT'S... A WORK IN PROGRESS.

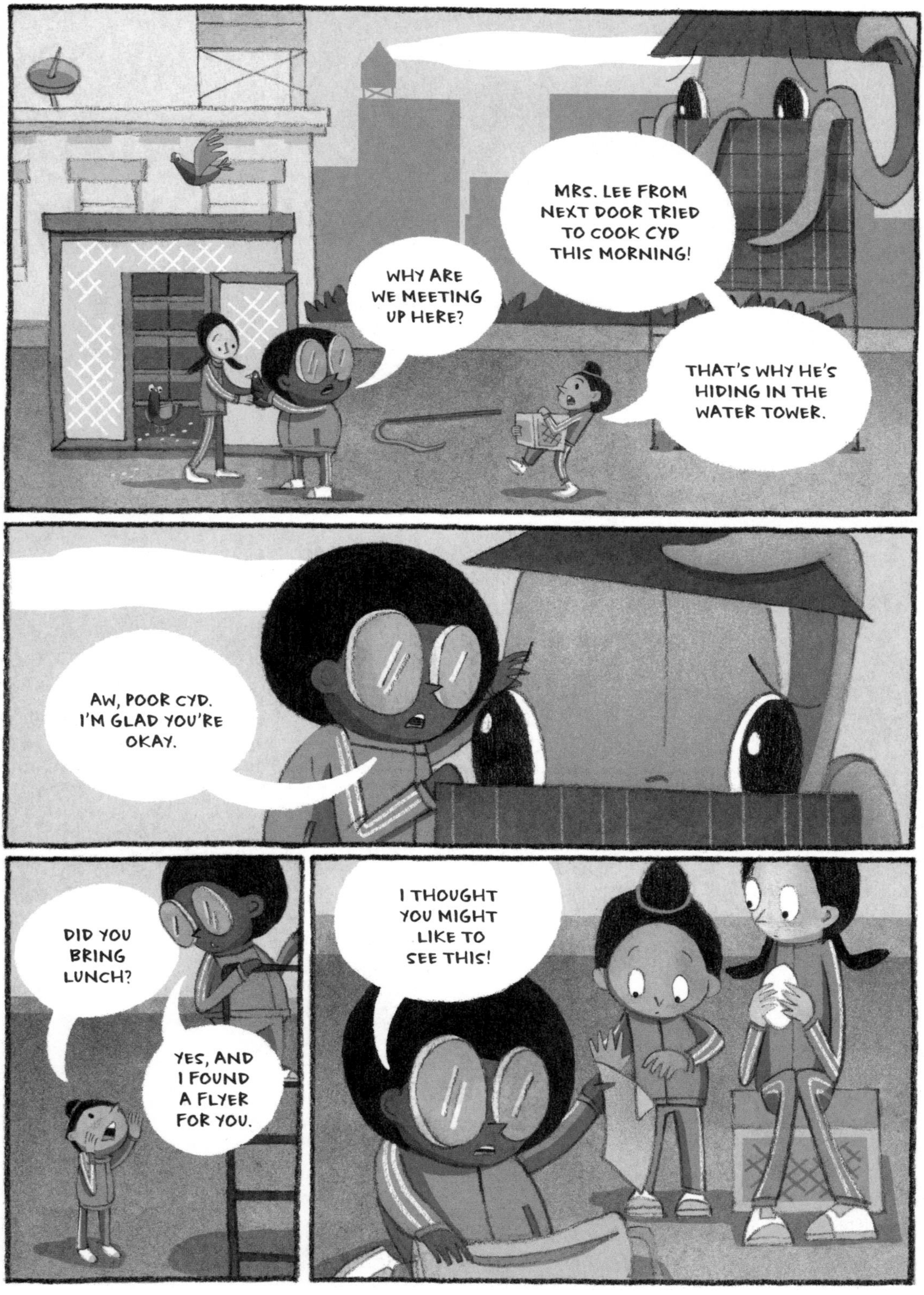
WHY ARE WE MEETING UP HERE?
MRS. LEE FROM NEXT DOOR TRIED TO COOK CYD THIS MORNING!
THAT'S WHY HE'S HIDING IN THE WATER TOWER.
AW, POOR CYD. I'M GLAD YOU'RE OKAY.
DID YOU BRING LUNCH?
YES, AND I FOUND A FLYER FOR YOU.
I THOUGHT YOU MIGHT LIKE TO SEE THIS!

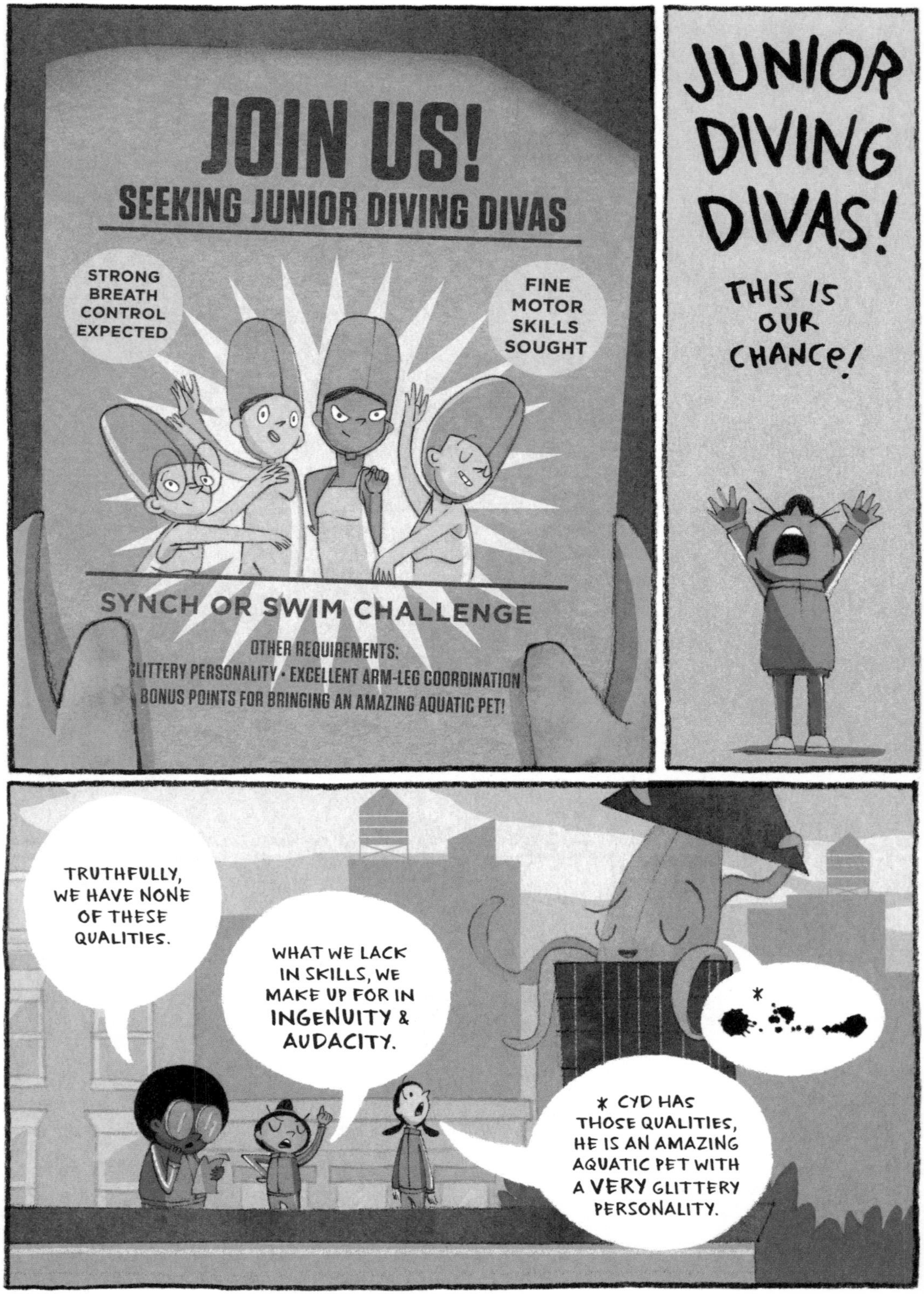
JOIN US!
SEEKING JUNIOR DIVING DIVAS
STRONG BREATH CONTROL EXPECTED
FINE MOTOR SKILLS SOUGHT
SYNCH OR SWIM CHALLENGE
OTHER REQUIREMENTS:
GLITTERY PERSONALITY • EXCELLENT ARM-LEG COORDINATION
BONUS POINTS FOR BRINGING AN AMAZING AQUATIC PET!
JUNIOR DIVING DIVAS!
THIS IS OUR CHANCE!
TRUTHFULLY, WE HAVE NONE OF THESE QUALITIES.
WHAT WE LACK IN SKILLS, WE MAKE UP FOR IN INGENUITY & AUDACITY.
*
* CYD HAS THOSE QUALITIES, HE IS AN AMAZING AQUATIC PET WITH A VERY GLITTERY PERSONALITY.

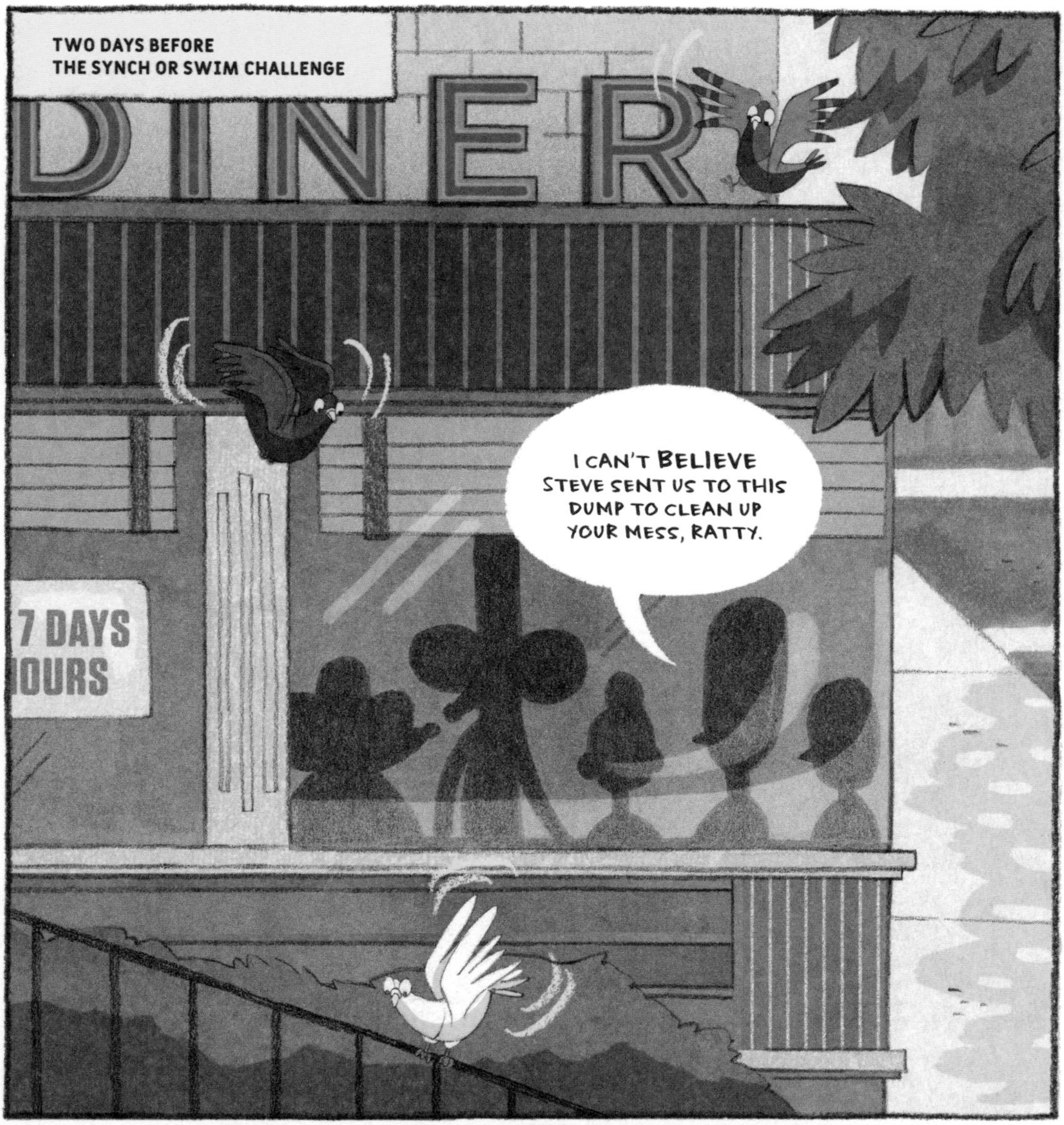
TWO DAYS BEFORE
THE SYNCH OR SWIM CHALLENGE
DINER
I CAN'T BELIEVE STEVE SENT US TO THIS DUMP TO CLEAN UP YOUR MESS, RATTY.
7 DAYS
HOURS

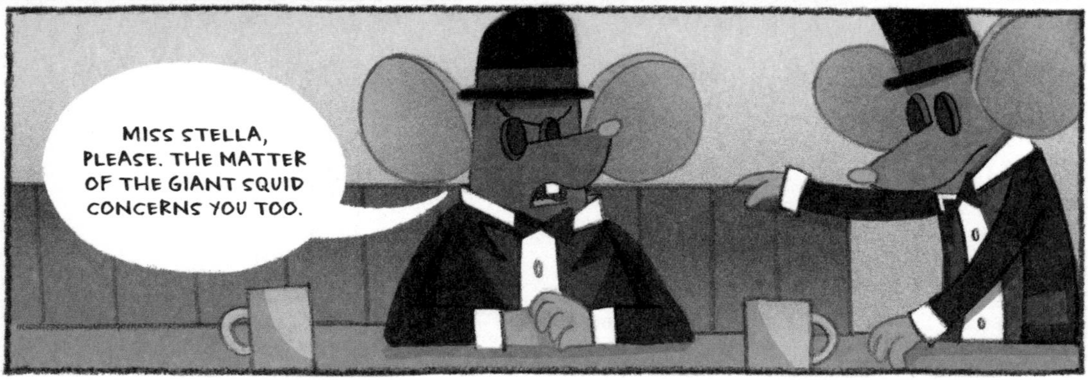
MISS STELLA, PLEASE. THE MATTER OF THE GIANT SQUID CONCERNS YOU TOO.

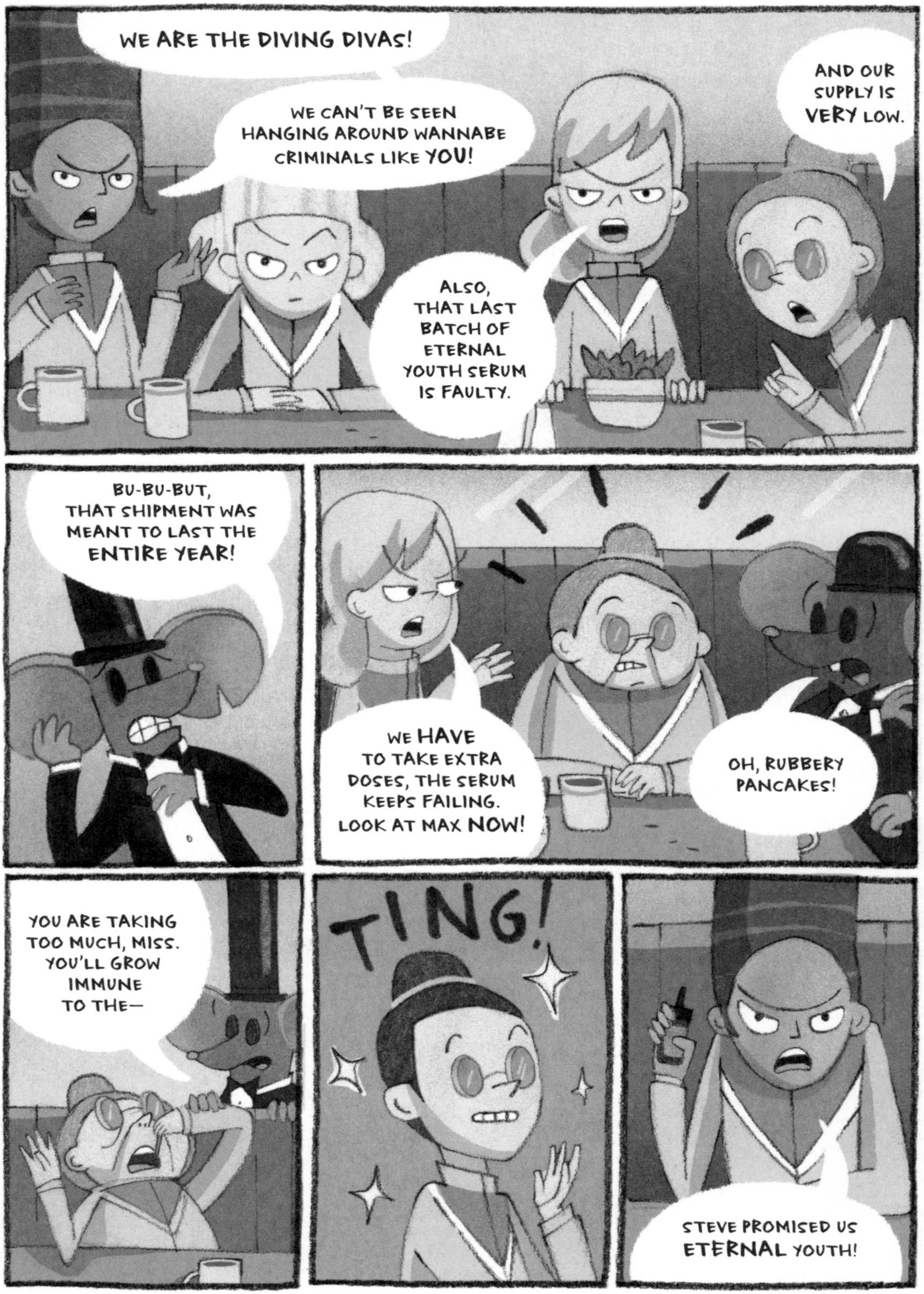
WE ARE THE DIVING DIVAS!
WE CAN'T BE SEEN HANGING AROUND WANNABE CRIMINALS LIKE YOU!
AND OUR SUPPLY IS VERY LOW.
ALSO, THAT LAST BATCH OF ETERNAL YOUTH SERUM IS FAULTY.
BU-BU-BUT, THAT SHIPMENT WAS MEANT TO LAST THE ENTIRE YEAR!
WE HAVE TO TAKE EXTRA DOSES, THE SERUM KEEPS FAILING. LOOK AT MAX NOW!
OH, RUBBERY PANCAKES!
YOU ARE TAKING TOO MUCH, MISS. YOU'LL GROW IMMUNE TO THE—
TING!
STEVE PROMISED US ETERNAL YOUTH!

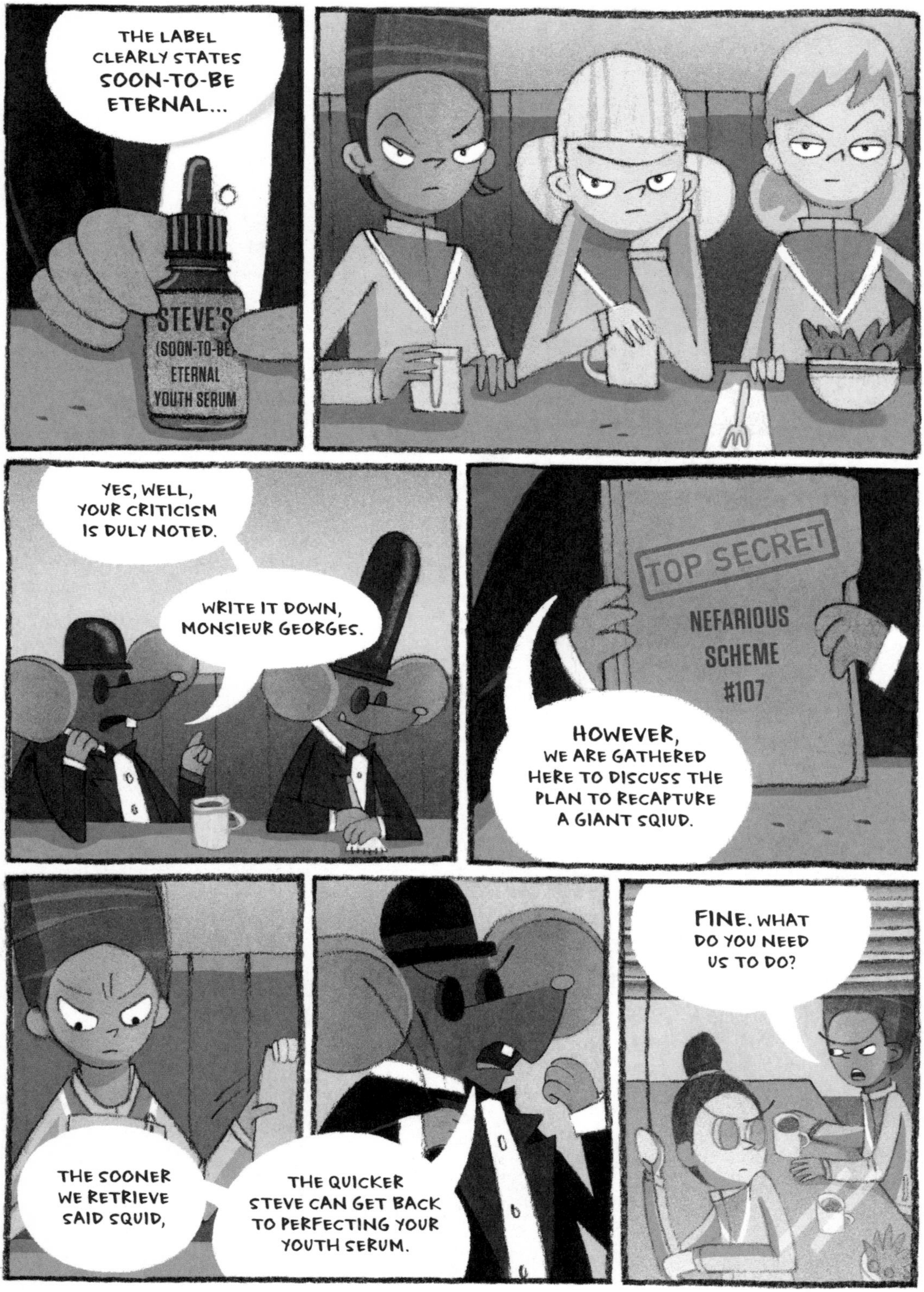
THE LABEL CLEARLY STATES SOON-TO-BE ETERNAL...
STEVE'S (SOON-TO-BE) ETERNAL YOUTH SERUM
YES, WELL, YOUR CRITICISM IS DULY NOTED.
WRITE IT DOWN, MONSIEUR GEORGES.
TOP SECRET
NEFARIOUS SCHEME #107
HOWEVER, WE ARE GATHERED HERE TO DISCUSS THE PLAN TO RECAPTURE A GIANT SQIUD.
THE SOONER WE RETRIEVE SAID SQUID,
THE QUICKER STEVE CAN GET BACK TO PERFECTING YOUR YOUTH SERUM.
FINE. WHAT DO YOU NEED US TO DO?

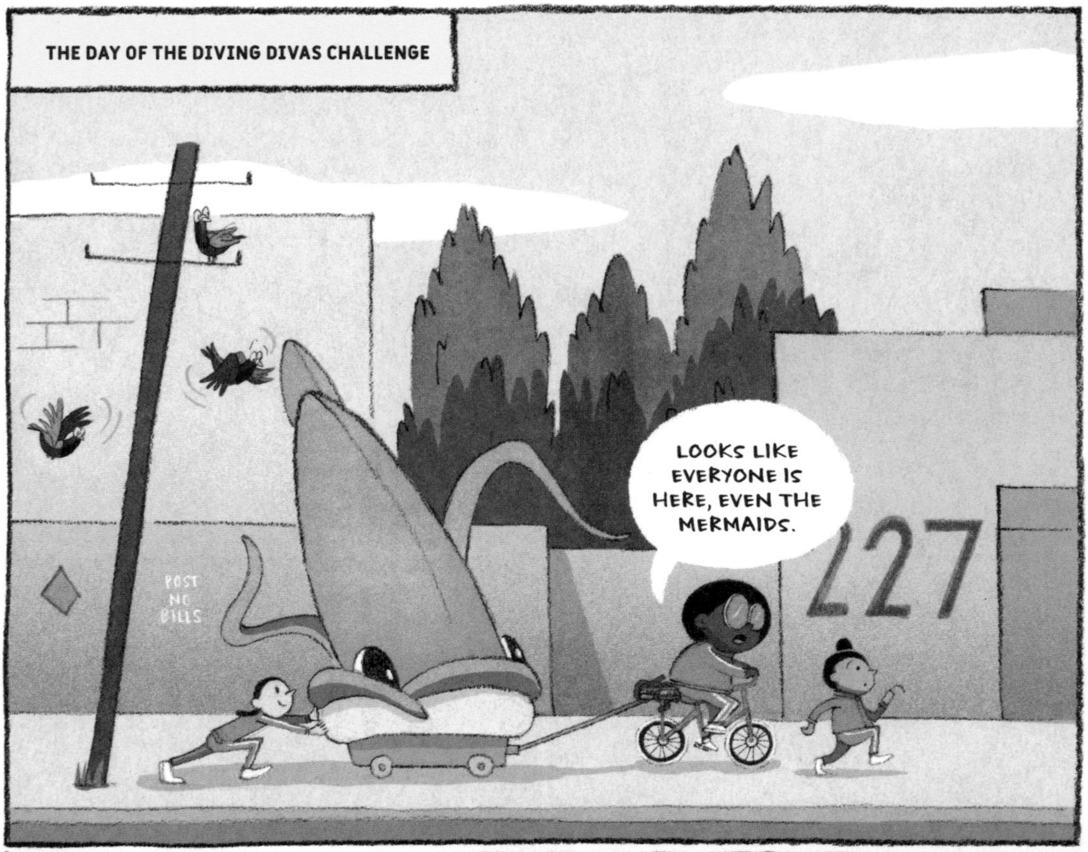
THE DAY OF THE DIVING DIVAS CHALLENGE
LOOKS LIKE EVERYONE IS HERE, EVEN THE MERMAIDS.
POST NO BILLS
227

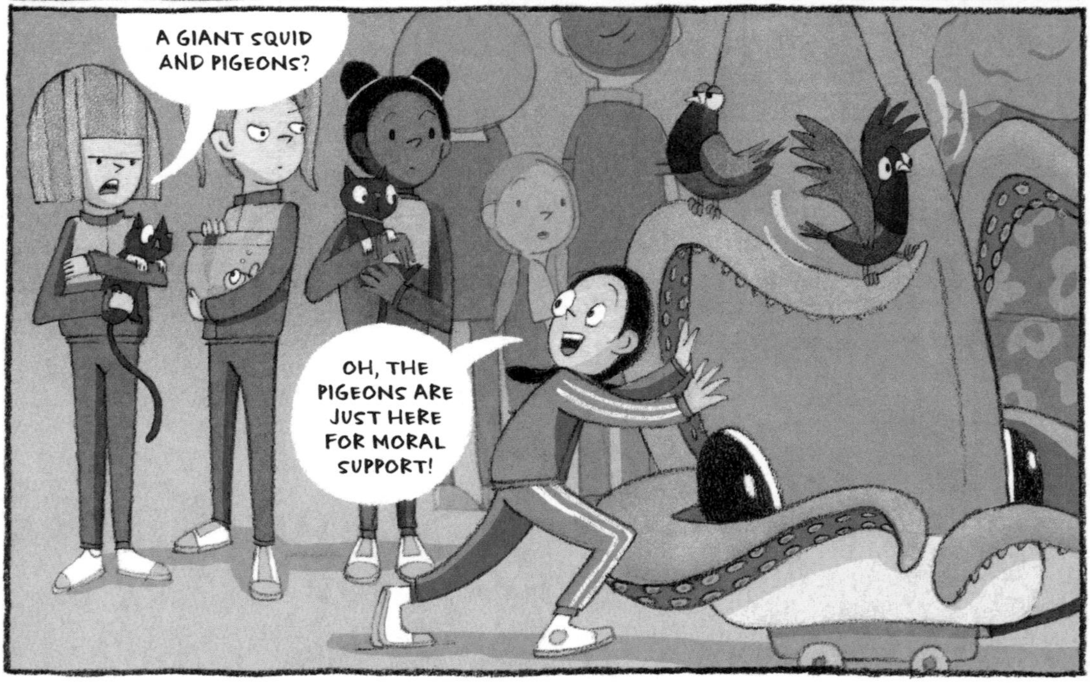
A GIANT SQUID AND PIGEONS?
OH, THE PIGEONS ARE JUST HERE FOR MORAL SUPPORT!

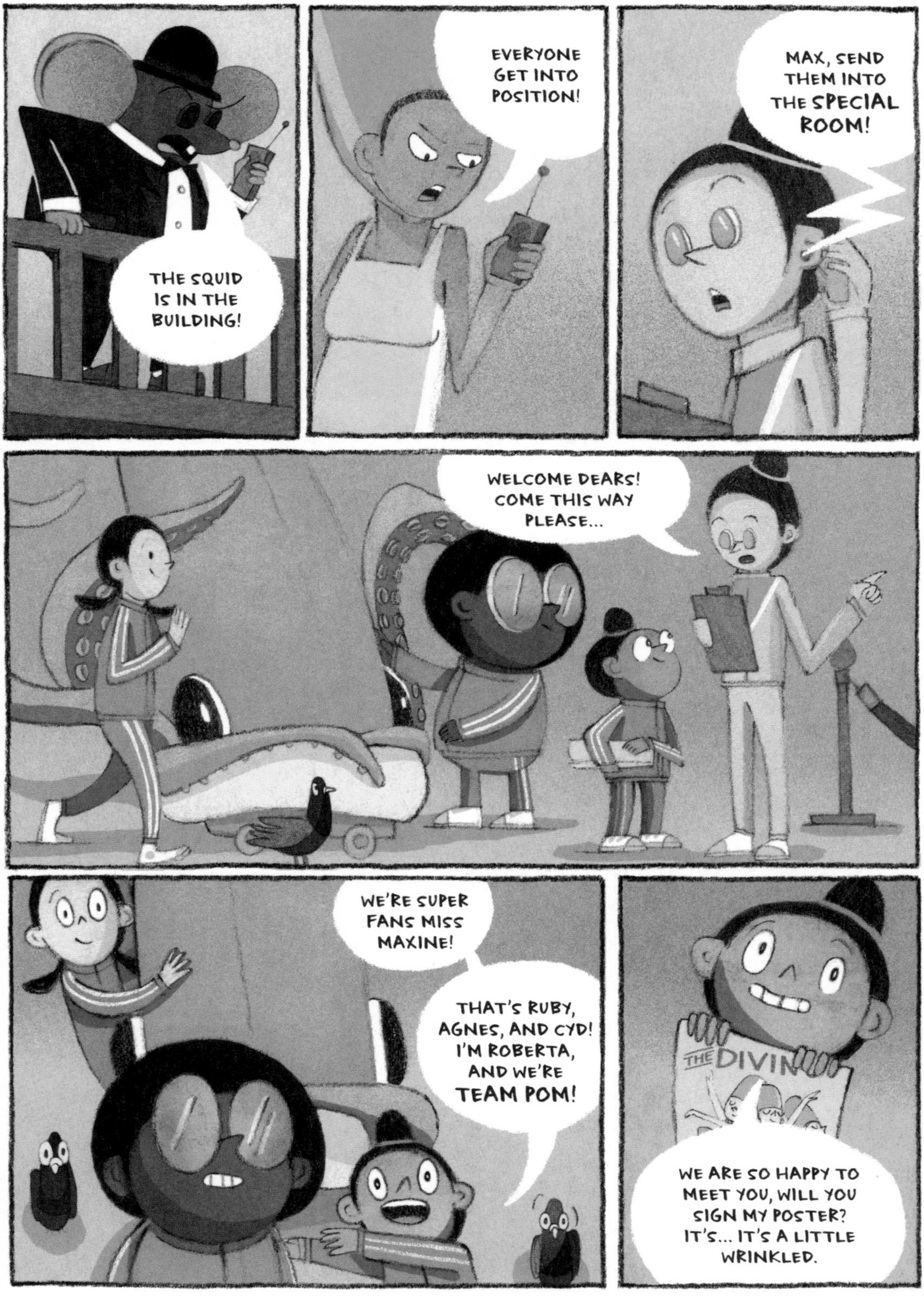
THE SQUID IS IN THE BUILDING!
EVERYONE GET INTO POSITION!
MAX, SEND THEM INTO THE SPECIAL ROOM!
WELCOME DEARS! COME THIS WAY PLEASE...
WE'RE SUPER FANS MISS MAXINE!
THAT'S RUBY, AGNES, AND CYD! I'M ROBERTA, AND WE'RE TEAM POM!
THE DIVIN
WE ARE SO HAPPY TO MEET YOU, WILL YOU SIGN MY POSTER? IT'S... IT'S A LITTLE WRINKLED.

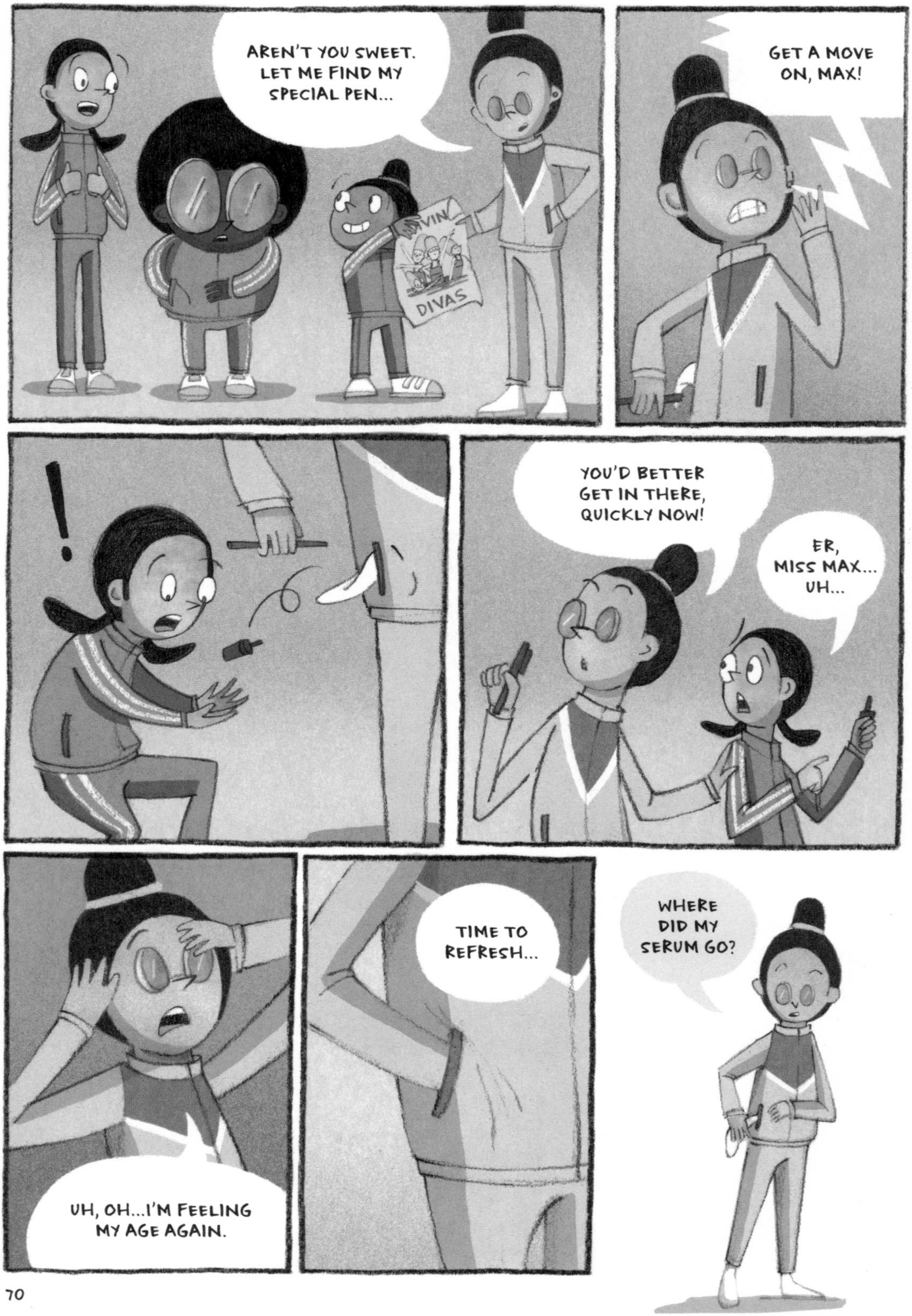

AREN'T YOU SWEET. LET ME FIND MY SPECIAL PEN...
VIN
DIVAS
GET A MOVE ON, MAX!
!
YOU'D BETTER GET IN THERE, QUICKLY NOW!
ER, MISS MAX... UH...
UH, OH...I'M FEELING MY AGE AGAIN.
TIME TO REFRESH...
WHERE DID MY SERUM GO?

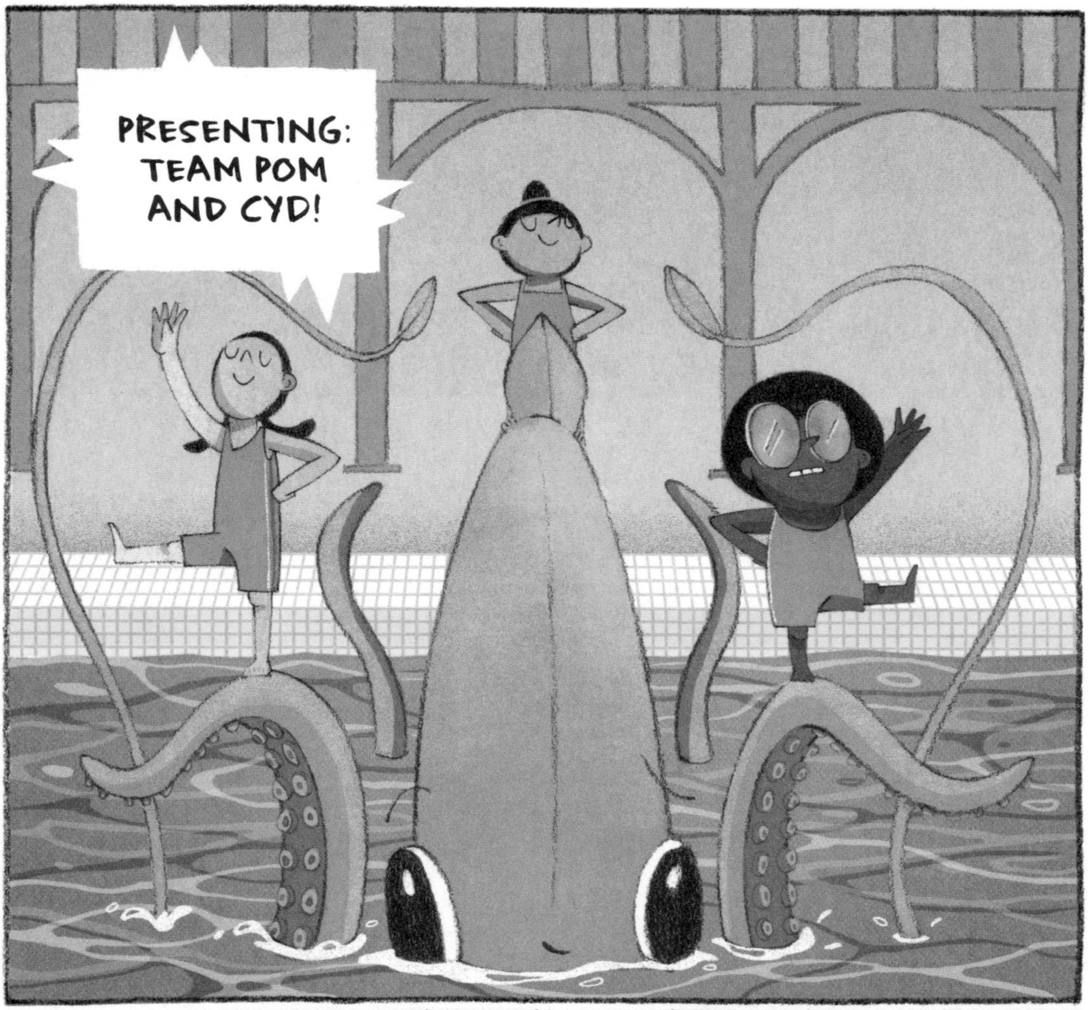
PRESENTING: TEAM POM AND CYD!

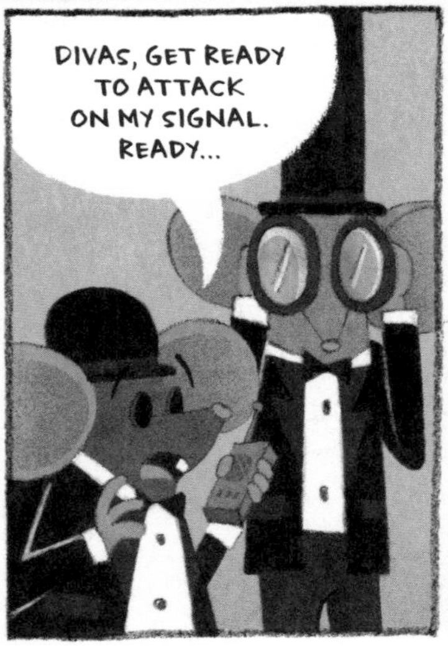
DIVAS, GET READY TO ATTACK ON MY SIGNAL. READY...

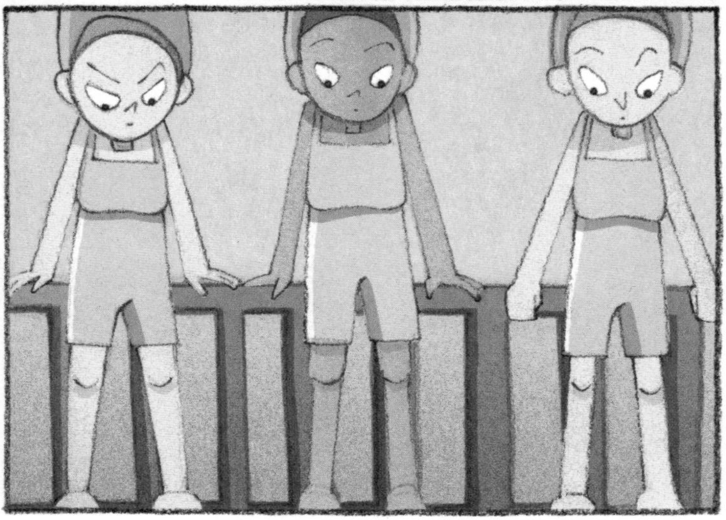

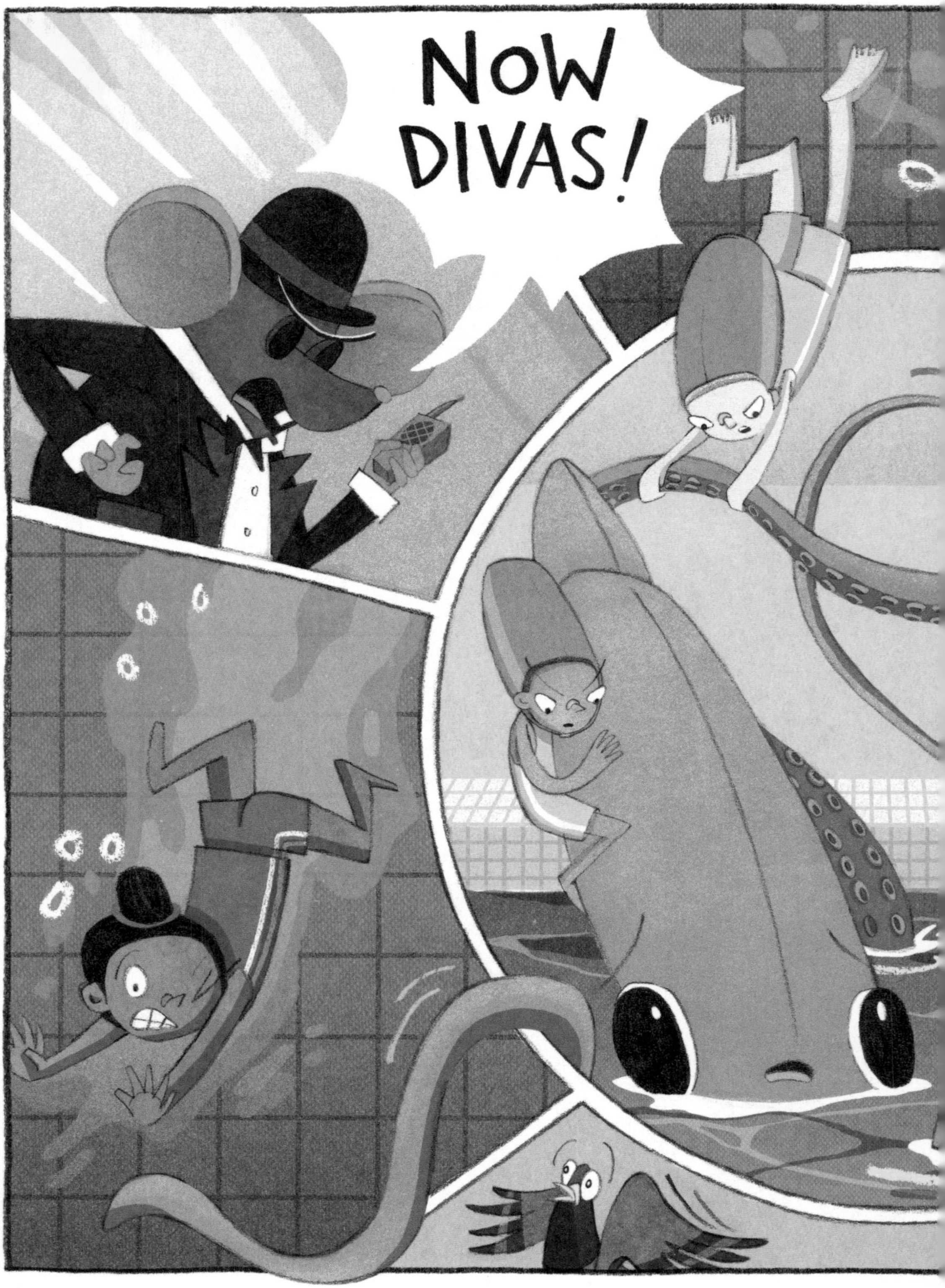
NOW DIVAS!

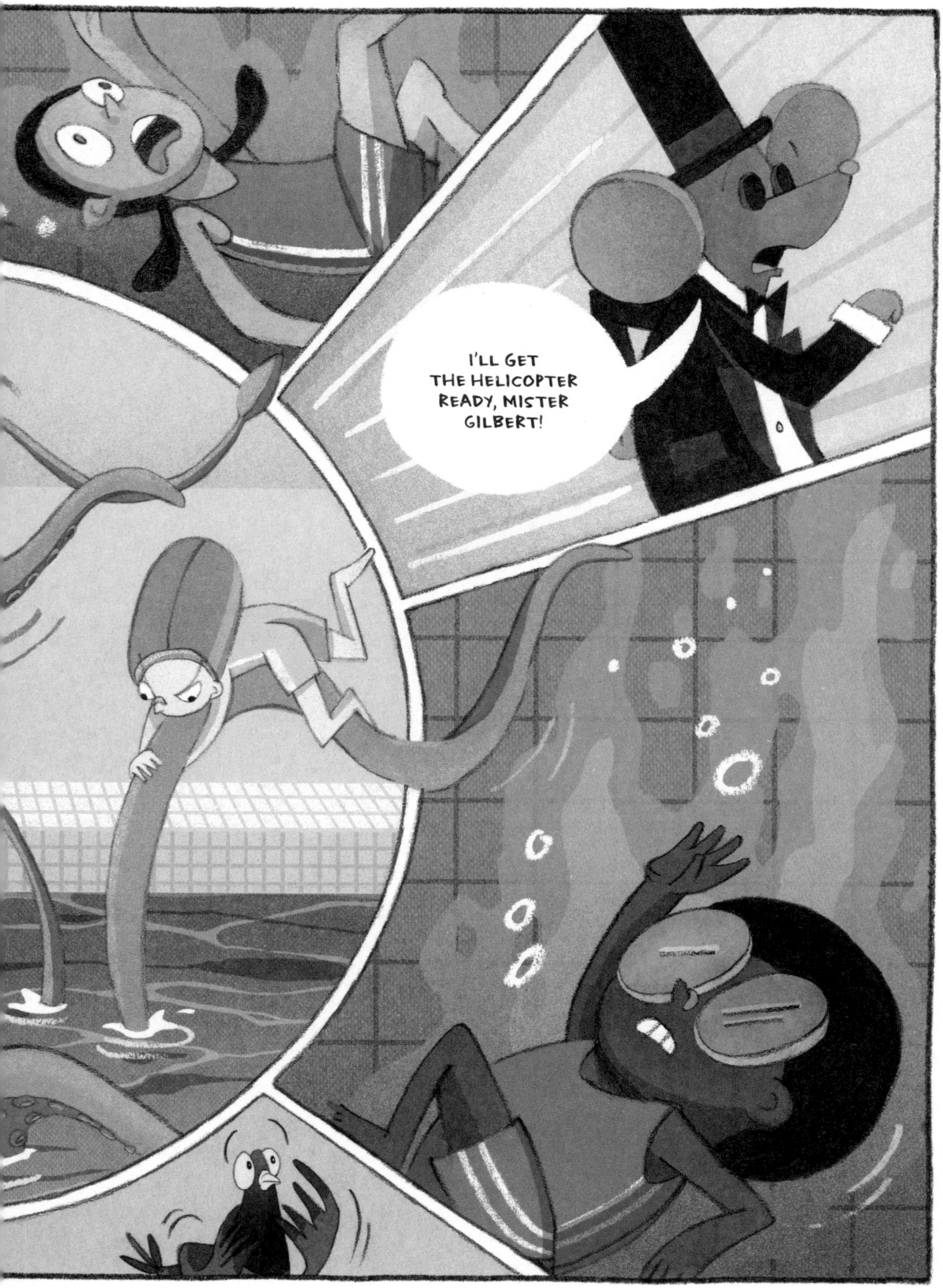
I'LL GET THE HELICOPTER READY, MISTER GILBERT!

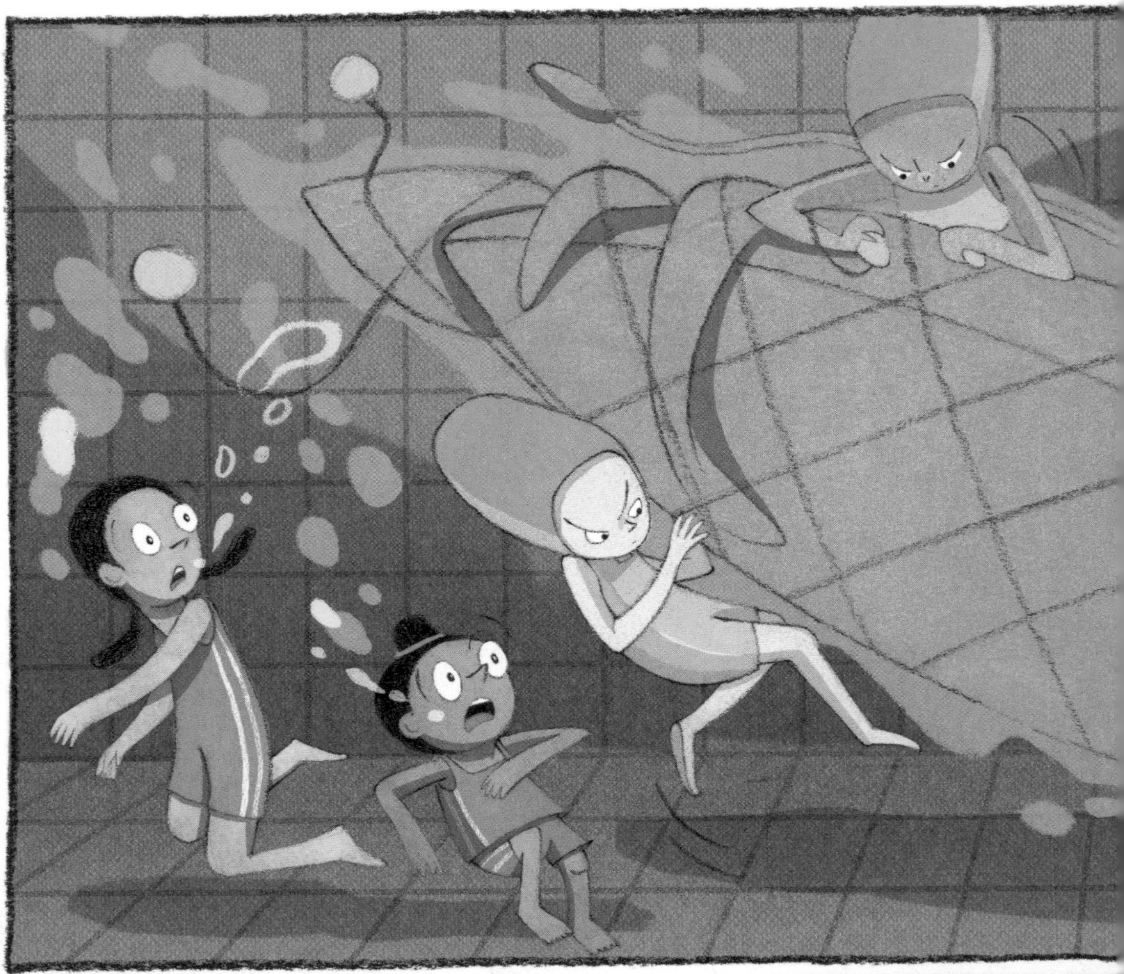

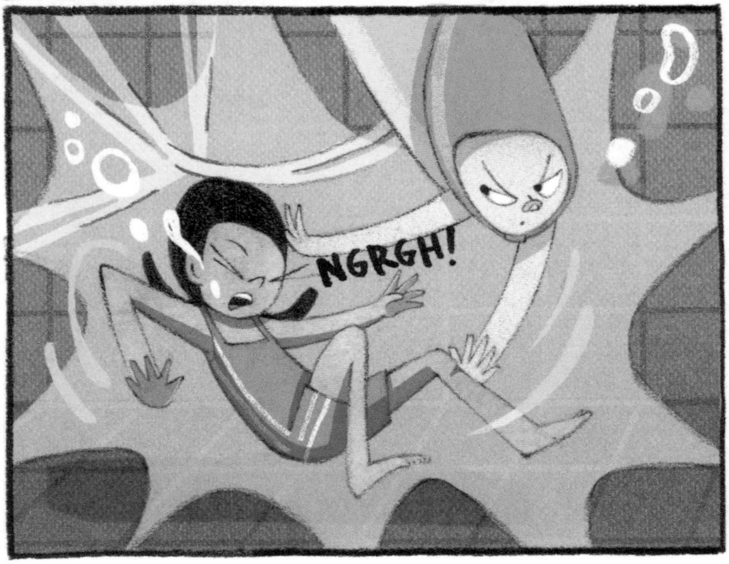
NGRGH!

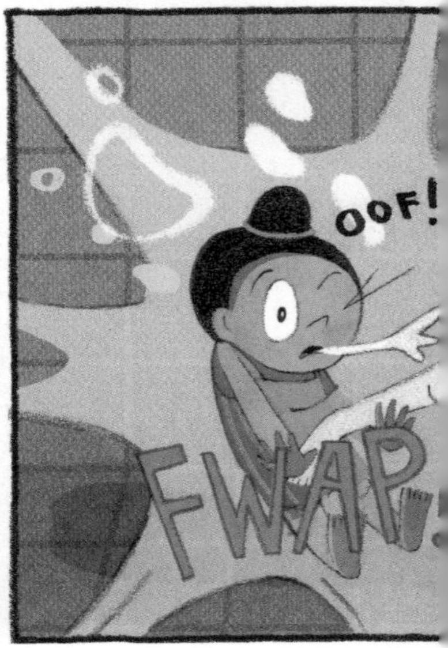
OOF!
FWAP!

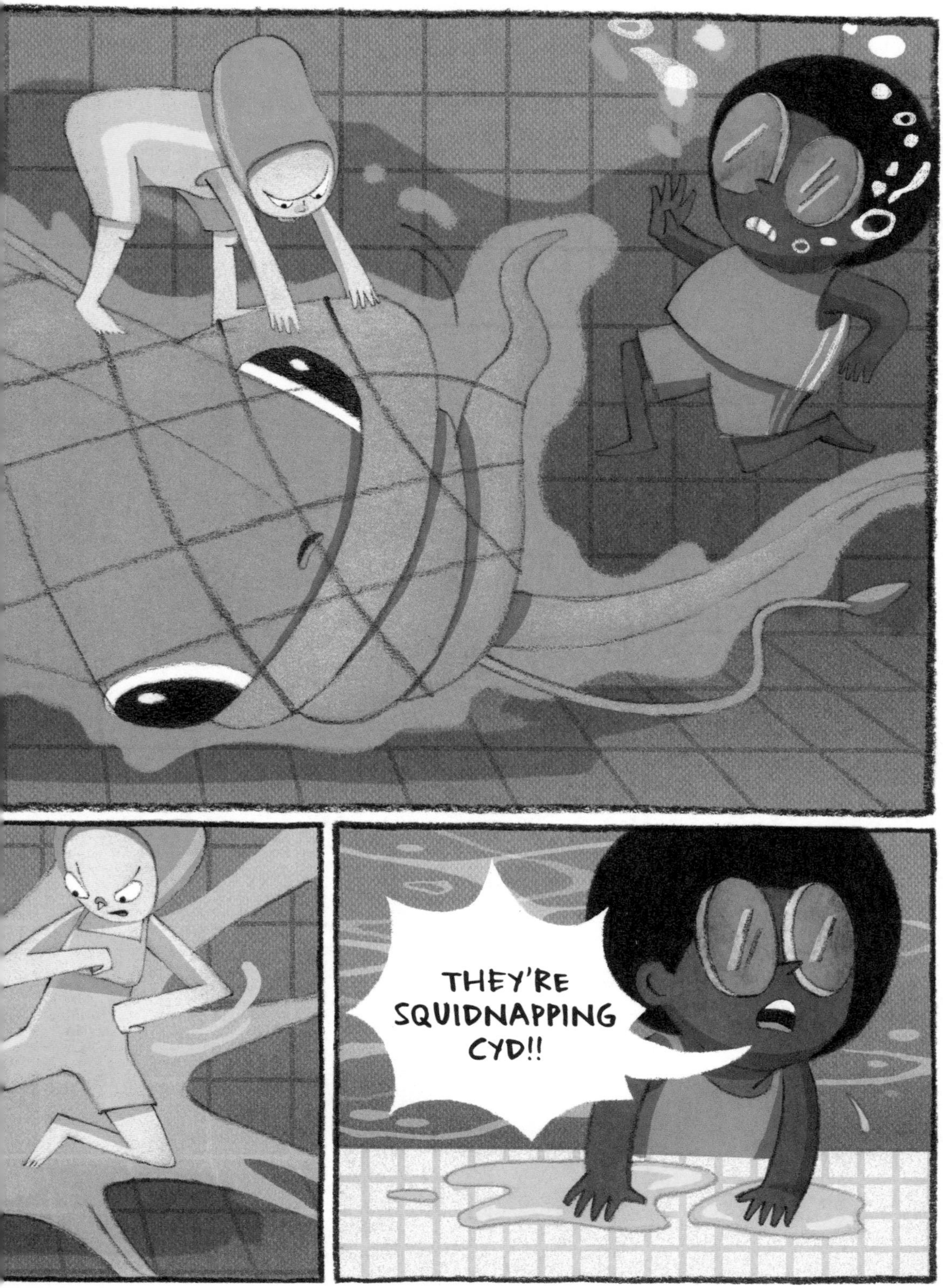
THEY'RE SQUIDNAPPING CYD!!

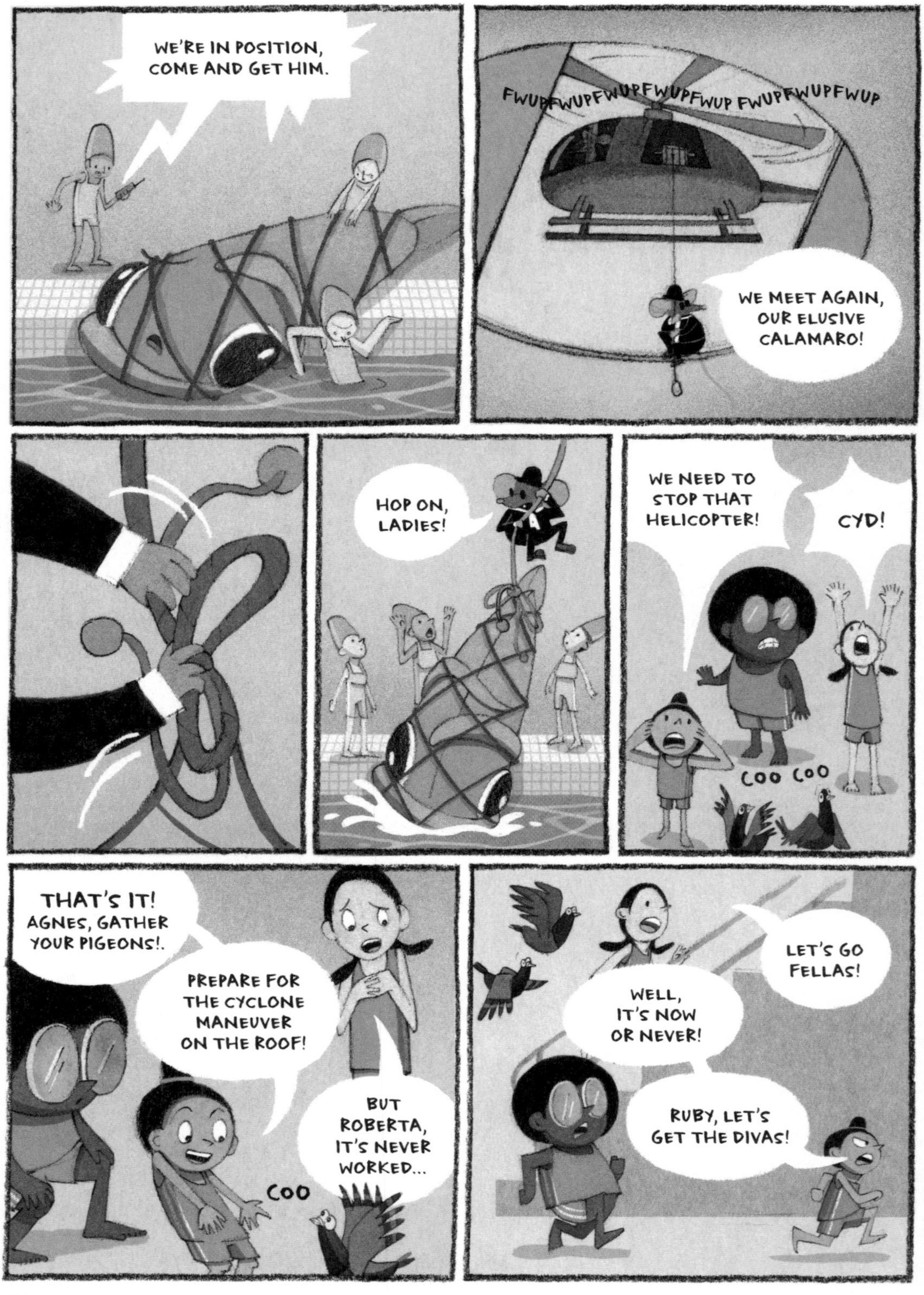
WE'RE IN POSITION, COME AND GET HIM.
FWUPFWUPFWUPFWUPFWUP FWUPFWUPFWUP
WE MEET AGAIN, OUR ELUSIVE CALAMARO!
HOP ON, LADIES!
WE NEED TO STOP THAT HELICOPTER!
CYD!
COO COO
THAT'S IT! AGNES, GATHER YOUR PIGEONS!.
PREPARE FOR THE CYCLONE MANEUVER ON THE ROOF!
BUT ROBERTA, IT'S NEVER WORKED...
COO
LET'S GO FELLAS!
WELL, IT'S NOW OR NEVER!
RUBY, LET'S GET THE DIVAS!

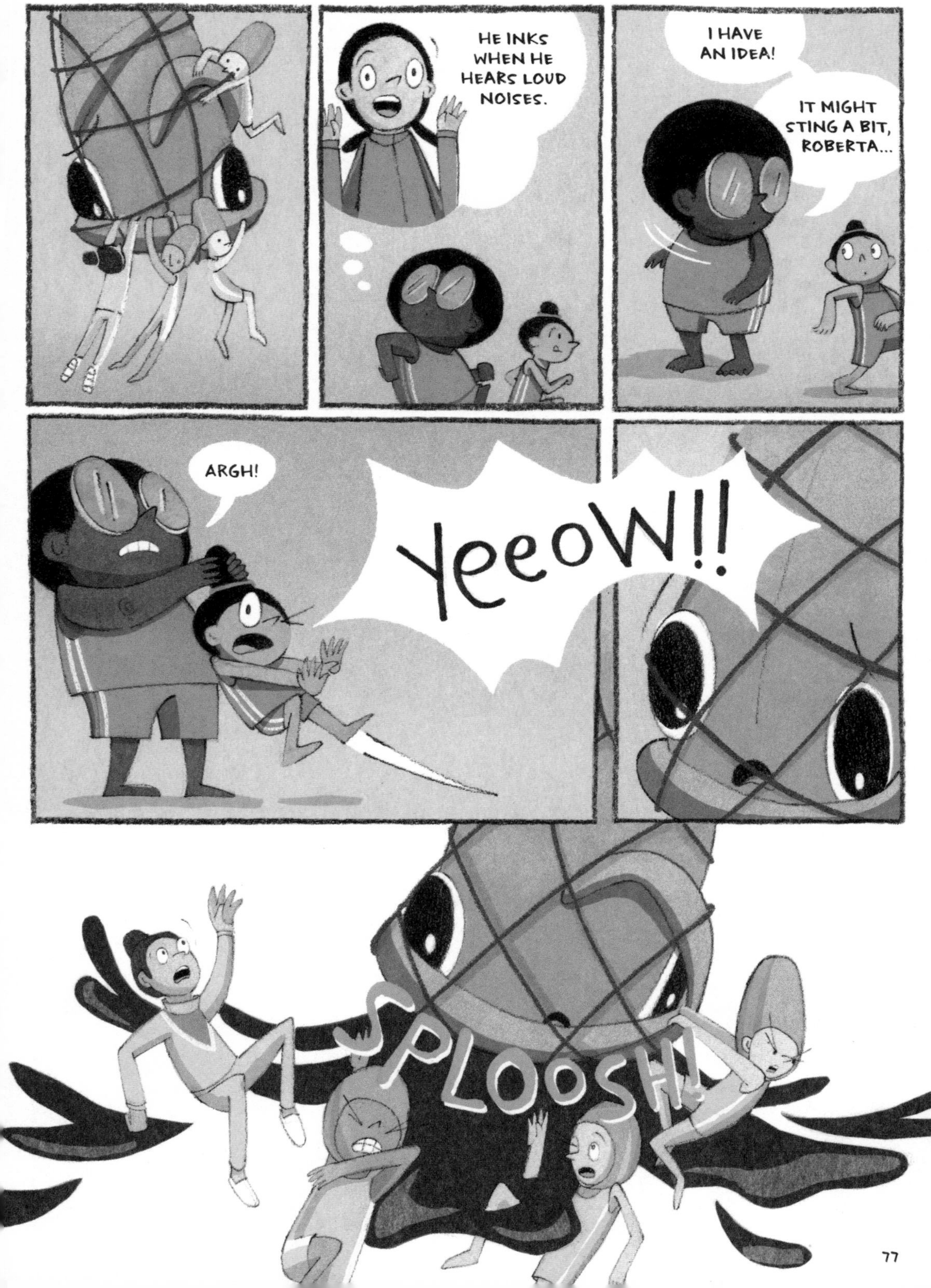
HE INKS WHEN HE HEARS LOUD NOISES.
I HAVE AN IDEA!
IT MIGHT STING A BIT, ROBERTA...
ARGH!
YEEOW!!
SPLOOSH!

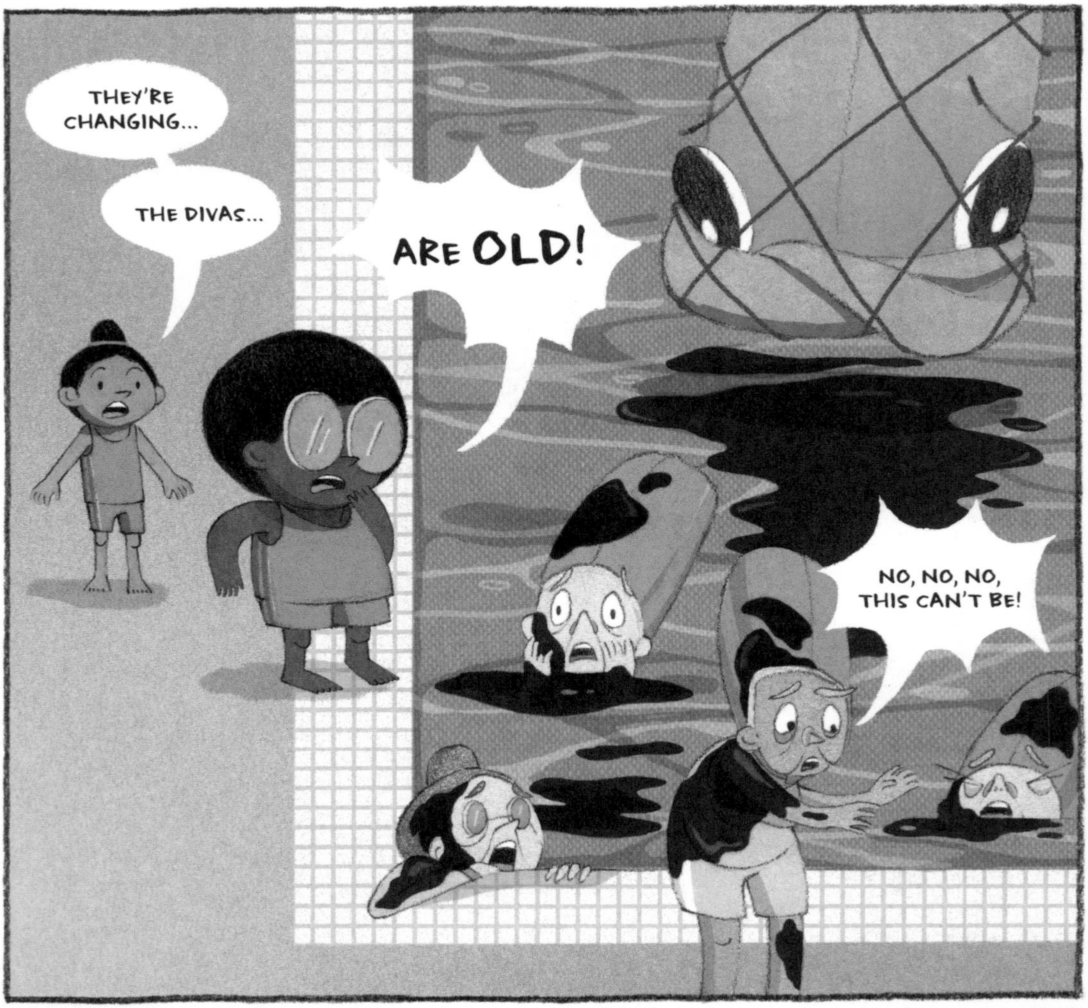
THEY'RE CHANGING...
THE DIVAS...
ARE OLD!
NO, NO, NO, THIS CAN'T BE!

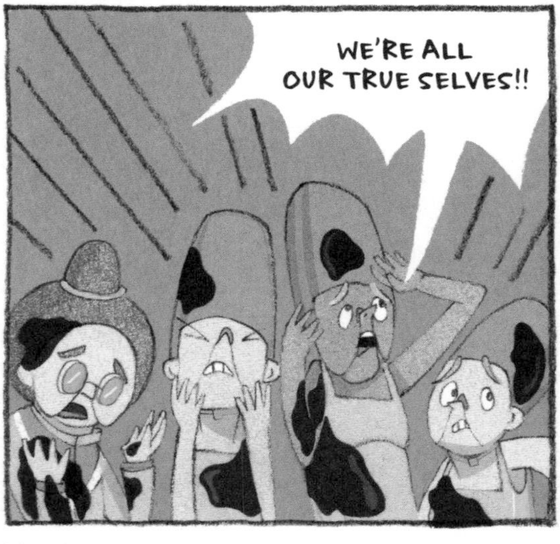
WE'RE ALL OUR TRUE SELVES!!

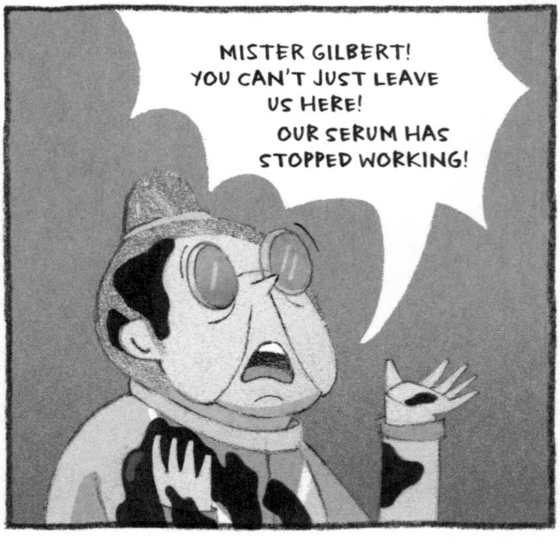
MISTER GILBERT! YOU CAN'T JUST LEAVE US HERE!
OUR SERUM HAS STOPPED WORKING!

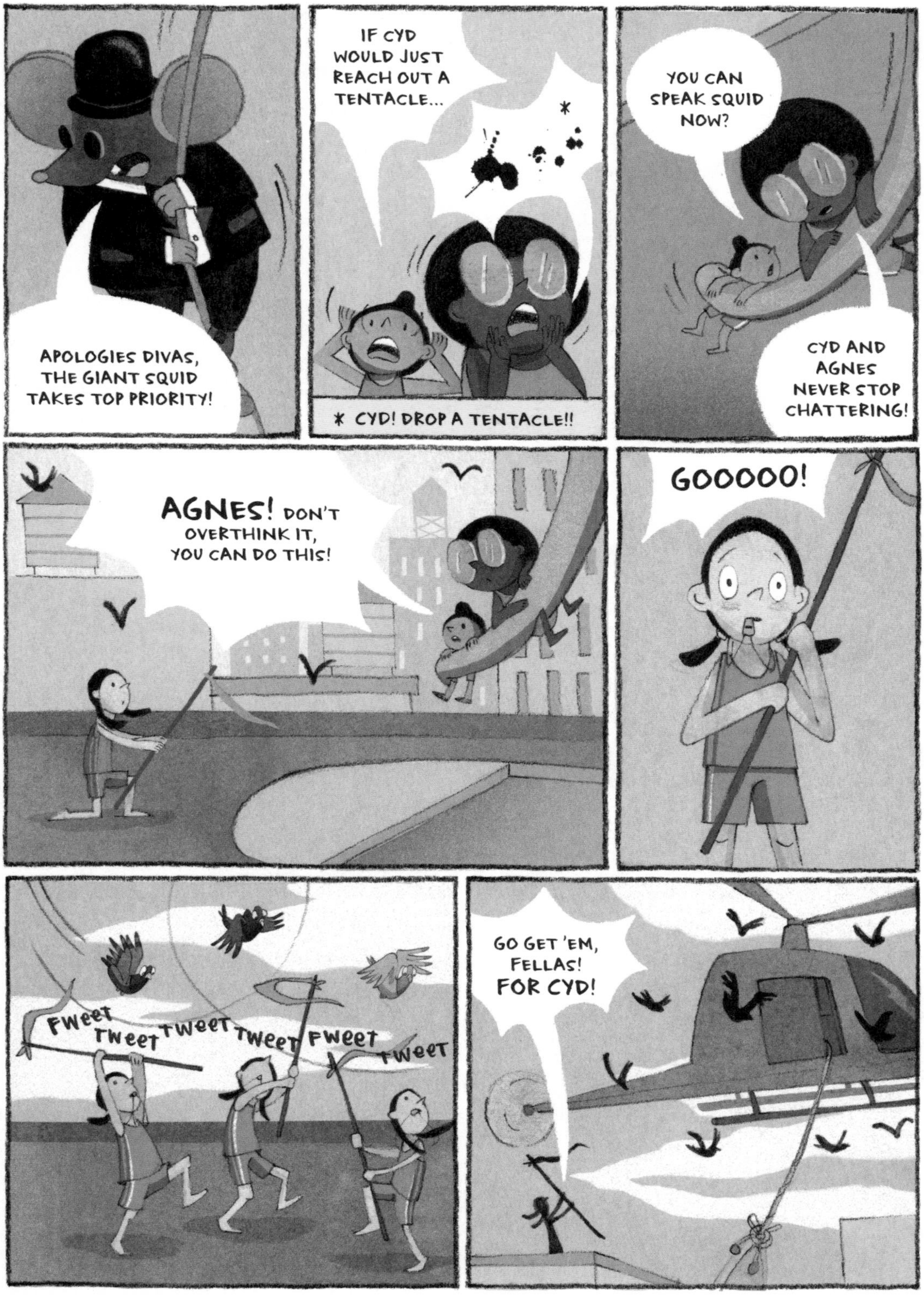
APOLOGIES DIVAS, THE GIANT SQUID TAKES TOP PRIORITY!
IF CYD WOULD JUST REACH OUT A TENTACLE...
*
* CYD! DROP A TENTACLE!!
YOU CAN SPEAK SQUID NOW?
CYD AND AGNES NEVER STOP CHATTERING!
AGNES! DON'T OVERTHINK IT, YOU CAN DO THIS!
GOOOOO!
FWEET TWEET TWEET TWEET FWEET TWEET
GO GET 'EM, FELLAS! FOR CYD!

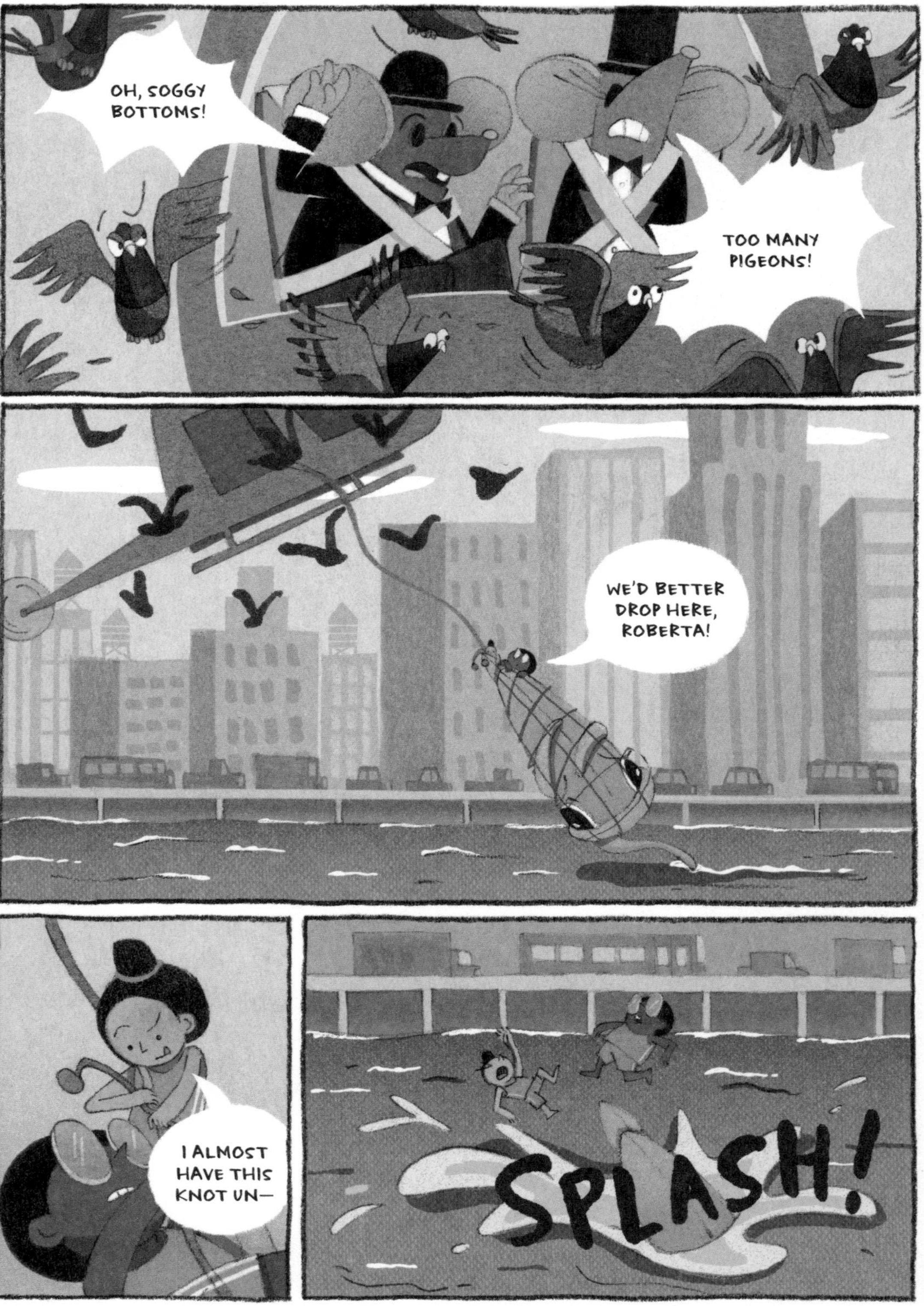
OH, SOGGY BOTTOMS!
TOO MANY PIGEONS!
WE'D BETTER DROP HERE, ROBERTA!
I ALMOST HAVE THIS KNOT UN—
SPLASH!

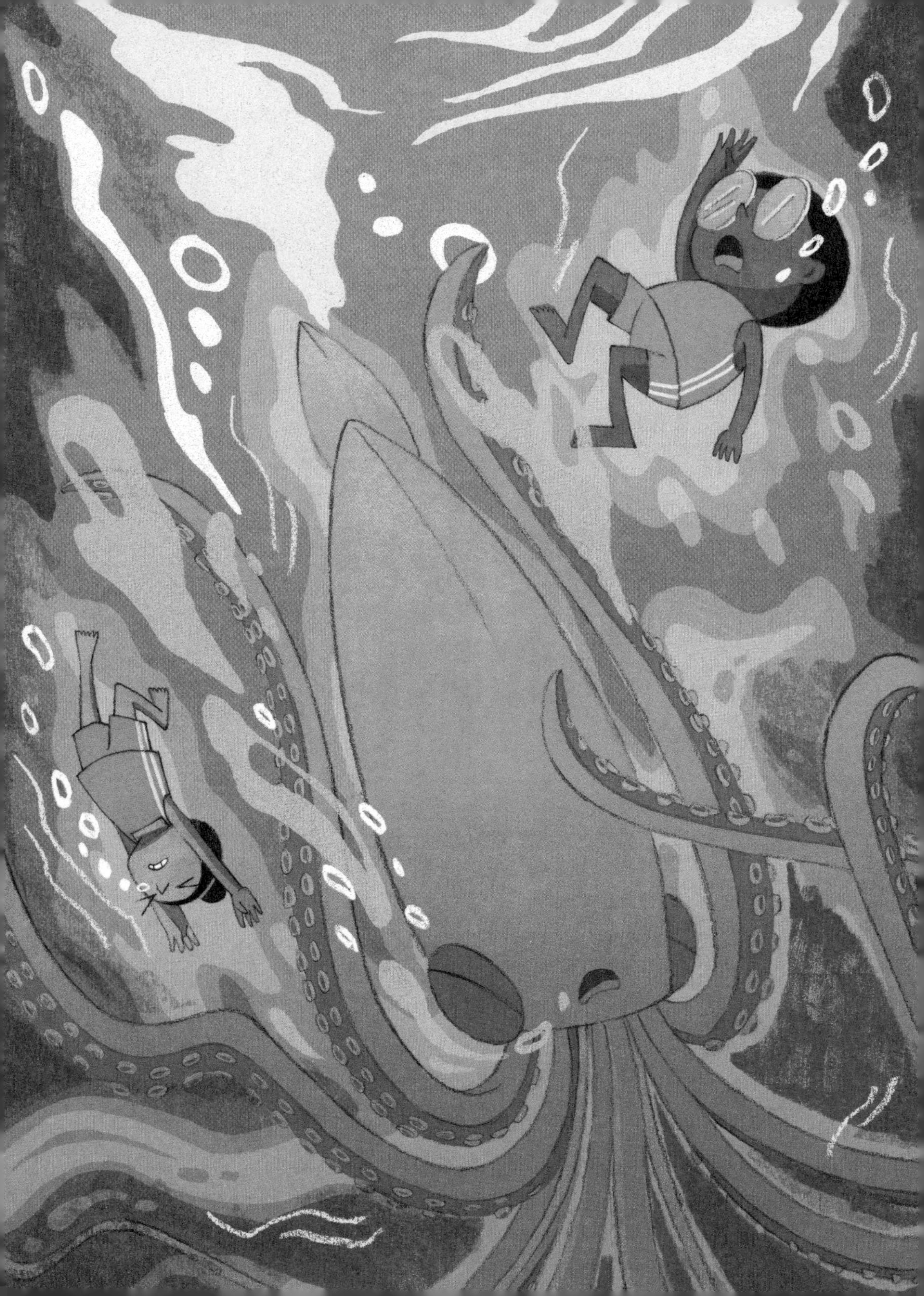

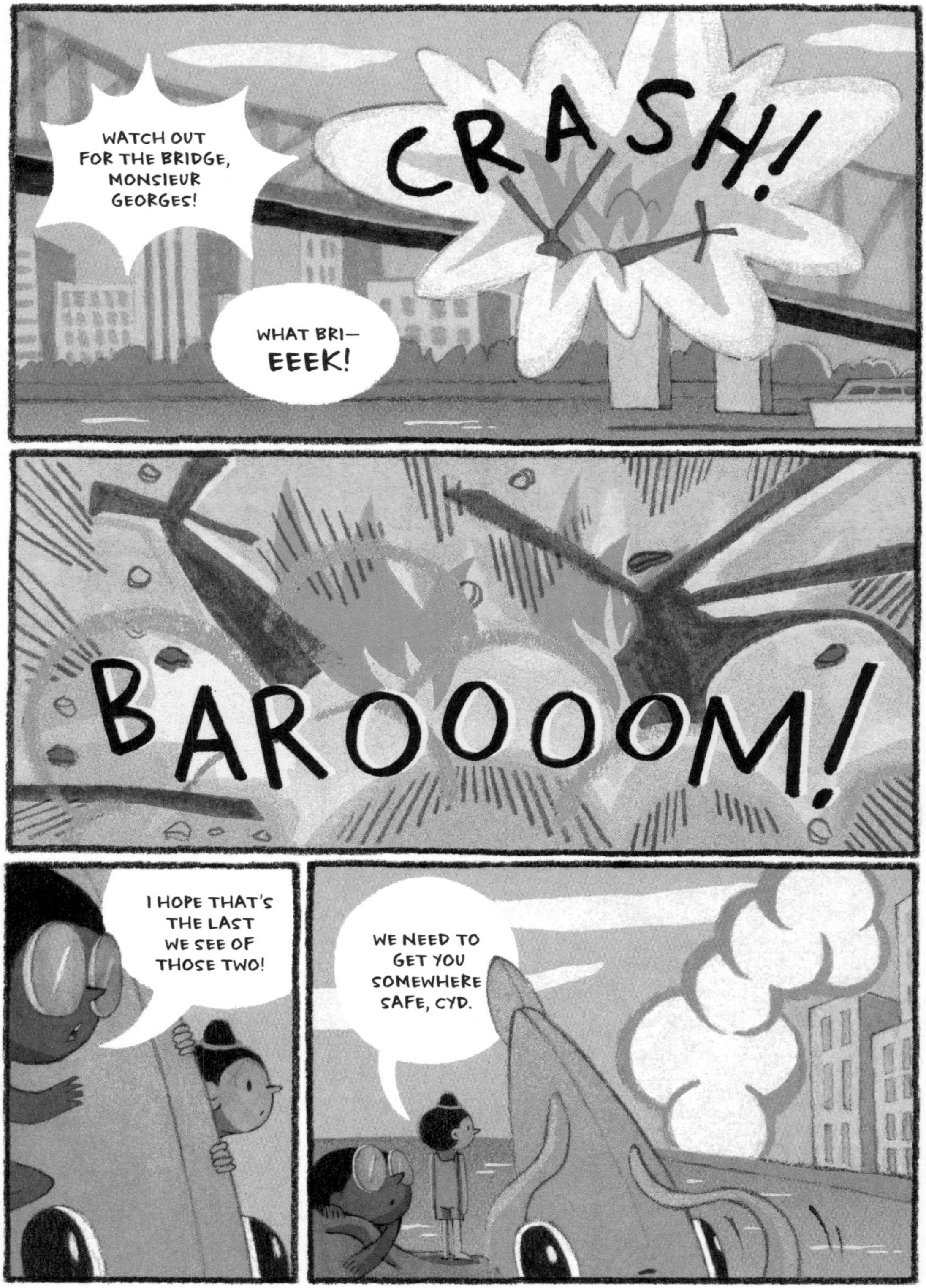
WATCH OUT FOR THE BRIDGE, MONSIEUR GEORGES!
CRASH!
WHAT BRI— EEEK!
BAROOOOM!
I HOPE THAT'S THE LAST WE SEE OF THOSE TWO!
WE NEED TO GET YOU SOMEWHERE SAFE, CYD.

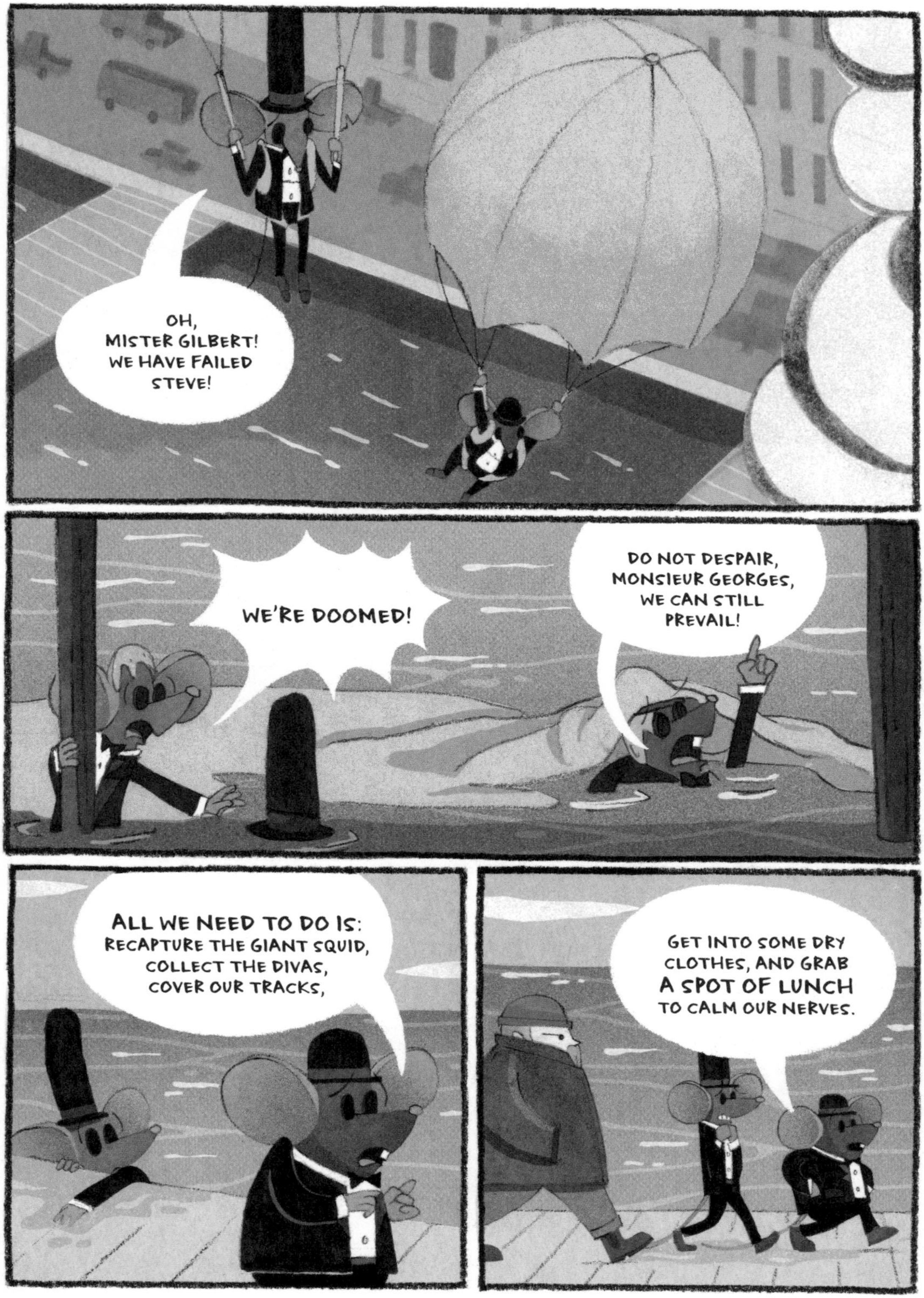
OH, MISTER GILBERT! WE HAVE FAILED STEVE!
WE'RE DOOMED!
DO NOT DESPAIR, MONSIEUR GEORGES, WE CAN STILL PREVAIL!
ALL WE NEED TO DO IS: RECAPTURE THE GIANT SQUID, COLLECT THE DIVAS, COVER OUR TRACKS,
GET INTO SOME DRY CLOTHES, AND GRAB A SPOT OF LUNCH TO CALM OUR NERVES.

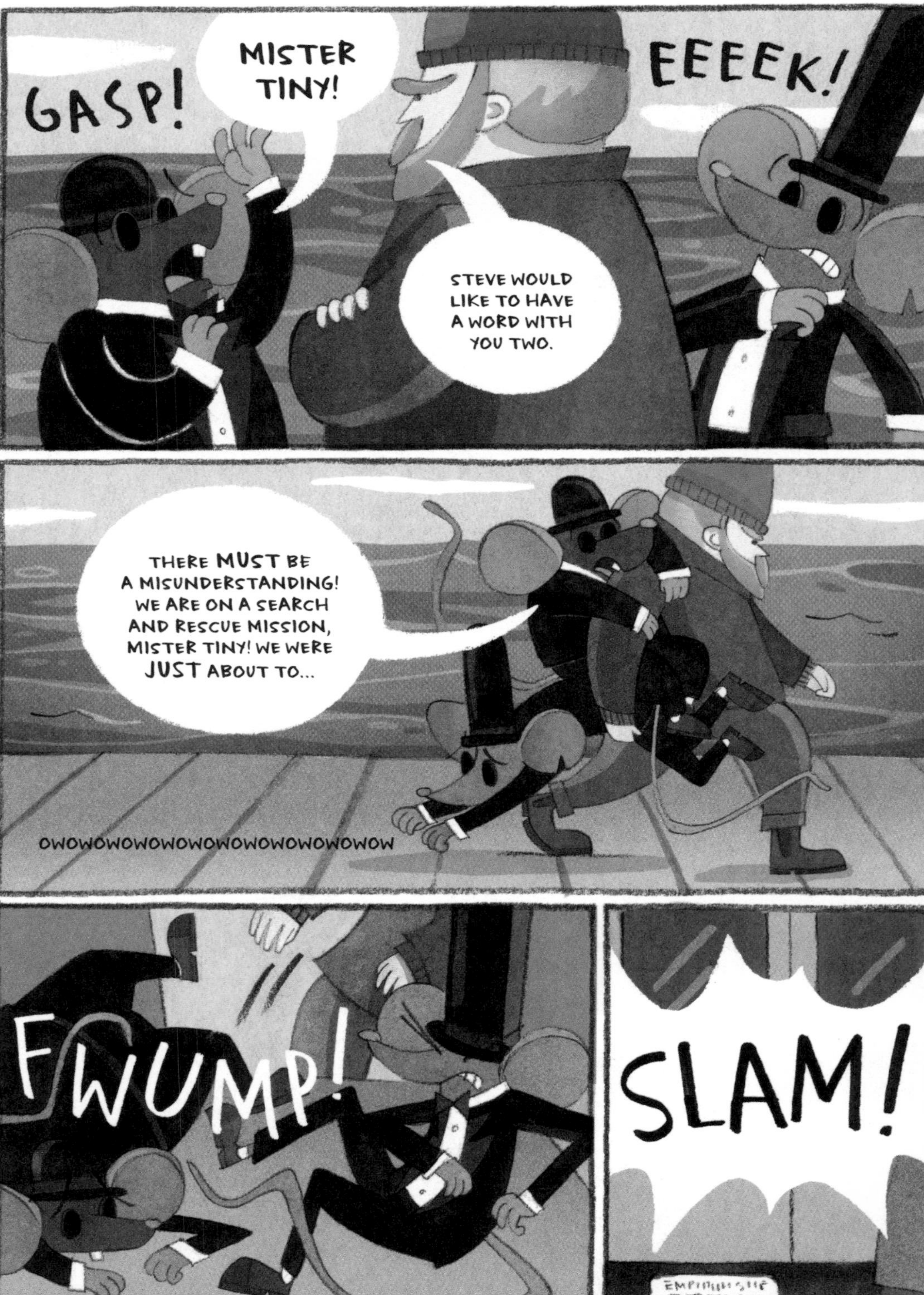
GASP!
MISTER TINY!
EEEEK!
STEVE WOULD LIKE TO HAVE A WORD WITH YOU TWO.
THERE MUST BE A MISUNDERSTANDING! WE ARE ON A SEARCH AND RESCUE MISSION, MISTER TINY! WE WERE JUST ABOUT TO...
OWOWOWOWOWOWOWOWOWOWOWOWOWOW
FWUMP!
SLAM!
ST3V3

CHAPTER 6

A FAREWELL TO TENTACLES

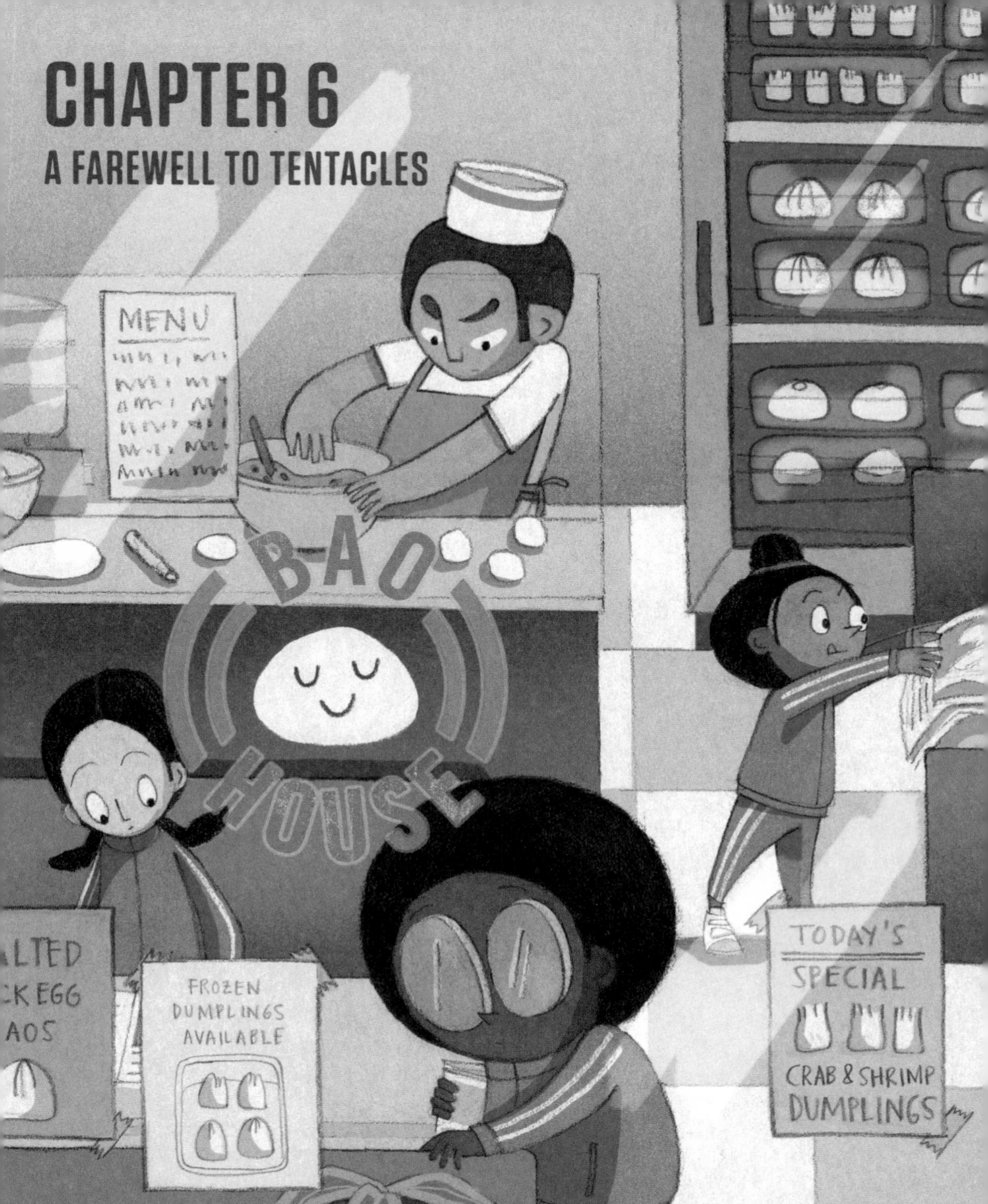
MENU
BAO HOUSE
ALTED
CK EGG
AOS
FROZEN DUMPLINGS AVAILABLE
TODAY'S SPECIAL
CRAB & SHRIMP DUMPLINGS

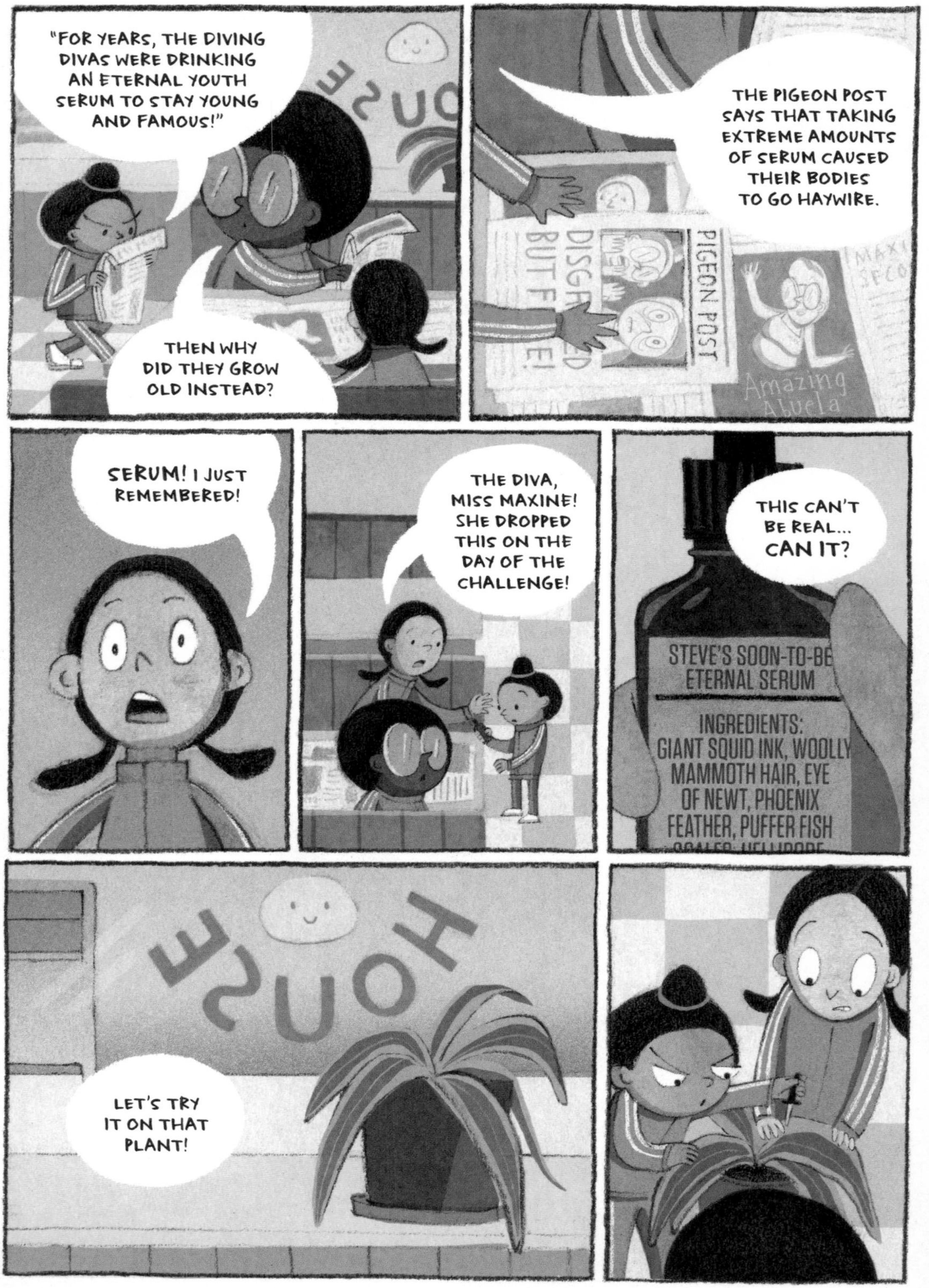
"FOR YEARS, THE DIVING DIVAS WERE DRINKING AN ETERNAL YOUTH SERUM TO STAY YOUNG AND FAMOUS!"
THEN WHY DID THEY GROW OLD INSTEAD?
THE PIGEON POST SAYS THAT TAKING EXTREME AMOUNTS OF SERUM CAUSED THEIR BODIES TO GO HAYWIRE.
PIGEON POST
Amazing Abuela
SERUM! I JUST REMEMBERED!
THE DIVA, MISS MAXINE! SHE DROPPED THIS ON THE DAY OF THE CHALLENGE!
THIS CAN'T BE REAL... CAN IT?
STEVE'S SOON-TO-BE ETERNAL SERUM
INGREDIENTS: GIANT SQUID INK, WOOLLY MAMMOTH HAIR, EYE OF NEWT, PHOENIX FEATHER, PUFFER FISH
LET'S TRY IT ON THAT PLANT!

WE REALLY NEED TO LEARN MORE ABOUT THIS STEVE...

YOUR BAOS ARE READY, ROBERTA!

THANKS, UNCLE BEN!

DO YOU SOMETIMES WISH WE COULD'VE KEPT CYD?

ABSOLUTELY. WE WOULD HAVE BEEN UNBEATABLE!

BUT HE BELONGS IN THE OCEAN.

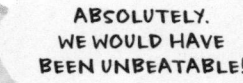

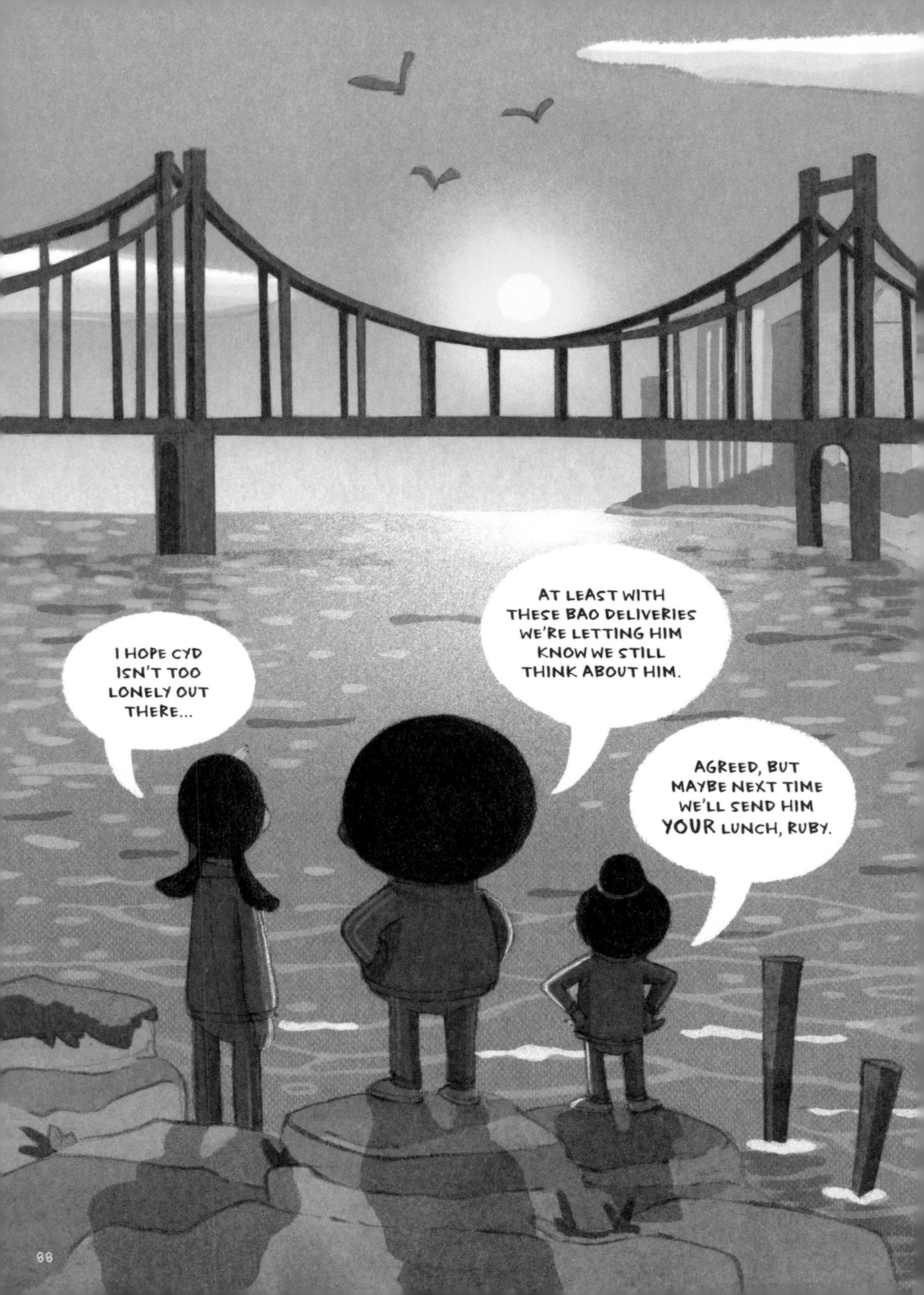
I HOPE CYD ISN'T TOO LONELY OUT THERE...
AT LEAST WITH THESE BAO DELIVERIES WE'RE LETTING HIM KNOW WE STILL THINK ABOUT HIM.
AGREED, BUT MAYBE NEXT TIME WE'LL SEND HIM YOUR LUNCH, RUBY.

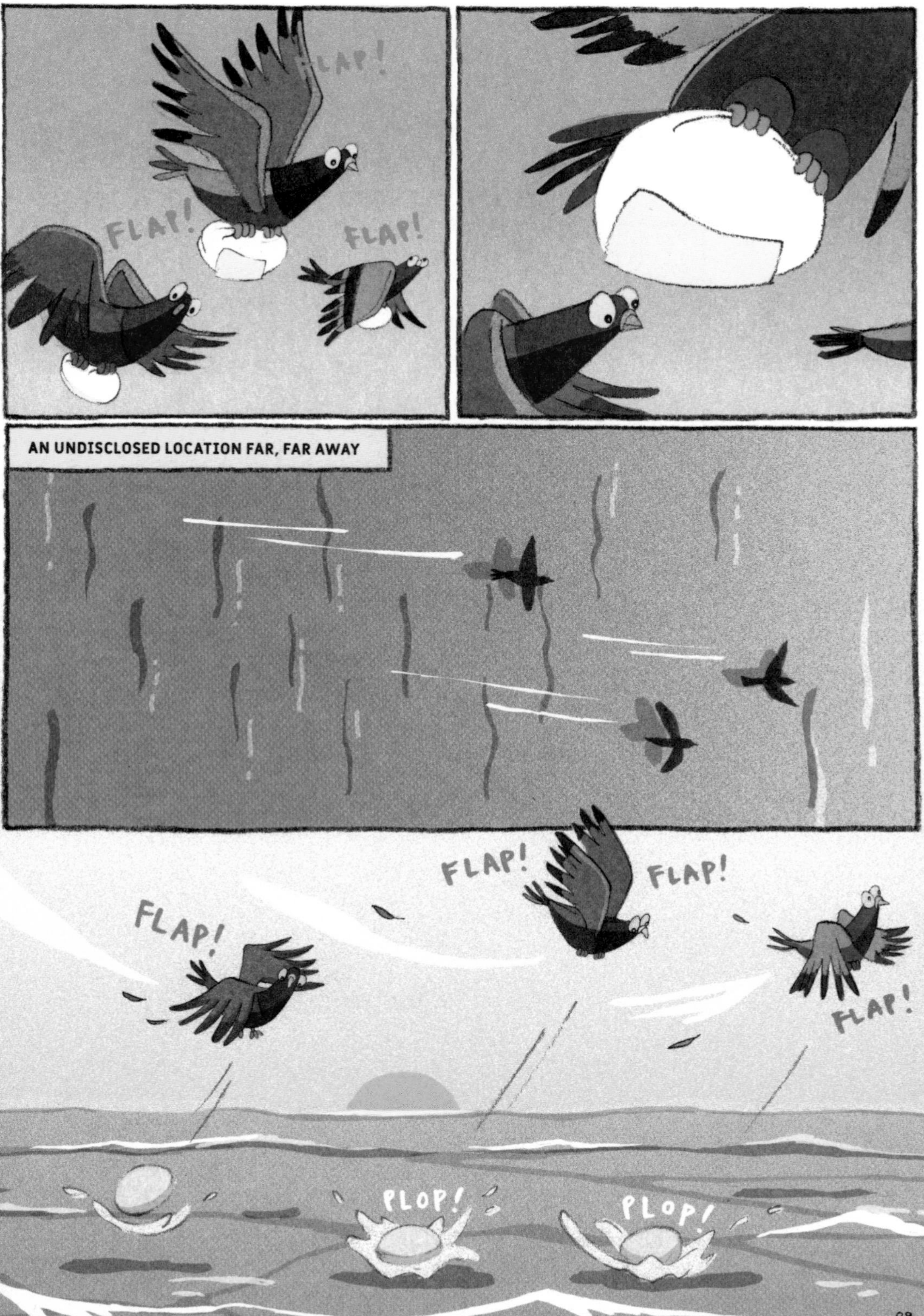
FLAP!
FLAP!
FLAP!
AN UNDISCLOSED LOCATION FAR, FAR AWAY
FLAP!
FLAP!
FLAP!
FLAP!
PLOP!
PLOP!

EPILOGUE

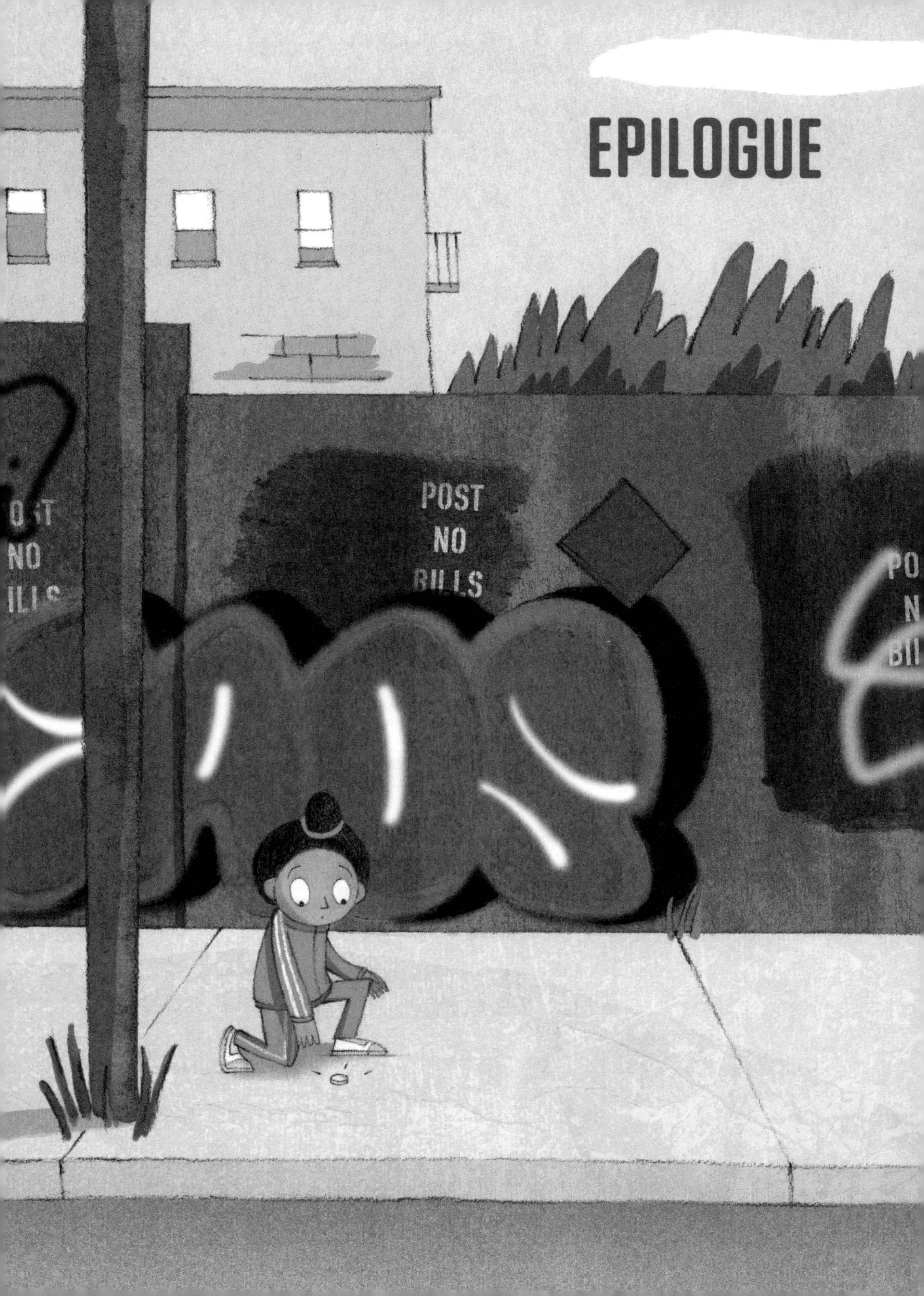
POST
NO
BILLS

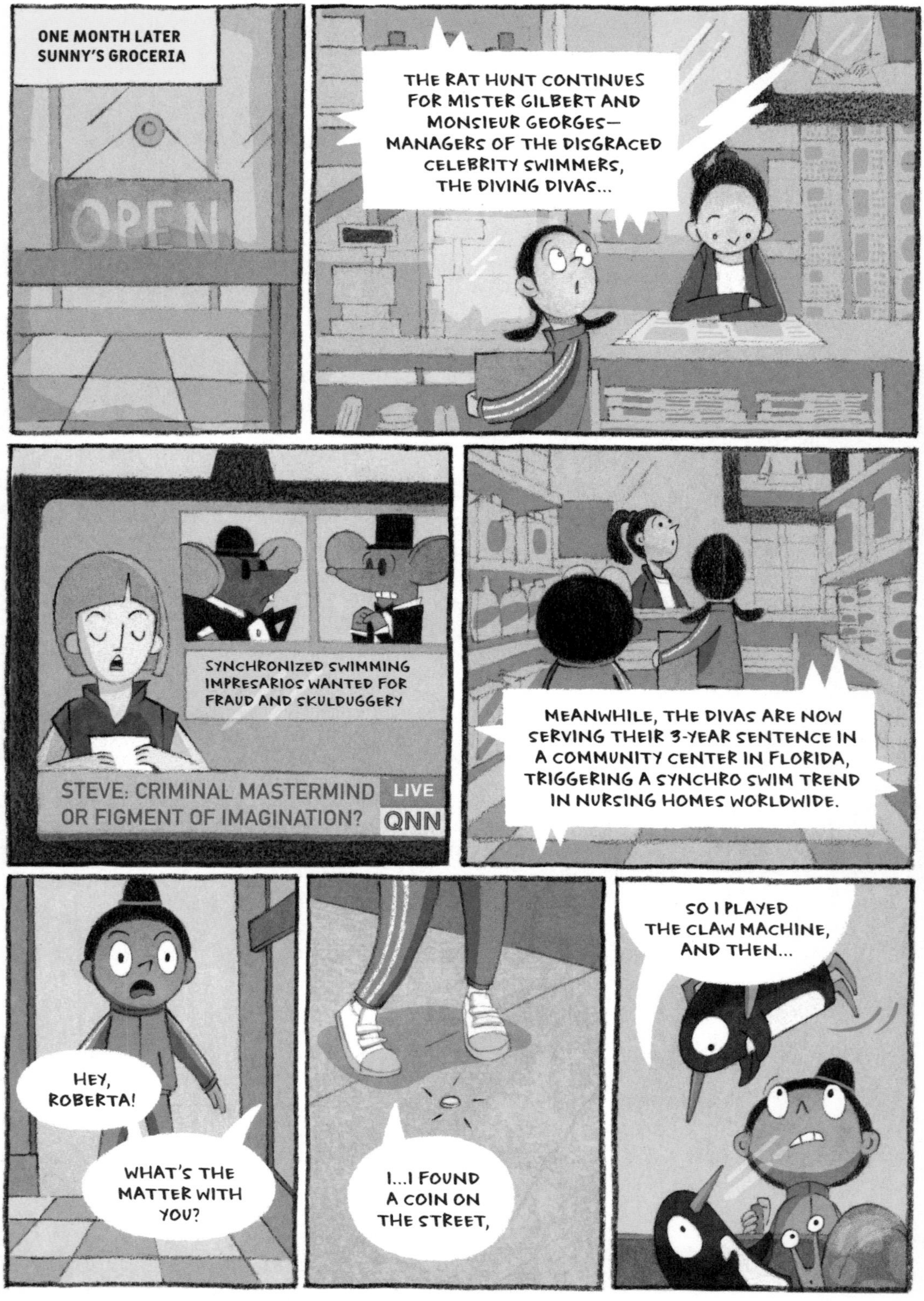
ONE MONTH LATER SUNNY'S GROCERIA
OPEN
THE RAT HUNT CONTINUES FOR MISTER GILBERT AND MONSIEUR GEORGES— MANAGERS OF THE DISGRACED CELEBRITY SWIMMERS, THE DIVING DIVAS...
SYNCHRONIZED SWIMMING IMPRESARIOS WANTED FOR FRAUD AND SKULDUGGERY
STEVE: CRIMINAL MASTERMIND OR FIGMENT OF IMAGINATION?
LIVE
QNN
MEANWHILE, THE DIVAS ARE NOW SERVING THEIR 3-YEAR SENTENCE IN A COMMUNITY CENTER IN FLORIDA, TRIGGERING A SYNCHRO SWIM TREND IN NURSING HOMES WORLDWIDE.
HEY, ROBERTA!
WHAT'S THE MATTER WITH YOU?
I...I FOUND A COIN ON THE STREET,
SO I PLAYED THE CLAW MACHINE, AND THEN...

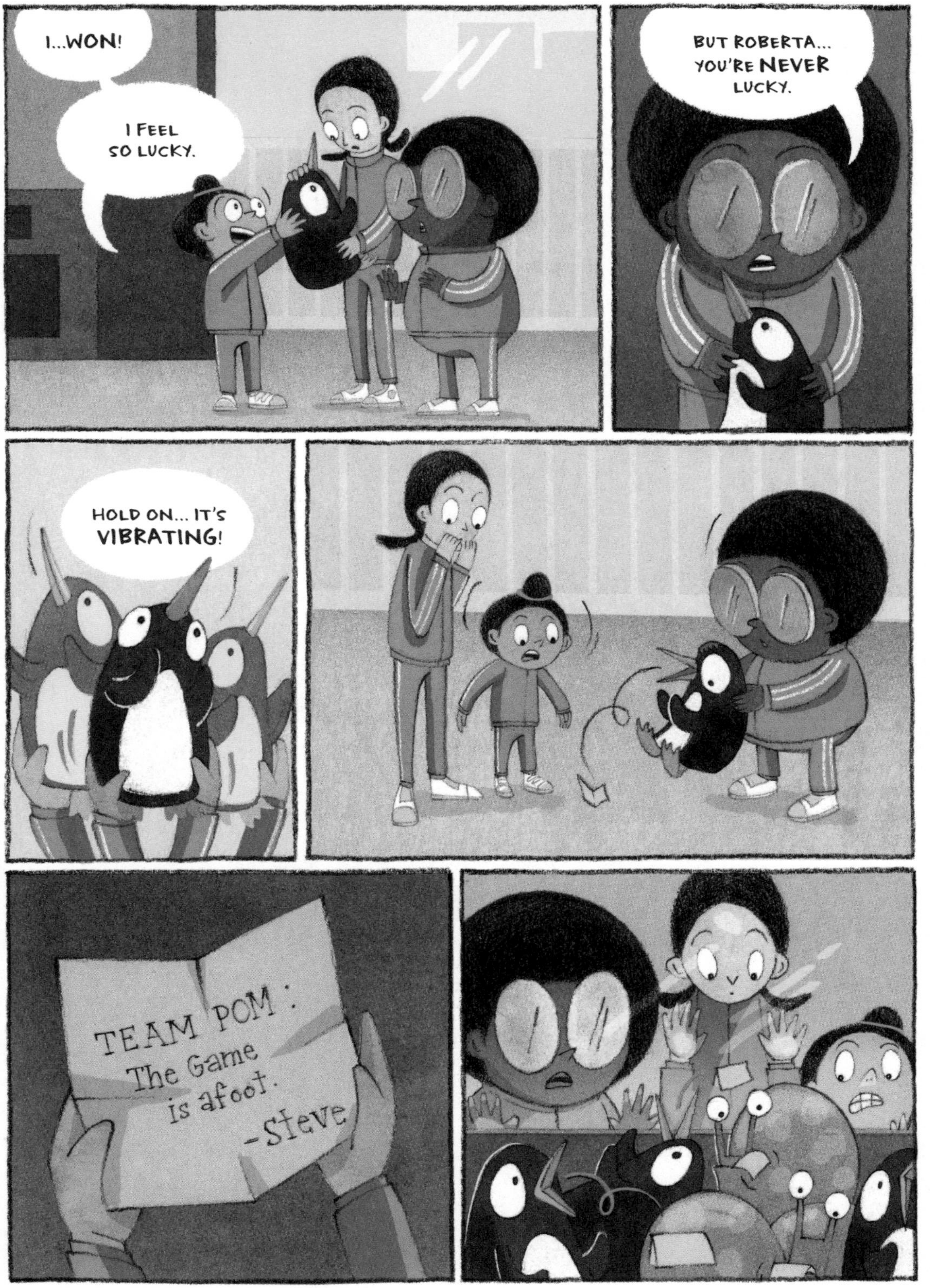

I...WON!
I FEEL SO LUCKY.
BUT ROBERTA... YOU'RE NEVER LUCKY.
HOLD ON... IT'S VIBRATING!
TEAM POM: The Game is afoot. -Steve

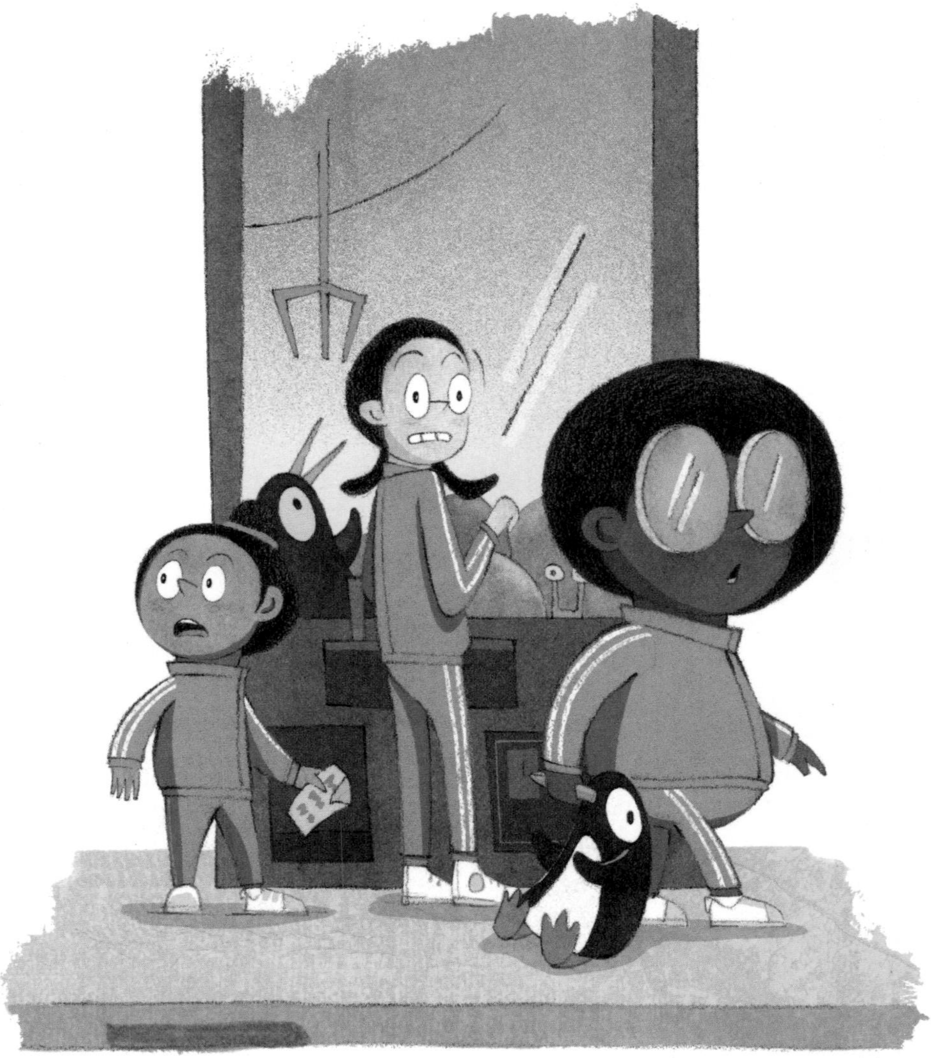